Praise for Sheryl Nantus and the Blood of the Pride series

"[W]ell wrought and very engaging. Owing to top-notch writing from Nantus...Rebecca Desjardin rivals Sue Grafton's Kinsey Millhone as an interesting female PI. Recommended for both fans of the genre and newbies to paranormal romance."
—*Library Journal* on *Claws Bared*

"A really good read that kept me guessing till the end. I loved the romance between Rebecca and Brandon."
—*www.BookLiaison.com* on *Claws Bared*

"This is a shifter series that I will definitely be following."
—*TomeTender.blogspot.com* on *Claws Bared*

"If you're a fan of strong female characters and mysteries with a paranormal twist, this is a real winner."
—*Reflections on Reading Romance* on *Blood of the Pride*

"The story moves at an even pace and the mystery is slowly revealed as the romance of Rebecca and Brandon develops. All in all, Sheryl Nantus' BLOOD OF THE PRIDE is a shifter romantic mystery that paranormal fans should find quite satisfying."
—*Love Romances & More* on *Blood of the Pride*

"Well-written urban fantasy with a strong, appealing heroine."
—Nicole Luiken, author, on *Blood of the Pride*

SHERYL NANTUS

CLAWS BARED

CARINA
PRESS™

CARINA PRESS™

PLEASE RECYCLE

THIS PRODUCT IS RECYCLABLE

Recycling programs
for this product may
not exist in your area.

ISBN-13: 978-0-373-00215-3

CLAWS BARED

Copyright © 2013 by Sheryl Nantus

www.CarinaPress.com

Printed in U.S.A.

Dear Reader,

Anyone who's been in a relationship knows there's a breaking point—a time and place when you have to figure out where you're going and how you're going to get there. When do you continue "just" dating, shift into a dedicated partnership, move in together, get married?

When do you cut the connection and move on, hoping for something better?

It's a question we've all had to deal with. And Rebecca Desjardin's no different than the rest of us, aside from being a Felis—a feline shape-shifter who can't shift.

Relationships between humans and Felis aren't forbidden, but the need for secrecy adds another level of tension that often breaks down even the strongest of feelings. Reb's headed for that point at a run and needs to figure out where her relationship with Brandon Hanover, her human boyfriend, is going.

Add in a murder case involving a male stripper and his possible Felis lovers, a Felis suitor for Reb's hand, and a whole lot of testosterone...and you've got a powder keg waiting to blow.

The big question is: How far do you go before making a commitment to each other? And if you don't make a commitment, are you willing to let go?

Sheryl Nantus

For my husband, Martin,
who doesn't flinch when I wander around
the house mumbling plot points to myself
and forgetting to make dinner because
I'm on a writing roll—coming up on twenty years
together and he still "gets" me!

And for Jazz—you are still loved and missed,
you sweet fuzzaloid...

CLAWS BARED

ONE

I HADN'T ORDERED any airline tickets.

I looked inside the open envelope with a mixture of surprise, dismay and confusion.

The bike courier let out a loud cough, covering his mouth with a gloved hand. I paused for a second, trying to figure out what he wanted. I'd already signed his clipboard and accepted delivery, expecting to find a court subpoena—I was used to having to testify on the stand both for and against my clients. Being a private investigator meant doing almost as much court time as investigating—the movies tend to leave that less glamorous part out.

Airline tickets weren't even on my radar.

He coughed again and wriggled his fingers. I caught on before he had to explain his chronic illness.

I dug in my pocket and found enough spare change to not embarrass myself. Handing it to the courier, I turned my attention back to the envelope.

The young man stuffed the coins into his pocket and threw me a jaunty salute before sprinting off through my small yard. He yanked his bike away from the rose bushes lining the front and jumped back out into traffic, the tires leaping in the air like some warped rearing horse.

I grimaced at the sound of screaming brakes coming from around the corner. Not hearing anyone calling for an ambulance, I closed the door and headed for my work desk. Running your business out of your home had certain advantages—like not having to worry about getting fully dressed for work. I wriggled my bare toes and sat down.

The drab brown envelope from a local travel agency held tickets from Toronto, Ontario, to Pittsburgh, PA. Open return, one person in my name. Leaving that evening. I sat down at my desk and scowled at the elderly white cat sprawled over the file folders.

"This is your doing, isn't it? Revenge because I wouldn't let you be a little piglet and get sick on that tuna."

Jazz turned her steady gaze on me for another few seconds before licking her paws.

I turned my attention to the envelope. Standard brown envelope with nothing inside other than the travel agency's business card. No mention of who had sent it or who had paid for it.

I had a pretty good idea.

I lifted the envelope to my nose and inhaled. Human scent, nothing out of the ordinary. Multiple humans including my stinky messenger and a woman who wore way too much perfume.

The phone rang.

I snatched up the receiver, blowing away a wayward tuft of white cat fur. Jazz gave a short trill of approval.

"Reb." I clenched my fist at the low voice purring my name. "Glad to see you're home."

"Hi, Jess. Yes, just in time to receive this envelope." I tapped the thick folder on the varnished desktop. "I assume you've got something to do with this."

"Maybe."

"So why shouldn't I drop this into my shredder?" I snapped, harsher than I'd intended.

I was missing Bran something awful.

Jazz dropped from the desk and trotted out of the room, picking up on my mood.

"Reb, is that any way to talk to a Board member?" The snarl in her voice sent phantom pains over my back, where the scars were. I resisted the urge to sit up straight in my chair.

"Is that any way to talk to an outcast? I do you one favor and suddenly I'm on your mailing list? I'm not part of the Pride and I don't have to answer to you." I kept my voice steady despite the butterflies in my stomach. "You declared me outcast twenty years ago and threw me into foster care, banished me from the family. I haven't forgotten that."

Or forgiven. The scars throbbed, reminders of the

thrashing I'd gotten at Jess's claws in a final test of my ability to Change.

I'd failed. Spectacularly.

"Oh, snap. Is that the way it's going to be, then?" The jovial tone didn't trick me. Jess hadn't earned and kept her position without having invisible wheels turning in a thousand different directions. "Do I have to thank you again for helping us find out who killed Janey Winters?"

"It wouldn't hurt." My eyes flickered to my check-book sitting nearby. I'd burned through the Pride's "appreciation" check already, thanks to some over-due bills and being head-over-heels in love, which didn't leave much time for taking on new cases.

"I can't go to the United States." I waved the tick-ets in the air. "I don't have a passport."

"It should be there within the hour. Took a bit lon-ger to get it approved than usual. You know these paper pushers, always making sure the *t*'s are crossed and the *i*'s dotted."

"I never applied for one." I ground my teeth to-gether. I'd forgotten the extent of the family's reach.

"Sure you did, you just forgot." Each word dragged fingernails over a mental blackboard. "Un-derstandable, given that you're coming up on your three-month anniversary. I take it you're still see-ing the human."

The throbbing behind my left eye started. "His name is Brandon Hanover and yes, we're still together. He's on assignment right now for his newspaper and why am I telling you something you already know?" I rubbed my face with one palm, resisting the urge to throw the phone across the room. "Jess, why are you bothering me? I've got work to do."

"No you don't." The invisible claws came out, ready to sink into my hide. "You've got nothing on your schedule at present and you need work. Coincidentally we need someone."

I didn't have to ask who "we" were.

"And if I say no?"

"You say no." I heard the shrug over the phone line. "But I thought you liked seeing justice done."

I glanced at the stack of unpaid bills on the desk. Good loving didn't keep the creditors away.

"Okay, give me the details." I grabbed up a pencil and a yellow legal pad.

"Small town about two hours south of Pittsburgh, name of Penscotta. You're going down to see Police Chief Carson. Dax Carson."

I chuckled. "Nice name. Sounds like a science-fiction hero."

Jesse's tone didn't shift. "He's on the Board of the local Pride and he has a problem."

"Something they can't handle on their own?" I kept the surprise out of my voice. If I recalled correctly it took a major event to ask for help from another Pride. We tended to keep as much as we could in-house for the sake of secrecy.

"A dead human." The slight scorn vibrated through the lines. "They want a neutral investigator because it's likely one of their own who did the killing." Her tone changed. "The Grand Council's been alerted and they're watching too. Bad for them, bad for us. Good for you."

I frowned. The Grand Council helped develop and direct policy for all the Prides, deciding what was best for the Felis as an entire species and leaving the local decisions to the individual Boards. Recently the Council had been alerted to the existence of half-breeds, thanks to my work, and was still discussing how to deal with them. The biggest worry was, as with the Winters case, of an orphaned or abandoned Felis half-breed running free without any restraints or concerns about exposing the family to public scrutiny.

Killing a human was a rare event in the Felis world. We avoided fighting with anyone other than other Felis on principle, our inherent feline skills giving us an edge few humans could match. If we had a beef we would walk away and risk being called cowards rather than take the chance we'd lose control and kill a human.

Now someone had lost control and we could all pay the price.

I rubbed the tip of my nose. "What's my fee?"

"Send me an email with your terms. We'll agree, pay and extract the money from the other Pride."

I couldn't suppress a grin. "So sure I'm not going to rip you off?"

"I know you, Reb. Better than you know yourself. Chief'll meet you at the airport." The line went dead.

I dropped the handset back into the cradle and glared at the ticket. Jazz hopped up onto the table and strode across the envelope to headbutt me, forehead to forehead. My little sister always had a way of helping me feel better.

"Yeah. This is going to suck."

It took me a few minutes to start the kettle boiling for a fresh pot of tea, during which I went over my options.

I could shred the ticket. I had no obligation to the Pride that had thrown me out like trash so many years ago. Jess had no way of making me take this case; there was nothing she could offer me or threaten me with.

But a man was dead.

If I didn't try to find the killer, no one would. Carson might be a good cop but he was both Felis and a Board member. If it got too close to someone important in the Pride, he'd hide the evidence and bury the body forever. That's why the Grand Council wanted a neutral observer, someone without a stake in the hunt. Someone who wasn't afraid to drag one of our own into the light, no matter how blazing hot it could get.

That would be me.

I tossed the two teabags into the new Brown Betty, a replacement for the one I'd lost recently during a home invasion linked to the Winters case. Jazz trilled from below, winding through my feet.

"I know." I tossed her a handful of cat treats, the hard nuggets bouncing across the floor. "Don't say a word."

The kettle whistled and I filled the teapot, killing a few more seconds.

I went upstairs to start up the ancient monolith known as my home computer. It coughed and whined but carried me online without any problem.

Penscotta, Pennsylvania, was a little town sitting on the Monongahela River, an hour south of Pittsburgh. Built on the coal mining industry, it'd been socked with the same economic depression slamming into most of the state in the past few decades, pushing the town into survival mode. People bought cheap houses and commuted elsewhere to shop and work. High unemployment, medium crime and a lot of unhappiness. It was a common story in a lot of small towns, sad to say.

Despite the economic woes, Penscotta had a population of about ten thousand, enough to not only keep a police chief and his force busy but also to contain and nurture a Felis Pride.

I didn't bother trying to dig further about Carson. The information I needed wasn't going to be found online. The family kept secrets better than, well, the "other" family.

I strode back to the kitchen and grabbed a mug from the pile in the sink to wash out. I felt wrong, out of sorts. It was like having an itch I couldn't reach but I wasn't sure if I wanted it scratched at all—once I started I just might not stop.

Grabbing a ginger snap cookie from the bag on the counter helped settle me for a minute. I jammed it into my mouth while waiting for the tap water to move from arctic cold to tepid warm.

I just couldn't get used to not being single. I hadn't been a social butterfly before, leaping from bed to bed, but the last few months with Bran had settled me and…unsettled me. Having to share my life with someone was a strange experience, something I hadn't ever prepared for.

When I left the farm, thrust into the foster care system, I'd been alone. I'd built my life as an outcast, romance novels and the occasional one-night stand my only release for any pent-up sexual tension. I didn't need anyone and didn't necessarily want anyone in my life.

Now I had Bran. He'd muscled his way into my world and didn't seem to be leaving anytime soon.

It was strange to not be alone. And frightening.

I grabbed another ginger snap before I wiped the mug dry and filled it with hot tea and a dash of milk.

Jazz let out another merp as I carried the warm

white ceramic mug to my desk and settled into the wooden chair.

The doorbell rang.

I headed for the front door, sure I'd find another messenger there with a brand-new Canadian passport. My right hand dug into the front pocket of my jeans and toyed with a two-dollar coin for a tip.

I swung the door open and held out the coin, the gold and silver disk shining in the morning light.

"Ooh." Brandon Hanover reached out and plucked the coin from my fingers. "I don't usually charge by the minute but in your case I could make an exception." He held up a thick padded envelope. "And I intercepted this in the front yard."

I scowled, letting him walk past me into the house. "I thought I had to sign for that. It's a damned passport. They're not supposed to give those away to anyone in the area."

"I have my ways. She was in a hurry." He dropped his satchel and leather duster on the couch. Jazz took no time jumping up and curling into a white ball on the soft black jacket. "So what do you need a passport for?"

"Jess wants me to go down to Pennsylvania and help out a police chief with a murder investigation." I pointed at the envelope on my desk. "Plane tickets, and you've got my freshly printed passport."

He tilted his head and shot a grin at me, the red hair and obvious Irish heritage threatening to take me down without so much as a move on his part. "Now you're their lapdog?"

The hairs on the back of my neck snapped to attention. "Not."

Brandon smiled and moved toward me. "And not even a kiss for me being away on assignment for so long?" His white dress shirt had mustard stains dotting down the front like an avant-garde tie.

"You were gone for two weeks," I grumbled.

"A lifetime for some people." His hand cupped my chin, pulling me up to look at him. "I missed you."

A flash of panic ran through me when I realized how much I'd missed him. Two weeks of moping around the suddenly too-large house. I'd refused to wash the sheets, not wanting to wipe his scent away.

I had it bad.

I turned my face away, hoping he hadn't seen the shock on my face. "Still not forgiven for the lapdog crack."

"Ah, well. Your loss." He released me and then looked down at Jazz. "Let me try my charm out on you. You been behaving yourself?"

I let out a snort. "She threw up twice on the kitchen floor. Hairballs the size of a streetcar."

Bran bent down and stroked her thick, bushy fur, encouraging the old girl to roll onto her back and demand a tummy rub. She let out a trill and curved into a half circle.

"I see I'll have to work a bit harder for your mistress's affections." He dug into his satchel. "How about some authentic, fresh-off-the-plane Montreal smoked meat?"

The man knew my weaknesses.

My nose twitched, seeking out the rich smoked spices.

I swallowed when he flipped open the bag and pulled out a small insulated pouch. Sure, I could buy some from my local grocery store, but nothing like the real thing, fresh and ready to be slapped on rye with a splash of mustard.

"Straight from the deli on Saint-Laurent Boulevard." He held the foil package over his head, a devilish smile spreading on his face. "Forgiven?"

"Maybe." My mouth started watering, betraying me. "Gimme."

He raised one eyebrow. "Forgiven?"

I crossed my arms and pouted.

"Don't do that." He laughed and handed it to me. "Surprised you didn't smell me a mile away with this, wrapped up or not."

I pulled the pouch open and inhaled deeply. "I was busy being Jess's lapdog."

Bran wrinkled his nose. "I'm not sure I'm happy with you taking work from them."

Anger spiked in my gut, spilling over into my words. "I'm not sure I'm happy with the way you just said that."

I didn't bare my teeth. I didn't have to.

His eyes went wide. Bran took a step back and lifted his hands in surrender. He looked over at my mug. "Tea still hot?"

"Help yourself." I followed him into the kitchen and put the smoked meat into the near-empty refrigerator. The flash of annoyance vanished, replaced by embarrassment.

This wasn't me. I didn't snap like this before.

I drew a deep breath, trying to center myself.

I didn't know who I was anymore.

It took only a few minutes for him to make up his own cup, adding a squeeze of honey from the bottle on the counter and passing on the milk.

I leaned back on the counter and watched him, letting my temper settle.

The white dress shirt worked to escape his jeans on one side, tempting me to grab the loose fabric and do something with it.

I licked my lips. It'd been a long two weeks.

"Quiet workday?" Bran studied me over the top of his mug. His brown eyes caught mine. It wasn't a retreat; it was a move-and-regroup before the next attack.

"Quiet enough that I have to take Jess's assignment." I glanced at the dishes in the sink, suddenly feeling guilty they were there. "Bills are piling up and I need to work."

"I can spot you if you'd like." He added more milk

to the half-empty mug. "If you really don't want to take the job I'll carry you until something comes up."

I shook my head. "A man's dead and if I don't check it out nothing's probably going to be done about it. I can't let that happen." I rubbed the back of my neck, pushing down the thin hairs. "I don't need your money."

It came out sharper than I'd intended, slicing the air between us.

"I wasn't offering to support you for the rest of your life." He stared at the floor. "This isn't exactly what I'd planned after being away for two weeks."

"I'm sorry." I rubbed my eyes. "I'm just, I'm still getting used to us being...us."

He took a sip of hot tea and placed the mug on the counter. "Us?"

"This. You, me, together." I flapped my hands in the air. "I'm just not used to having someone in my life."

He crossed his arms, a confused look on his face. "Don't you want me here?"

"Yes, God yes," I said. "I just don't... I just don't play well with others." I sighed. "Does that make sense?"

"Yes and no." A mischievous look came into his eyes. "But now that you've mentioned playing, why don't we discuss this in a more appropriate location?"

Without warning he grabbed me around the waist and lifted me up over his shoulder, his hands tight on the backs of my legs. "Let's see if I can apologize better in bed."

"I have work to do," I weakly protested. "I've got a flight to pack for. It leaves in three hours."

"Then I'll be fast." The muffled reply against my thigh was accentuated by a slap. "Now let me grovel like a good little boy on my hands and knees."

TWO

AN HOUR LATER Jazz padded her way across the bed, making sure to step on every soft spot and joint on both of us before settling up by my head in a purring ball of fur.

"Ugh." Bran rolled over to face the ceiling. "That's getting old."

I patted the elderly cat and sat up. "She's an old gal. She gets to do what she wants."

"Okay, but the first time she stomps on my 'special bits,' I reserve the right to scream like a girl and ban her from the bed."

I rolled my eyes as I swung my feet off the bed, leaving the sheet behind. "She's not likely to hit such a small target."

Bran mimicked an arrow thudding into his chest.

"Drama queen." I jerked a thumb toward the bathroom. "Sit here and pout or help me pack." I waited a minute for dramatic effect. "After I shower."

He sprung to his feet, tossing the sheets everywhere. Jazz let out an annoyed trill when the mattress rocked under her.

I couldn't help admiring his sleek form as he

grinned at me, his hands on his hips without an ounce of awkwardness at his nudity. His red hair stood up in peaks, giving him a punk look.

"I assume I'm forgiven."

"For now." I headed for the shower. "I still have to figure out what I'm going down to Pennsylvania for."

"For?"

"Nothing is ever what it seems where the Felis are involved. Wheels within wheels."

"You think the cops are bad?" Brandon strode into the shower stall and reached for the hot water tap. He twisted it hard, sending steamy tentacles all around the small bathroom.

"Maybe not bad, but definitely plagued by divided loyalties. If he's the chief for the town and a Board member, that's got to be a handful and a half when it comes to keeping peace on both sides of the line." I sighed, exhausted at the mere thought of traveling. "I'll need you to take care of Jazz." I stepped under the hot spray and reached for the bar of soap. "I don't mind leaving barrels of food out for her but I'd like someone to check in with her and make sure she hasn't run out of water or knocked something over and caused a mess."

The hand brushing against the small of my back stilled. "Do you want me to come along?"

I turned, suddenly feeling very much crowded in the stall. "I thought you had a story to write?"

Bran shrugged and plucked the soap from my

hand. He rubbed the sliver between his palms, generating a handful of foam. "I can write anywhere. There's this thing called a laptop and wireless internet."

I chewed on my lip, studying the water dribbling down the drain between our feet.

"But you don't want me down there with you, right?"

I turned back around and lifted my face to the strong streaming water. "It's nothing personal. I mean, I missed you too. I don't want to go away right after you get back."

His soapy hands moved over my back, the strong fingers tracing my scars. "But it's Felis business and you don't want to show up in strange territory with a strange human."

I flinched, but not from his touch. "You're catching on to this political stuff a lot faster than I thought you would."

"Doesn't mean I have to like it." Bran spun me around, hands gripping my waist. "But I'll respect it. How about a compromise? I'll stay home for a day or two finishing up the story and taking care of Jazz, and then I'll come down." His dark brown eyes locked with mine. "I'll relocate her to my condo. She'll be safe at my place."

A few months ago I'd had a home invasion connected to the case that brought us together. Jazz hadn't been hurt but I still hated leaving her alone even for overnights at Bran's.

I let out a contented sigh. "Don't you have another assignment yet?"

"Not until I turn this one in. And I can afford to take a break. Maybe there's a freelance story waiting in Pinata."

"Penscotta."

"Whatever." His head dipped down, teeth nipping at my neck. "Okay?"

"Ah." I realized I'd lost the argument before we'd even stepped into the shower. "Okay."

"Good. Now let me show you how to survive a TSA security scan."

FIVE HOURS LATER I stood in a Pittsburgh airport and wondered exactly what god I'd tweaked to inflict so much excitement into my otherwise boring life in such a short time.

People surged by me as I stood there with my duffle bag at my feet. One man raced by, sweating exclamation marks of fear. Two women sauntered down the hall, their perfumes battling for dominance. A mother with a baby in a stroller stalled by the washroom, the baby in dire need of a diaper change and whining in a high-pitched tone.

I spotted Carson before he spotted me, his uniform sticking out like a sore thumb in the middle of all the travelers.

His nose twitched as he approached. I knew what he saw. A blonde woman just barely over five feet high with indistinct, generic features—not homely but not drop-dead gorgeous either. Cold steel for eyes and copping a definite attitude. I crossed my arms and waited for him to approach me.

The long leather coat, a recent present from Bran, helped my image. First impressions were important but doubly so for Felis. The animal was never far from the surface.

The stout man walked up to me. "Miss Desjardin?"

I nodded.

Carson stretched out his hand. "Dax Carson. Pleased to meet you." His eyes were a shade of darker blue, verging on navy. The uniform jacket was tight over his belly but well worn on the elbows.

He squeezed my fingers in a classic show of Felis strength.

I held my own, gritting my teeth as I worked through the pain.

He released my hand. "Jess said nothing but good things 'bout you. Hope you can help us."

I hoped the first was the truth. I wasn't sure about the second.

"My car's over here." He picked up my duffle and hoisted it onto his shoulder, the fluorescent lights bouncing off his bald pate. "You travel light."

"You've got stores down here, don't you?" I

grinned. "I don't mind contributing to your local economy."

Carson laughed a deep, rolling belly laugh. "And we appreciate your money. It'll be about an hour's drive down to the hotel, so I can brief you on the way."

We hit the highway, and the trappings of civilization fell away within a few minutes. Nothing but a cement road and trees, trees, trees.

It was glorious. I took deep breaths, inhaling a thousand scents and smells, the local flora and fauna smashing into my senses.

I'd forgotten how much fun the wilderness was. A good run through the forest at dawn, maybe stop and grab a rabbit for brekka.

My back ached, forcing me to squirm in the uncomfortable generic cop car passenger seat and reminding me why I didn't do morning hunts anymore.

"I've got you a room at the Super 6 Hotel. It's comfortable and got good room service, not too far out of town. Hope you don't mind small rooms." He scratched his chin as he swerved from lane to lane. The siren and lights weren't on but traffic parted around us out of fear. "The body's still in the morgue. Family's in Ohio and still making funeral plans, so we have a bit of a window before we have to ship it out."

"Jess wasn't too forthcoming with all the details. Let's take it from the top." I winced as a pickup truck jumped from lane to lane in front of us, an NRA bumper sticker about to fly off the tailgate and slap us in the face.

Without taking his eyes off the road Carson reached down and pulled out a file folder from a thick stash rammed beside his seat. He handed it to me.

I flipped it open to see a color photograph of a dead man. The deep gouges across his neck went almost to the spine, giving him a second mouth.

What was left of his bare chest gaped open, giving me an almost clinical view of his internal organs. The claws had ripped across his ribcage, the scratched bones clear evidence of the vicious attack. The photographs continued a gory expedition through the insides of a human body.

"Dead man's name is Michael Hansa. Died of blood loss, shock, fill in the blank for your horrific death of choice. We're reporting it as a bear attack."

"Wait. Bear?" The word stuck in my throat. I lifted a hand and flexed my fingers. "As in, a bear?"

"Yep." The patrol car slid between a pair of tractor trailers with ease. "Fortunately for us we've had bears in the area before, even had one or two relocated when they got into peoples' garbage and caused a fuss." He shrugged. "Claw marks are claw marks are claw marks."

"Yes, yes they are." I shook off bad memories. "Why couldn't you scent the body? You should have been able to identify the Felis who did this within a few seconds."

Carson chuckled. "Michael Hansa worked at a nightclub as a stripper."

"Oh." I felt my cheeks go hot.

"Club's pretty popular with the Pride's women."

I saw where this was leading. "So he's got all sorts of Felis trace over him."

"Oh, yeah." Carson chortled as we pulled off the highway onto a side road. "At least a dozen. I've made up a list." He poked a finger toward the official file. "It's at the back, clipped to the folder."

Which made it easy to remove, the unspoken words went, when it moved into the official filing cabinet.

I couldn't blame the chief—it'd be hard to explain to any non-Felis law enforcement how a list of women ended up on the suspect roll call because of their scent on a dead man.

The car slowed down enough to let me crack the window without my hair flying all over the place. The vibrant spring colors and smells offset the migraine starting behind my left eye.

A murdered stripper who was popular with the ladies. Ladies being Felis women who wouldn't be happy about being questioned about visits to the club. Felis women being the nastiest, back-biting-est species on the planet when it came to claiming and keeping their territory and their secrets.

There was a reason why it was called cat fighting.

"Oh, and I have to add that my wife's among the female suspects."

I considered throwing the door open and jumping. It'd be a fast death if I was lucky.

"Your wife?"

Carson shrugged. "She likes to go out with the girls to the club. We've got an arrangement—she gets to go to her club and I get to go to mine." His teeth were blindingly white and perfect as he smiled. "It works for us."

We pulled onto an even smaller road and cruised by a sign proudly proclaiming Penscotta, The Town with Heart.

"Where would you like to go first?" Carson slowed down and nodded to a pair of boys on bikes. "Morgue, crime scene, Hansa's apartment?"

I looked at the sky. Still enough blue to call it daytime. "Let's hit the crime scene first."

"And the crime scene is…"

"The nightclub."

"Of course." I resisted the urge to test the door and see if it was locked.

We turned off onto a side street. A second and third turn put us in an industrial area with warehouses and short, squat buildings lining the road.

"Not that close to town."

The chief nodded. "When the owners came into town a year ago and proposed the idea half the town was up in arms. The other half saw it as a great money-maker. Compromise was to put it out in the industrial parks so that you had to work to get there and kids could be kept away."

"Has it worked?

"As best as could be expected." He whistled through his teeth. "It's brought in money for the town. And plenty of employment for locals."

"Hansa a local?"

Carson shook his head. "None of the dancers are locals. Management figured it'd be good to out-source, get people who you weren't likely to have dated or gone to school with."

"Not a bad idea," I replied. "Could make it awkward to see your former teacher shaking it up on the stage."

"I don't know." Carson gave me a wide grin. "I wouldn't mind seeing some of my old teachers up there."

"And Hansa?" I brought the conversation back down to reality. "Where did he come from?"

"Hansa moved in three months ago. Came over from Columbus, Ohio."

"Who found the body?"

"Karl Rice. Veteran patrolman, was doing the usual nightly sweep of the area." He shifted in his seat. "He's not family. He radioed in an animal attack, called the ambulance, and I came running. You know the rest."

I nodded, keeping my thoughts to myself. If it hadn't been a human finding the body Mike Hansa might have become one of the missing, disappearing into the woodwork without a trace.

The family kept secrets, no matter the consequences.

We drove into a parking lot next to a large warehouse. The garish blue and yellow neon cartoon cat's face winked at us. Flowing letters spelled out Cat's Meow in the same color scheme.

"You've got to be kidding me." I got out of the car and stared at the flashing lights. It was just dark enough for the bold colors to wash over us in a never-ending flash dance.

"Sort of an inside joke. Owner's not even Felis. She came up with that on her own. No one tried to stop her." Carson stepped around the vehicle. "It's closed tonight, sort of a memorial to Hansa."

"I'm touched." There was a pink teddy bear sitting against the locked red double doors and a handful of burnt-out candles with melted white wax cementing them to the ground. "Where did it happen?"

"Out back by the Dumpster." He pulled the large flashlight from his belt and pointed it at the ground. A jab of his thumb sent the light disc skittering along the gravel. "Just 'round the corner."

I followed him to a green metal Dumpster tucked just behind one corner of the renovated warehouse.

The worn metal cube balanced precariously on warped wheels.

"Story is that the bear came to scrounge through the garbage." Carson tapped the edge of the Dumpster with his flashlight. "Leave the lid open and lots of wild things come a-calling."

I frowned. "Where's the…" I gestured wildly, trying to find the right word.

"Yellow tape? Fingerprint dust?" Carson shook his head. "It was a bear attack. Ain't no crime scene for a bear attack."

I rolled my eyes. Any evidence here had probably been compromised to the point of uselessness. Bitten again by the need for secrecy.

"We found him about here." Carson stepped over to the edge of the curb where the concrete ran out and the short grass began. "You can see a bit of the blood there."

I knelt down where a few puddles of dried blood stained the grass. The dirt was saturated, the few strands of untouched grass pleading for relief.

"We figure the bear came out of the woods to scrounge in the Dumpster and ran into Hansa out here for a smoke break between shifts," Carson said, his voice a bit too loud for casual conversation.

I caught the human scent when the wind changed.

"That's too bad." I looked up to see the two women walking toward us, swaying as one on matching delicate stilettos.

"Police Chief Carson." The first woman offered her hand. She was an older woman in her late forties, wearing a dark blue power suit. "I called the station and they said you were at the airport meeting someone important." Her dark eyes narrowed as she zeroed in on Carson. "Then I drive by here and see your car in the parking lot."

"Mayor Langstrom." Carson straightened up. It wasn't quite a snap-to-attention but it was evident who topped whom.

"Hello, I'm Dale Langstrom." She ignored Carson and offered me her hand. I stood up, reflexively wiping my hands on the leather coat.

"Rebecca Desjardin." It was a replay of the handshake at the airport. Except she wasn't Felis and seemed to have bigger balls.

"And you are…" She tilted her head to one side and leaned in.

"Insurance investigator." I pointed at the club. "Mr. Hansa had a life insurance policy."

Her forehead furrowed. "You investigate bear attacks?"

"Oh, yes. I mean, it's obviously an accidental death but we always like to check these things out in person, especially when it's something so unusual." I smiled, putting on my best bored and blank expression. "It's just a matter of paperwork. We're curious as to whether Mr. Hansa had any part in his death."

"Like rubbing raw meat all over himself?" The second woman stepped forward, glaring at me.

I chuckled. "Not quite. If he was drunk or under the influence of illegal drugs and taunted the bear or something along those lines it would go into my report."

"And you wouldn't pay out to the recipient?" Langstrom asked.

"Oh, no. We'll be paying regardless. A man has died, after all." I held up my hand, stalling another question. "It's just the paper pushers who like their statistics. How many die each year from this sort of thing, what were they doing and all that. Helps out when they do up the yearly reports for the shareholders to have as many variables covered as possible."

I studied the second stranger. She was a shade taller than me, rocking back and forth on ankle-breakers, hands stuffed in the front pockets of her jeans. I didn't immediately dislike her but I knew she'd be trouble. "And you are?"

"Cassie Prosser." She didn't offer her hand. "I run the local paper. Editor-in-chief, top reporter, whatever you want to call it." She jerked her head toward Langstrom. "Came by and saw her pull into the parking lot beside the police car. Figured there might be a story here." Her upper lip twitched. "Other than a bear attack."

"Ah." I didn't have to be Felis to feel the hatred rolling off her in waves. She didn't like me and she didn't like Carson. She barely tolerated the mayor. "Did either of you know Mr. Hansa?"

Langstrom drew back. "No." The words worked their way out through clenched teeth. "I never come here and don't plan to start."

"What company did you say you worked for?" Prosser snapped at me.

"I didn't." I looked at Carson. There wasn't anything to be gained by pissing too many people off the first few hours in town. "I think I'm done here." I nodded to the pair. "Ladies."

The police chief didn't say anything as I headed for the parking lot, leaving him behind.

I leaned on the hood of the cop car for a few minutes, listening to the bickering around the corner. There were times when having extra-sensitive hearing sucked, especially when living in a big noisy city.

This wasn't one of those times.

"Who is she?" Langstrom hissed.

"She told you," Carson answered.

"Bullshit. Did you check her credentials? The last thing we need is some goddamn tabloid reporter sneaking around looking for some gossip. We've worked too hard to have this screwed up by some trashy exposé looking for small-town smut."

I couldn't help smiling at the irony, given that I'd met Bran when he was working for the *Toronto Inquisitor*, a rag that put the "oy" in tabloid. My skin tingled, eager for his touch. I gave myself a shake and kept listening.

"I checked. She's legit." Carson held his ground. "She's only going to file a report and get the paperwork done for the family to collect the money."

I heard Langstrom grinding her teeth. "I didn't want this business here in the first place and I sure as hell don't need any trouble. She gets in, she gets her information and she gets out of town. I'm holding you responsible for this."

Prosser interrupted the mayor's rant. "Are we sure it was a bear attack? If she says different it's going to be big news." There was a hopeful lilt in her voice as if she wanted me to find otherwise.

I filed Cassie Prosser away under "trouble" in my mental cabinet. If she suspected there was more to Hansa's death, I might have a war on two fronts. Maybe Carson's Pride hadn't been as secretive as they thought they were.

Carson's low, calm drawl was like pouring honey on panicked ants. "She's nothing to worry about. No one cares about a bear attack and it's all going away in a few days. Won't be reflecting negatively on the town."

"It better not." The click-click of Langstrom's expensive shoes stung my ears. "I'm trying to save this town. I won't have some rag printing stuff about dead strippers and killing even more investment opportunities. This damned club…"

She came around the corner, ignoring me as she headed for her car. A second later Prosser followed, climbing into her own dark red Jeep.

The dark sedan spun out of the parking lot. The Jeep followed, spewing gravel at us as it fishtailed back onto the paved road.

Carson strolled toward me. He shook his head and spat on the ground.

I jerked a thumb at the disappearing vehicles. "Small-town love."

"Yep." He pushed back his uniform cap. "Dale's pissed 'cause the club brings in money to the area but it's not a respectable business. Cassie's pissed 'cause she put the paper against the club and lost. Hansa's death is the worst possible thing right now to hit this town—animal attack or not, it's going to make news and there's no way to spin it good."

"Neither one of them are family."

He tilted his head to one side with a sly grin. "Nope."

"Could have surprised me." I got inside the car. "Got enough claws and fangs."

Carson pulled out onto the empty street. "Nice one about the investigation."

I shrugged. "I've done some insurance work so it's not a total lie. They can check me out and it'll stick."

It was getting dark. And by dark I don't mean different shades of grey. I mean pitch-black, grab-the-cute-guy-next-to-you-for-support black, deep

mine shaft black. If I took my eyes off the road illu-
minated by the car's headlights, it was like looking
into a black hole.

"Next?" Carson asked.

"How about the morgue." I squinted into the wilderness, waiting for my night vision to kick in. "Still
open?"

"They never close." Carson laughed at his own
joke. He plucked his cell phone from his pocket.
"Henry? Hey, yeah. Listen, I've got the PI here and
she'd like to see the body now." He paused a minute.
"Cool. We'll be there in a few."

A scattering of streetlights led us to the hospital,
a small three-story building I would have mistaken
for another warehouse if not for the large H signs
all over the place. A helipad circle on the front lawn
convinced me we were in the right place.

It was a radical shift from the busy downtown
hospitals I was used to. No screaming ambulances,
no hysterical hookers screaming for their pimps, no
strung-out addicts looking for a fast hit.

It was like going from a hundred miles an hour
to zero without an airbag.

"This way." He pulled into the single handicapped
spot in front of the sliding double doors. "We'll go
through the emergency. They lock all the other doors
after sunset."

The receptionist looked up from her newspaper
as we walked through the empty waiting room and

toward the elevator. She nodded at Carson and gave me a quick once-over.

"She's with me." Carson stabbed the button. "Going to see Henry."

"Have a good night." The elderly woman picked up a pencil and began working on the math puzzle.

The elevator doors opened and we got in. I couldn't help smiling—the surreal atmosphere was killing me.

"Quiet town," I said, stifling the urge to giggle.

The elevator lurched as we began to descend.

"Yep." He took off his uniform cap and ran his hand over his bald pate. "The worst we get is DUIs when the local university starts up. Murder isn't exactly our forte."

The doors shuddered open. We walked out onto cold concrete floors that hadn't seen paint in the past decade. The grey scabs followed us down the corridor, dodging in and out with bare cement.

"Henry's the coroner and one of us. So don't be afraid to ask the tough questions," Carson said as we approached a set of double doors.

"Good." The last thing I needed right now was to worry about parsing my words.

Henry turned out to be a senior who could have been my grandfather. A small crown of white hair hovered over bright blue eyes that screamed elderly wisdom. He clucked his tongue as he led us to the examination table, hands tucked into the pristine white hospital coat.

"Soon as I heard you was coming down I pulled him out of the freezer. Didn't cut him up or anything, wanted you to see him as good as the pictures. As soon as you're done I'll do the official autopsy." A yank brought the white sheet flying off, bunching at the corpse's feet. "He's a bit cold so don't mistake the skin color."

I blinked. I'd been in morgues before, seen dead bodies, but this one…this one made me glad I'd eaten before leaving Toronto. The Montreal smoked meat sandwich seemed a long, long way away right now.

"Healthy as a horse. Dead as a doorknob." He winked at me. "Enough metaphors for you?"

"Maybe." I looked down at the naked man. Chewing on my bottom lip helped hold back my combination of curiosity and dismay as my eyes headed south of his waist, seeking some area of unmarked skin to steady myself away from the mutilated torso.

He was amply qualified for the position of exotic dancer. Maybe even overqualified.

I swallowed back a giggle, glad it wasn't the smoked meat sandwich returning. "Let me guess the cause of death."

Henry raised an eyebrow as I pointed at the deep gouges across the body, still gaping open. "You're a smart one."

"That's why they pay me the big bucks." I steeled

myself, leaned in and took a sniff. Carson was right. More scents than I had fingers. I could identify Carson and the coroner, but that wasn't surprising considering they'd both had to handle the body.

There were also a scattering of human traces, both male and female, but they didn't concern me.

Mr. Hansa had been a busy, busy little boy.

"If you asked me to say which cut was the lethal one, I couldn't tell you." Henry shook his head. "The throat might have been the first or the last. Either way he bled out quickly enough once the cut was made." His long slender fingers hovered over the destroyed skin. "It was a clumsy attack, this first one. Maybe in the heat of passion or anger. Sloppy. Just enough to start the blood flowing but not much weight behind it."

"Then she picked up the pace and hit him again, deeper and harder," I murmured. "Bloodlust or panic, passion or fear." I studied the wounds again. "Was it a fast death?" I envisioned the man falling to his knees, trying to stem the flow of blood as it gushed out between his numbing fingers.

Henry frowned, his tongue rolling over his bottom lip with a low whistle. "Couldn't say. It'd take a few minutes but I can't say he was conscious or not. There's a nasty smack on the back of his head from when he hit the ground; could have knocked him out before he knew what happened." He pressed his lips together before continuing. "I only hope he was out before she started on his belly. Doesn't get more painful than that."

"Can you roll him over, please?" I didn't touch the body.

Henry took hold of the man's hip and shoulder, expertly rolling him halfway.

There were no bruises or footprints on Hansa's back. It was pure bronzed skin, unmarred and pristine. I knew it was a long shot to hope he'd have a specific shoe-size imprint on his back or the tattooed name of his Felis lover, but stranger things had happened.

"No tats. Guy kept himself in shape," I murmured. "Probably hit the tanning salon three times a week." I resisted the urge to reach out and stroke the smooth skin.

"Except for that dying thing he's in great condition," Henry quipped. We shared a quick grin.

Henry glanced over to the side where Carson stood. "Okay to clean him up now? His family's not going to want him looking like this. Sew him up, make him respectable and all that."

Carson looked at me.

"Give me one more look." I winced as we turned the body back over, the stiff flesh falling back on the cold metal table.

I studied the deep gouges and gashes in his flesh, the discolored edges starting to turn grey. He'd been sliced to pieces, no doubt about that.

Now I just needed to find the claws that did it.

I stretched out my hand, imagining the Felis claws jutting out from between my knuckles. Long, sharp nails much like your average house cat, like Jazz sitting back in my house and demanding treats from her obedient house slave Brandon.

The deep incisions didn't match exactly but they were close enough. An angry attack, as well. Nothing clean about this, nothing planned. Emotional, savage and intense.

I nodded. "Go ahead—I've got the photos in his file. Thanks for holding him on ice."

Henry's attention went from me to Carson and back again. He cleared his throat, pulling my attention away from the body.

"I heard that you, ah—" He frowned as he fumbled for words. "I heard you couldn't Change."

"Nope." My stomach twitched, wrestling again with the half-digested sandwich. I closed my hand into a fist. "Is that going to be a problem?"

Henry chuckled. "Take more than that to spook me, kit. But I had to ask. Just sort of curious about it all." He pulled off the blue latex gloves and rubbed the tip of his nose. "From a medical point of view it's interesting to me." He licked his lips. "Any chance we can talk sometime in the future about it?"

"Sure. But it'll have to wait until I'm done here. Then we can sit and chat and I'll give you all the blood samples you want."

He grinned like I'd given him a precious gift. "Thank you. I know it may seem sort of morbid but I'd like to see if this is hereditary. It might skip generations and it'd be interesting to track this back and see if there's any other cases 'round the country."

My mind raced back to my parents, dead for many years. "Ah, you'll have to check with Jess on that. She's got all the bloodline records." I rolled my shoulders, feeling the scarred tissue pull and tense. "I never knew it happened to anyone else."

"Well, so far I haven't found any other cases." Henry gave me a grandfatherly smile. "But that doesn't mean it hasn't happened. And if we can find a cure, well…"

I opened my mouth to say something and stopped, my stomach churning with a mixture of fear and panic. All I could cough out was a mumbled mouthful of words in support.

Henry nodded. "Thank you." He gestured at the sterile, empty room. "There's not a lot of people doing medical research on problems inside the family. I know it's a sore spot but we have to get the information."

"Like knowing we can breed with humans." That bit of revelation had come at the cost of one woman's life and two families shattered with the news.

He nodded, wearing a sad, knowing smile. "Yes."

I turned to Carson. "My…difficulty. Is this going to be a problem for you?"

He shrugged. "Jess said you were the best for the job so I don't care. Hell, you could still have your tail and I'd want your help on this."

Henry pulled the sheet up over Hansa's face. "Crime is a crime. Justice needs to be done."

"Right." I shook my head. "As long as we're all on the same wavelength. Where's his personal effects?"

Henry pointed at a transparent plastic bag on the far counter. "I'm no cop but I can tell you he wasn't killed for his money."

I pawed over the contents after receiving a nod from Carson. Wallet with all his identification and a hundred dollars in small bills, handful of wrapped candies, a receipt from the local gas station, car keys.

"Where's his car?" I shook the bag, listening to the jingle. "And no cell phone?"

"Still in the parking lot when we found him. Now it's in the police impound lot," Carson answered. "And we didn't find any cell phone on him or nearby. Guess the bear took it." He didn't crack a smile.

"Anyone call the cell?"

"Out of service. I figure the phone's already in a landfill somewhere." Carson scratched his chin. "Bet he kept a lot of information on it, which is why it disappeared."

"Yeah." I glanced at the sheet-covered body. "Damned things these days can hold everything from videos to text messages to books."

Carson nodded. "Where to now?"

I spotted the generic office clock hanging over a set of stainless steel cabinets. It was just past nine o'clock.

"I'm ready for the hotel now." I wanted to sit and read the file, process what I had so far before tearing into Hansa's apartment. There was no use in going in guns blazing if I had no idea of what I was looking for.

Not to mention dumping my police escort. He was a nice guy but he had his own reasons for finding Hansa's killer—and they could crash into mine at any minute. Pride justice often had very different goals and punishments than the justice system humans used. My scars were proof enough of that.

"Roger that." Carson touched his index finger to the brim of his cap. "'Night, Henry."

The coroner tucked his hands into the lab coat pockets. "'Night, Dax." His bright blue eyes met mine. "Call me if you need anything."

We walked back through the empty emergency room and into the parking lot. The streetlights highlighted the handicapped parking sign.

"Why did you call Jess?" I stepped around to the passenger side of the car. "Could have gotten others to help. State, federal cops." I knew we had family in law enforcement and almost every area of life. There was no restriction on what you could do with your life as long as you kept what you were a secret.

Carson unlocked the door with his key fob. "I

heard 'bout the problem you helped them with. Thought having you down here would help keep things above ground, keeping things honest. Keep it all above board without anyone questioning your loyalty."

Except to the Felis, my inner voice added.

"The other Board members didn't give you a hard time?" The streetlights marched down the street in unison, tugging us along the empty concrete.

"Never seen a Pride operate without a lot of politics butting their way into everything," Carson replied. "As soon as I saw the body I knew there'd be trouble. Plussey and McCallum, they got all antsy as soon as I mentioned scenting April on the body. Wasn't like I could hide it—if I hadn't mentioned it Henry would have."

He cleared his throat. "We're not used to having murders in this town, much less a human by a Felis. Family's getting nervous, looking at each other strange. Bad business all 'round." He sucked his lower lip. "I'm not going to say everyone's happy with having you down here. Once word got out, some wanted to keep it internal, not even report it to the Grand Council. Get rid of the body and let things be."

"Would have been easier," I said. "Not right, but easier."

Carson tapped his badge. "Problem is, secrets never keep. Sometime, somewhere, story would come out. Best to nip that in the bud before it gets too far."

We pulled into the parking lot of a small hotel tucked just off the main highway we'd come in on, a scattering of cars filling the slots. A giant neon sign announced the Super 6 Hotel with the stereotypical flashing Vacancy announcement. A single-level long, flat *L* stretched out into a grove of trees barely visible from the handful of safety lights at the emergency exit doors.

Continuing his previous habit of chivalry, the chief carried my duffle into the lobby of the hotel and placed it by the front desk. "Can I get you anything before we turn in for the night?"

"Right now, food and sleep." The sandwich had been good but it wouldn't hold me until morning. An evening snack would help me focus on the task ahead and banish the last vestiges of the morgue.

"That we can do. Order what you want from room service. You're fully comped. They make a great Italian hoagie." He patted his belly. "I can testify to that."

"Good." I smiled. "Whatever a hoagie is."

"I think it's what you call a submarine sandwich. Ernie, here's the lady I made the reservation for," Carson said to the young man behind the counter. His eyes went wide as he looked from me to the police chief and back again. A bit of peach fuzz on his chin signaled his triumphant entry into manhood, probably last week.

"Young kit," Carson said in a stage whisper. "First real job."

The kid licked his lips, his cheeks turning a bright pink.

"Well, I like 'em young." I stepped forward and took the cardkey from his hand, enjoying the mixture of terror and sudden lust in his eyes. "But not that young."

Carson laughed as I picked up my bag. "Oh, the Board's going to love meeting you tomorrow."

THREE

I LOOKED AT him. "The Board?"

"Board meeting tomorrow morning at nine. I'll pick you up at eight-thirty; take you to the diner where we have breakfast." He headed for the door. "Just want to lay down a few ground rules and all that."

He vanished into the night.

My good nature disappeared in a burning flash of annoyance, centered in my chest. The kit, sensing my change of mood, busied himself with the crossword puzzle in the newspaper spread across the desk.

"Please send one of those hoagies and some cola to my room," I snapped before heading down the hall.

My room wasn't far from the lobby and within minutes I was busy booting up my laptop. My duffel waited patiently on the bed while I snarled at the free wireless taking forever to connect.

Pride politics. It never changed. Meetings, committees and discussions. Everything I despised wrapped up in a breakfast burrito of Felis fun.

A stack of fliers lay on the small table, advertising the local sights. A regional festival starting up this weekend, some sort of Ren Fair. A county fair going off in two weeks. An art gallery offering old photographs of the area.

The Cat's Meow was the last one, the full-page spread of the male dancers posed as provocatively as they could without being obscene. A middle-aged redhead stood in the center, drawing her long pink fingernails across multiple arms and pecs, just hard enough to draw red streaks on the bare skin. I read the listing at the bottom, curious who she was.

Sophia Martin, the owner of the club. I'd look that happy too if I were surrounded by gorgeous men like that day in and day out, tanned and oiled skin by the square foot.

Almost made me want to switch occupations.

I spotted a familiar face in the crowd.

Mike Hansa stood beside her wearing a grin and a g-string the size of a computer mouse covering his privates.

He looked a lot better alive.

A knock came at the door. I frowned and checked my watch.

Either the hotel employed the fastest cooks alive or someone had come calling—and I doubted it was the Welcome Wagon.

I peeked through the eyehole.

Dale Langstrom stood there, still wearing her power suit and looking like I'd just peed on her leg.

I opened the door a crack. "Can I help you?"

Her deep ruby lips pulled back over ivory white teeth. "I need to talk to you."

I paused for a second before swinging the door open, just long enough to see her left cheek twitch with annoyance. "Come on in."

I strode over to the small office table and sat down in one of the two chairs.

She followed, settling herself opposite me.

I waited.

Ten seconds.

Twenty.

"I've got food coming. I wasn't planning to share." I studied my fingernails, making a mental note to cut them when I got home.

"I ran a fast check on you. You're from Canada." She pronounced it kah-nah-dah.

"Yep." The mini-bar was within reach. I wondered if my comp included draining every bottle and can inside.

"You're a private investigator."

"Yep."

She chewed on her lower lip for a second, threatening to smear the perfectly applied lipstick.

I checked my watch again.

"You're legit, according to my research." She drew a deep breath. "I hope you're here for the right reasons."

"I'm here about Mike Hansa's death."

It wasn't a lie.

She nodded. Her long manicured fingernails, painted bright pink, began to rattle on the tabletop. I resisted the urge to reach across and slap her hand down.

"I want you to know that we're a good town, good hard-working people."

"I never thought otherwise." I glanced at the door, feeling the first pangs of hunger.

Langstrom grabbed a loose strand of blond hair and wrapped it tight around her finger. "Do you think Mike's death was connected to the club?"

"He worked there. He died there." I chose my words carefully, negotiating the minefield. Some people might find it easy to lie but I'm not one of them. "I don't think he was targeted by the animal because he was a stripper." I put up my hand before she could reply. "And there's no reason for my report to say anything about the club or his occupation. As far as I'm concerned it's got nothing to do with his death."

The relief on her face almost snapped the makeup mask in half. A small, almost invisible bead of sweat appeared on her upper lip.

"We're good folk here," she repeated.

"Who have a strip club," I added, sitting back in my chair. My stomach rumbled but I wasn't going to pass up an opportunity to check some facts. "How does it stay open?"

Langstrom's expression changed from relieved to annoyed, a scowl stretching her botoxed skin. "They keep winning the votes. Five members on the council, three for a majority. Myself and Jan Redman keep voting to cancel their license. Other three keep voting to keep the club open."

"Because..."

"Because they think it'll lead to more business coming back." She crossed her legs, comfortable with political discussions. "They think people will start reopening stores and finding the money to spend on local products and employ local help." An angry toss of her head sent blond missiles flying around her. "Fools."

"You think it won't work."

"I think only a fool thinks stripping is going to bring in the type of business this town needs to survive." She checked her watch. "Excuse me. I've got to go. Early meeting tomorrow and I'm not allowed to be late." She stood up and brushed invisible wrinkles out of her power suit. "I'd appreciate if you let me know if you find anything before you take it public. Just call my office. They'll put you right through." She pulled out a business card and threw it across the table. "Don't take it personally but I'll be glad to see you go."

"I get a lot of that." I escorted her to the door.

The kit was there in the hallway, standing to one

side with a large cardboard box in one hand and a
bottle of pop in the other. I knew he'd been listening.

The mayor glared at him.

He held his ground and looked at me. The flash
of defiance in his eyes vanished as Langstrom took
another step forward and then he melted against the
wall, a young kid working his first job.

Langstrom strode by, her heavy steps echoing
down the hall as she headed for the lobby.

"Good work." I plucked the sandwich box and bottle from the kit's hands. "A wise man knows when
to give ground and when to take it."

The flash of pride in his eyes before I shut the
door made me smile. I knew he'd be on the phone
in a few minutes, reporting back to the Board about
the mayor's visit.

I put the box on the table and opened the bottle.
The mouthful of needed caffeine helped as I held off
attacking the sandwich for the few minutes I needed
to unpack.

I'd just finished hanging up a few clean blouses
when my cell phone went off. It was the latest model
with all the bells and whistles, another gift from
Bran.

"Hey." His mellow tone stroked over my annoyance and shushed it into silence.

"Hey."

"So, solved the case yet?"

I sighed. "I wish." It took a few minutes to fill him in, during which I sampled the monster sandwich.

Carson was right. Darned good. I mumbled something to that effect into the phone.

"Wait. Hotel food that's edible?"

I let out another sigh, this one of contentment. "Hot salami, pepperoni and Italian dressing all over my fingers. Damn. Tastes so good."

"I can think of something else I'd like to be tasting."

My cheeks burned. "Yeah, well. That's not happening for a few days."

"No phone sex?"

A mozzarella cheese bridge dipped and danced between the sandwich and my lips. "Dream on."

"Well, yeah." He chuckled. I could imagine him in his fancy condominium, stretched out on the black leather couch with television remote in hand. "By the way, Jazz loves to hog the sheets. Takes after you."

"You could always push her to one side."

"And hurt your sister's feelings? Never." His tone changed. "This sounds like a bad movie. A male stripper and plenty of Felis women pawing him over?"

"Don't forget to add in the welcome wagon of grumpy locals and a mayor who'd like to see me gone," I grunted through a mouthful of lettuce and tomato. "And tomorrow morning a Board meeting."

"Ouch." I could hear him wincing. "I know you love those."

"I live for it." The cell phone display blinked. "Damn. Jess is calling. I've got to take this."

"Phone sex?" The hopeful tone made me smile.

"With Jess? I'll ask her but I don't know if you're her type."

Bran snorted. "Spoilsport. I've got the first draft done and I'll call tomorrow night to see how things are going."

"Right. Love you."

"Love you too."

I tapped the tiny button and flipped connections.

Jess's gravelly voice killed my romantic mood. "Took you long enough."

"Had to give Bran a quickie," I deadpanned.

"Typical human. No stamina." I couldn't tell if she was serious or not. "I called to see how things were going."

I scoured the empty box, looking for any scraps. "I haven't solved it yet, if that's what you're asking."

"No." The smooth tone unnerved me. "I'm asking what you think about the situation."

"I think someone killed someone who didn't deserve to die." I drained the last of the soda from the plastic bottle. "Hansa being a male dancer sort of complicates things. Could have used that info before I flew down."

"Didn't think it was relevant. Besides, would you have changed your mind?"

I chewed on that for a second. "Probably not." I decided to cut through the crap before my meal turned sour in my stomach. "What's this call all about? I don't think you're calling to read me a good-night story."

"I understand you're going to a Board meeting to-morrow. I'd like you to report back to me what your feelings are on the situation down there."

I scowled. "You want me to spy for you. On another Pride."

"No." Jess's tone shifted from silk to steel. "There've been concerns from the other Boards about this group being a little too prominent in the area. Small town, large Pride."

I brushed a crumb off my shirt onto the grey carpet. "That's not their fault."

"To a degree, it is. They could force their kits to move away, head for a large city and blend in."

"Like you've done." I couldn't keep the snark out of my response.

"It's worked." Her voice shifted again. "Look, the police chief is on the Board. There's a Felis on the local council, one of five spots. They're not control-ling the politics down there but they're darned close with that setup."

I wrestled with a slice of lettuce stuck between my front bottom teeth. "There's no rules against Felis taking on public service jobs, if I recall correctly. We've got enough politicians and police at all levels."

"You remember right. But at a certain point you have to worry about priorities clashing. Like here," she said. "Police chief's wife is a suspect. Will he have the balls to turn her in if she did it? Is he going to destroy evidence to keep her safe?"

"Carson seems pretty straight to me." My words sounded weak to me.

A little voice in my head pointed out it'd been hours since the crime—if Carson was going to do anything like taint the crime scene or muck up the apartment he'd have done it long before picking me up at the airport.

"Carson's not the only one you have to worry about," Jess continued. "Hansa didn't kill himself. No matter which way you slice it there's a killer down there."

"And I'm starting way behind the rest of the pack."

In my mind's eye I could see Jess at her desk, tapping her long fingernails on the polished surface. "Just keep your eyes open at the Board meeting tomorrow. I'm not asking for a word-for-word transcript. Just keep an eye open and give me your thoughts on the situation. Good luck on finding out who killed the stripper." A trace of humor crept into her words. "Enjoy the research."

I cut the connection before my temper won out and I said something I regretted.

A few minutes of banging around the television dial found me nothing but outdated movies and bad porn.

The digital clock on the small side table caught my eye. I could call Bran back.

My nose twitched as I weighed the options. He'd want to chat and I'd miss him and I'd go to bed even more frustrated that I was right now. Not a good idea.

Not when I had to decide where to go with this relationship.

I decided to cut my losses. I left a wakeup call at the main desk and went to bed.

The next morning I woke up hungry and alone, two conditions I hated. After a fast shower I tugged on my well-worn jeans, running shoes and a white blouse before grabbing my leather coat and heading out to the hotel lobby.

Carson was waiting for me, his fingers tucked into his belt. "Good morning."

I nodded. "Morning." The kit wasn't behind the desk, having been replaced with a young blonde who studiously ignored the two of us in order to keep texting her posse.

"Mayor came to see you last night." He opened the passenger door for me.

It wasn't a question.

"Nothing important. The usual 'be careful in my town' speech." I slid across the leather seat.

"Langstrom's a good woman and a good leader." Carson got in. "But sometimes she forgets the forest for the trees. Might be a problem in the future."

I didn't respond.

We started down the main street and ended up ten minutes later at a small diner on the outskirts of town. The chief nodded to someone inside the windows as we got out of the car.

The diner was a short, squat shiny rectangle sitting on an acre of wilderness, cars surrounding it as if it were under siege. The smell of fried food hit me across the face, making me drool. The hoagie was a long-lost memory at this point and I needed something in my belly before starting my own hunt.

"Good food?" I asked, a hopeful lilt in my voice.

"Best." Carson tapped the side of his nose with his index finger. "Steak and eggs is their specialty."

I picked up the Felis scent on both sides of the counter as I walked in, the handful of tables filled with morning customers. In the corner a large booth held two men with place settings for four set up in front of them. There was a quiet space around them, a respectful circle of silence.

A few heads turned as I walked by, noses twitching. I kept my head high and strode with authority—I wasn't here to make friends or find a new playmate.

"Miss Desjardin." The first man dragged out the

word to make it sound like he had swallowed a bee-hive. He rose up to shake my hand. "Harris McCallum. This here is Lionel Plussey. Please, have a seat."

The second man stood up as well, brushing a hand down the front of his shirt. They could have been twins. Both were in their sixties and had white short-cropped hair. No beer bellies here; I had no doubt each could give me a run for my money in the field.

I slid in beside McCallum. Carson sat on the other side, giving me an easy exit if I needed it.

I knew that was on purpose. No Felis worth their salt would allow themselves to be boxed in with strangers, kin or not.

"Hungry?" Plussey asked. His bloodshot blue eyes had a murder of crows feet, giving him a wise look.

"Ravenous." I glanced toward the kitchen in the back. "I hear the steak and eggs is great."

"Al makes the best." He grinned. "Medium rare?"

I smiled. My stomach let out a happy growl.

It was good to be among family and not have to explain my food preferences. Brandon never complained but I knew he flinched now and then when we were out and I ordered the meat barely warmed over the grill.

Plussey waved over the waitress, who refilled the two coffee mugs and added two more while taking our orders. She was family as well, dipping her head just enough to acknowledge the Board members. I got a curious look and an extra scribble on her notepad.

"We were wondering how you intend to proceed with the investigation," McCallum said. His meaty hands went around the coffee mug with plenty of room to spare. His cheeks were bright red, reminding me of the classic Santa Claus image.

"I saw the crime scene last night and the body, as Chief Carson can attest to."

Plussey nodded. "So we've been told."

I spotted Carson's left eye twitch, an almost invisible reaction. He didn't like being here either.

"And the mayor decided to visit me at the hotel."

"We know." Plussey's tone reminded me of Jess's. The hairs on the back of my neck started to snap up as I resisted the urge to tell them all to screw off and then head back to the airport.

"I thought I'd interview all of the women who saw Mr. Hansa that night and—" I pursed my lips, searching for the right words, "—and who, ah, may had a reason to come into contact with him." It felt dirty to talk about women stuffing dollar bills into g-strings over breakfast with men who could have been my father's age.

McCallum nodded. "Figured that. We thought it'd be a little less confrontational if you do it at the monthly run later on this evening. Come out to the farm and chat with the girls without dragging them to the station or parading them into the hotel." He looked at Plussey and received a nod of approval.

Carson didn't say anything, studying his cup of coffee.

I licked my lips, contemplating telling him what I thought of men who called fully grown women "girls."

The waitress approached with a balancing act worthy of Cirque du Soleil, stifling my anger with the rich smells of a hearty breakfast.

The plates soared onto the table, four orders of medium-rare steak and scrambled eggs. I was the first to the hot sauce, putting enough on the eggs to make them bleed heat.

"I thought I'd just visit their homes. Fast, quiet visits." I picked up the steak knife and attacked. The bloody slab of meat was fork-tender, needing little force to split it into small bite-sized pieces. Soon the entire plate swam in red. "You know, like I usually do."

McCallum shook his head. "I think you'll understand we don't want an investigator racing around town, knocking on doors. It's a small town and people see things. People gossip about things." He waved a fork at Carson. "He's managed to put it away as a bear attack and your presence as an insurance investigator. Not going to look good if you're sniffing around personal residences, riling up curious neighbors." He shook his head again. "No, we've already set it up. We have a get-together once a month at our farm, put it under a social club title. Have us a nice cookout, have a bit of a run and all that. Be best to do your talking there."

His tone shifted from fatherly to dictatorial.

I ground my teeth down on a large piece of steak, choosing my response carefully. "The longer the time from the murder to the interviewing of the possible witnesses and the murderer, the more likely it is that people either forget, fix or reinvent their stories. I've already lost a day between the murder and my arrival—any further delay could seriously impede the investigation."

"Very possible." Now it was Plussey's turn to muddy the waters. "But it's the best we can do. We can't have you running wild. People will talk and when there's talking, there's questions." He looked at me over a forkful of scrambled eggs. "We've done fine in this area keeping our secret. We're not going to give that up for you to find out who killed Hansa."

"Because he's 'only' a human?" I drained the last drops of coffee from the mug.

"No." Carson's words were sharper than the steak knife. "A death is a death is a death, Felis or human. But we're not going to sacrifice the Pride to find the killer. Needs of the many and all that."

I finished the steak and eggs before responding, putting my rage into eating.

It wasn't hard given the excellent food. I would

have licked the plate if I hadn't been annoyed at the men around me. "What are my restrictions until the meeting tonight?" It took a concentrated effort to keep the snark out of my voice.

Plussey chewed on a forkful of eggs before responding. "Go around and do your thing. Check out Hansa's apartment, go back to the morgue if you want to, putter around town and buy some souvenirs. Go do that computer stuff from your hotel room. But don't go to personal residences."

McCallum let out a polite burp and rubbed his stomach. "Excuse me. Gall bladder's being a bitch these days." He nodded at Carson, who slid out from the other side of the table, leaving part of his breakfast uneaten. "Dax'll take you back to the hotel. There's a rental car there waiting for you. It's got a GPS system so you can't get lost."

And so you can track me, the little voice in the back of my head intoned. These boys weren't going to let me off the leash any further than they needed to.

McCallum lifted his hand and motioned to the waitress. "We'll send over instructions to the meeting."

I resisted the urge to kick the table over. Instead I moved into the narrow aisle. "Thanks for the briefing." I dug my wallet from my jeans pocket.

"On us," Plussey said.

"I'd rather not." I threw a twenty on the table,

knowing it'd cover more than just my share. "Consider it Canadian courtesy."

Before they could speak I headed for the door. Carson was behind me and I swore I heard a chuckle from the policeman.

I didn't look back at the diner. Neither did Carson as he unlocked the police car.

Carson stayed silent until we'd gotten back in the car and pulled onto the street. "I'm sorry 'bout the Board. I know it puts a lot of restrictions on you." He shifted on the faux leather seat. "It's hard to ride the line between both systems."

I let out a huff of annoyance. "How do you get anything done around here? If a Felis commits a crime do you just let them go?"

"Depends on the crime. Got a justice of the peace nearby who's family and understands how things work." The material squeaked under his weight. "We got a lot of people on probation 'round here if that tells you anything. But there's a lot of sore heads and bruises from farm 'accidents.'" He glanced at me for a second before turning his attention back to the road. "I'll understand if you want to go to the hotel and then just head back to the airport. Wouldn't blame you if you did."

I chewed on my bottom lip for a long minute even though I'd made up my mind back in the diner. "No,

I'm good. I understand why things are the way they are."

I didn't have to agree, just understand.

FOUR

THE FLASHY RED sedan in the hotel parking lot went a long way to assuage my ego. Carson grinned as I ran my hand along the hood, letting myself enjoy the luxury of a new car. My old Jeep was about to give up the ghost and it would be nice to drive something that didn't cough and burp every few minutes.

"Figured we'd have you travel in style." The cop touched the brim of his hat. "Any problems, call the station—number's in Hansa's file. They'll get hold of me right 'way."

"Roger." I hadn't stopped staring at the new car. "I'll see you tonight."

Carson laughed. "Key's at the front desk. Have a good day."

I headed inside the hotel as the police car drove away. A few morning stragglers were in the lobby with stacks of luggage as they checked out. I stood in line behind a family obviously doing the cross-country run. The two kids were nose-deep in electronic games on their computer tablets, ignoring everything around them as they threw digital birds at digital pigs.

Great way to see the country.

The father argued with the clerk for a few minutes over the hotel bill before walking away with a grunt, gesturing for mom and the kids to follow. They stumbled out into the parking lot and out of sight, the children still navigating by sound.

The young blonde behind the hotel desk passed me the keys with a wide grin before I could say anything.

"Cool ride."

"Ain't it, though?" I grinned as I headed back to my hotel room.

It'd been searched, as I'd expected.

A sniff of the air revealed two ham-fisted male Felis who had torn through my belongings. They'd tried to make themselves invisible and might have, to the average human. But not to me. My hairbrush was a fraction of an inch to one side, my laptop cord twisted behind the table where it'd been straight before.

It also didn't help that the bastards peed in the toilet and left the seat up.

I spent a few minutes reshuffling my clothing to make sure the perverts hadn't been sniffing my underwear before heading out. I might not be able to go straight to the source and start banging on some doors but I could do some tracking off the beaten path without tweaking anyone's whiskers.

THE LOCAL NEWSPAPER covered a good part of the passenger seat along with some handwritten notes I'd gathered from a few minutes chatting with the hotel clerk. Sometimes the best information can't be found online.

Penscotta was just like any small town, with the usual local hangouts. It held four churches and three bars, the fourth bar having been burnt down two years ago in a personal altercation between the owner and his partner. According to the clerk it'd been a difference in opinion regarding who was allowed to date a certain woman.

In the end she'd chosen a third man, a sanitation worker, and moved to Florida.

I loved small towns.

I spotted the green pickup tailing me before I got out of the hotel driveway. Tempted as I was to lose the poor fellow I figured there was no harm in letting him tag along. It wasn't like there weren't other Pride members around to report on my movements—starting with the hotel clerk who'd let the two thugs wander in and out of my room.

My first stop was Hansa's apartment. After a few wrong turns and at least one discovery of a one-way street going the wrong way, despite the adamant denials of the GPS system, I found it. The green pickup parked a few cars down, the driver slouching behind the wheel as I got out of my car. I left him there.

The small apartment sat above a bakery, the ongoing creation of edible delights filling the narrow stairwell with a thick doughy smell as I made my way up. A pair of elderly ladies nibbling on fresh croissants threw a curious look my way before returning to their discussion of the librarian's latest lover.

I knelt down and started the process of picking the lock with the slender metal tools I'd smuggled on the flight. It hadn't been hard to hide them in my checked luggage as part of my cosmetics. And no good investigator leaves home without his or her set.

My taser had stayed home—I doubted my skill to smuggle it across the border, and in a country where guns and ammo were plentiful, packing a taser would be like bringing a shot glass to a keg party.

A light click reached my ears, signaling the lock's surrender. You didn't have to be a Felis to be a good thief but it sure didn't hurt. With our heightened senses it was tempting to walk on the wild side and make easy money preying on the less fortunate humans around us.

I'd reached that branch in the road pretty early in life and chosen the lawful fork. I knew most Felis stayed on the straight and narrow, terrified of being trapped in a cage even for a short length of time for the slightest infraction of law.

We didn't do well in prison, but that didn't mean I couldn't hunt on the path less taken at times.

The door swung open.

I moved through the one-bedroom apartment as quietly as possible. The bakery below me sent vibrations through the floor as industrial-sized beaters smashed and kneaded dough.

I started with the bedroom. Shirts ironed and hung up in a neat line in the closet, a variety of running shoes, dress shoes and cowboy boots on a rack set on the floor. Socks and tighty-whities folded and laid out in rows in the top drawer of the generic furniture dresser. T-shirts from a dozen universities, all in excellent condition, sorted by color in the next drawer along with a handful of tees in neutral colors. Dress shirts of all hues, including a lovely salmon, pressed and waiting on hangars for use. A tie tree draped with a dozen neck stranglers in solids and stripes for every occasion. A handful of blazers and jackets in excellent condition—no rips or ugly patches on the elbows.

A snappy dresser. Considering he made his living taking his clothing off it was rather ironic.

Living room held a huge flat-screen television and DVD player with a stack of movies piled up on the floor in no particular order. His viewing habits consisted of documentaries, comedies and a few MMA shows. Furniture consisted of a black couch and coffee table with little wear and tear, a week's worth of the local newspaper sitting on the varnished wood ready for the recycling bin downstairs. No video games, no smell of spilt beer and popcorn. He didn't have the boys over for the Steelers games, in other words.

The refrigerator was stocked with a variety of healthy foods including enough types of lettuce to put a rabbit into ecstasy. Energy drinks filled the door rack. The freezer held neatly labeled packages of chicken and ground beef, sorted by date. Cans of soup and stew in the cupboard along with a handful of spice bottles completed the food inventory.

No dishes in the sink. He'd cleaned up before going to work and to his death.

I winced, thinking about what someone would find in my house if I died suddenly. The days-old dried jelly on the counter and withered apples in the crisper wouldn't impress anyone.

The bathroom was my next stop.

No double toothbrushes and no sanitary products hiding under the sink, no evidence of a stable girl-friend. Only one type of generic dandruff shampoo and bland soap bars in the shower and on the sink. A dirty towel sat in the laundry bin with clean ones hanging on the rack.

I headed for his computer desk, hoping to find something meatier. Right now Hansa was too good to be true. Neat, single and a healthy eater.

A grocery list—milk, bread, cereal. A mug sat on the counter, holding chewed pens and pencils.

I frowned and turned around in a slow circle.

There was no laptop. No tablet, no dock station, nothing.

Interesting.

It was a good bet anything regarding his girl-friends would have been electronically created and delivered. Text messages, photos, emails filled with sweet nothings.

I didn't think it was a coincidence Hansa's cell phone hadn't been found at the scene.

The drawers were filled with scrap paper, a few paperclips and pencils scattered around. Bank account had no strange large withdrawals or deposits according to his checkbook sitting on the desk, just small amounts going out to the local stores and a weekly paycheck that would pay my mortgage twice over.

This was too good, too pat. If Hansa was this neat and tidy he'd have been snatched up long ago by some lucky woman. He danced, he came home and hung out in a neat bachelor pad, he danced again. He watched porn, he watched sports and went back to work.

If he was schtupping any of the Felis women, he sure wasn't doing it here and he wasn't getting paid off to either keep quiet or deliver the goods.

He owned a pickup truck sitting now in the police impound yard. Maybe that's where all the hot and heavy action went on, 'cause his bedroom was spotless. There wasn't even a box of condoms in the bathroom.

Wherever Hansa was socializing he didn't do it here.

The only Felis I could scent were the two thugs who'd rifled through my hotel room this morning. At least the Pride was consistent, using the same enforcers. They had probably been here before my plane went wheels-up.

They'd been looking for clear evidence of guilt from a specific woman, Felis or human, trying to find a suspect for Carson to arrest and cancel my arrival.

Hadn't worked.

I reached over to the coffee table and picked up Hansa's day planner. It had nothing in it other than listing the length of his workouts at the local gym and his shifts at the Cat's Meow. No phone numbers, nothing.

The scene had been compromised to the point of uselessness. I wouldn't find anything here.

I locked the apartment and walked back to my car.

The green truck was still there, the driver's head lolling to one side. I resisted the urge to wave at him as I pulled away from the curb.

He caught up to me a block later, hanging back behind a minivan. The guy wasn't bad at this following thing. If I'd been in Toronto I'd be able to lose him in a few fast turns down the alleys, but this was his turf, not mine.

It was almost lunchtime and I mentally shuffled between the three bars, trying to judge which one to visit first. I settled on the closest when my stomach began to growl. I tapped the address into the GPS and followed the cute little voice's directions.

Harvey's BBQ had a full parking lot of battered pickup trucks. The aroma of freshly barbecued meat charged at me through my open window.

My watcher drove in as I got out, parking between a pair of vehicles a sneeze and a cough away from the scrap yard.

I headed for the front door of the square single-story shack doubling as a bar. No neon, nothing more than a hand-painted sign announcing the name of the place.

Vegetarians were definitely not welcome. The second I stepped in my senses snapped to full alert. The Felis scents mixed with the heady musk of human men on the prowl and a whole lot of raw meat on the bone. The ratio of women to men ran at about one to five, not counting the overworked staff.

The theme seemed to be "keep what you kill," judging by the number of deer heads mounted on the walls. A fifteen-point buck hung over the bar, dark glass eyes staring down anyone who asked for milk or water.

There was an open stool at the very end of the bar where I could put my back to the wall. Strange Felis in enemy territory—best place to be. Especially when I wasn't sure who was friend and who was foe.

I slid onto the faux red leather padding and took in a deep whiff of charred meat heaven.

The bartender waddled down toward me.

"What can I get you?" The plump woman smiled. She was maybe ten years older than me and every day showed in deep wrinkles and age spots. Her long red hair was pulled back into a tight ponytail and her faded blue T-shirt displayed some old rock band insignia. I caught a whiff of charcoal and cheap perfume. She wasn't family.

"What's on tap?"

She squinted and studied me for a minute. Finally she wagged a finger at me. "You look like a Yuengling girl. Local beer, good tasting." Her gaze darted to some of the men standing around. "Like some other items 'round here."

I spread my hands. "Make it so."

She laughed and grabbed a tall clean glass almost as long as my forearm from under the counter before expertly slapping the pull bar down to start the beer flowing. "You must be the investigator."

I clasped my hands to my chest in an exaggerated heart attack. "Are there no secrets in this town?"

"Nope. Not in this place." The foaming glass moved in front of me, daintily sitting on a cardboard coaster. "Sorry to hear about Mike. He was a good fellow."

I sipped the amber liquid. Damn fine beer. "Did you ever see him perform?"

"A few times." She shot me a saucy wink. "I appreciate fine man-meat."

I grinned. "Ever see him with anyone special outside of the club? A girlfriend?"

Her eyes narrowed. "I thought he got done by a bear."

"He did." I sipped the smooth lager, using it to lube up my lies. "Just want to make things clean for the family. They don't need someone showing up screaming paternity test in a few months, claiming Hansa knocked her up and now looking for a payday." I looked at her over the top of the glass. "He had very good insurance, if you know what I mean."

"Oh." She pulled out a menu from under the counter and passed it to me. "I can see how that'd suck. I don't remember him being with anyone, now that you mention it. He'd come in, grab a drink and that'd be it. Nice quiet customer, more of a listener than a talker." Her eyes darted to one side. "Could use more of those."

I smacked my lips as I scanned the laminated sheet. "What do you recommend?"

"The Penscotta Pig Out Special. Pulled pork sandwich. We put coleslaw and fries on it."

"On it," I asked. "On the sandwich itself?"

"And more fries on the side."

"Ah." My cholesterol clots gave a happy leap. "One Pig Out Special, then."

The customers surged and ebbed around me in waves as I waited for lunch. It was a working man's hangout, sweat and dust mixed in with plenty of well-toned muscles. Not that a few beer bellies didn't sneak in here, but they were attached to honored old men who perched on their favorite stools and gathered their audience around them like the ancient shamans of old, dispensing wisdom and dirty jokes in the same sentence.

There were Felis here but not in overwhelming numbers. They blended in and if they scented me they ignored me or at best gave me a short, curt nod and moved on.

The food arrived in a red plastic basket with checked wax paper holding back the biggest sandwich I'd seen in a long, long time. The scarlet sauce dripping over and out of the meat managed to choke my taste buds into submission as I wallowed in juicy goodness. The coleslaw dripped through, the white dressing blending with the sauce. French fries with just the right amount of crunch and crispiness clogged my mouth and sopped up the drool.

I could die happy right now. Given the amount of calories and saturated fat I was taking in, it could happen.

Any minute.

Without warning.

I didn't care.

My moment of happiness shattered when I caught a whiff of who'd just walked in the door. I remembered it from the night before and winced inside, hoping I'd get a few more seconds of culinary orgasm before having to deal with her.

Cassie Prosser made her way through the crowd and sat on the now empty stool beside me. She wore a dark brown blazer over a red blouse and jeans, her cowboy boots polished to a high shine. "Good food." She waved over the bartender and placed an order as I continued my love affair with the sandwich.

"Great food." I snatched up a handful of napkins, glad I didn't wear makeup as I tried to clean the spicy sauce off my face.

"I checked you out. You don't just do insurance investigations—you dig up all sorts of crap. Divorces, industrial spying—you do it all. And you're from Canada." Her nose wrinkled as if I'd just farted.

"Canada's nice." I dipped a fat French fry into the escaping sauce. "We have curling."

The bartender placed a draft beer in front of her, giving me a curious glance.

Prosser grabbed at the tall glass of beer like a dying woman at a life preserver, drinking a good mouthful before replying. "What are you really here for?"

"Just paperwork." I sipped my drink. "I'm just verifying the events before we pay out to the family."

"It was a bear attack." Her eyes locked with mine. "Wasn't it?"

"What else could it be?" I lobbed the ball back into her court. "You're a reporter. You tell me what you think it was if you disagree."

The left side of her face twitched, so small anyone else might have missed it. She wasn't buying the bear story.

The beer turned sour in my mouth.

"You knew Hansa?"

Her eyes narrowed. "I saw him at a benefit the club put on for some returning vets. Raised money to help renovate homes, make them wheelchair-accessible. Big story so we covered it."

"But you don't like the idea of a strip club in your town." I filled in the blanks.

"That club's been bad news since it opened." She took another sip. "They can hide behind good causes but it's still a black spot on the community."

"I hear it's been good for the area. Town council approved it, right?" I chomped down on a fry, giving her time to react.

Her tongue flicked out, wetting dry lips. "They're wrong. And I intend to prove it." She waved a hand at the crowd. "Small-town politics. Everyone's a player and everyone's got a price."

"Well, I'm not and I don't." I licked my fingers because it would have been gauche to lick the waxed paper. "If you've got anything else, feel free to share."

She nursed the beer for the length of time it took for me to finish my own, studying the condensation puddles on the wood.

I put a twenty down on the bar, tucking it under my empty glass. The bartender looked over and gave me a smile and a nod.

Cassie didn't say anything when I headed for the door.

The green pickup sat in the parking lot, watching me return to my car. A hot breeze sent the smell of freshly cooked beef over us.

I hoped the driver was starving.

The next bar had good coffee and bad chemistry. I sat there in the middle of a stack of youngsters bragging about their latest stock market conquests and wondered if I were in the same town. The neon colors of their shirts almost blinded me as I listened to the suits discuss things far, far over the head of a simple private investigator, such as stock trading and how to beat a drunk driving charge by chewing charcoal. A few Felis here as well, all snubbing me as if I had rabies. I lasted about a half hour before bolting for the door, feeling way too clean and leaving my seven-dollar latte half-drunk on the table.

My tail was still there. I had to give the guy points

for being persistent if not subtle. I waved at him and got no response.

I got rid of the clean feeling at the police yard. The guard gave me the keys and waved me through with a nod and a thumbs-up, another family member.

The pickup truck stayed outside, parked down the street. The guard glanced at it once before returning to the sports section of his newspaper and ignoring both of us.

I made my way through the handful of impounded cars before finding Hansa's truck in the far corner of the lot.

The remains of a dozen fast food meals cluttered the front seat, shredded paper wrappers and empty mustard packets everywhere. He sure hadn't romanced anyone here, unless they liked having mustard on their ass. It was an amazing contradiction, the man working out at the gym, frantically keeping his perfect form, and on the side stuffing his face with fast food hamburgers.

The different smells mixed in my mind. But there was only one person's scent—Hansa's.

He hadn't slept with anyone at his place or in his car. The likelihood of keeping a secret lover rendezvous at a nearby hotel was small, given the amount of locals working there. Someone would have talked.

If he'd been with any woman it'd been at her place, at her home.

It took guts to have sex when a husband/boyfriend/mate could walk in the door at any second. More guts than brains, but it'd been my experience that some women liked their men big and dumb.

I wasn't sure if Hansa was dumb but after seeing him naked I could testify to the "big."

I nodded to the security guard minding the police lot as I drove out.

The truck tailing me continued to hover in my rearview mirror, tempting me to slam on the brakes and confront the driver. I resisted, if only to tease him with the third bar and yet more food.

The last bar turned out to be not far from the diner where I'd had breakfast, with some of the same crowd I'd seen earlier shuffling over from coffee and pancakes to beer and pretzels. A handful of people filed in and out, grabbing takeout orders as I nursed a coffee at the bar.

The Felis bartender, a middle-aged man with a bit of a pot belly, eyed me again. He'd been slow to get me the first coffee, watching me like I was about to rob the place.

His meaty fingers tapped on the bar as he glanced left and right, sizing up his clientele. Finally he came over to me, rubbing his bushy beard with one hand.

"You're here about Hansa," he mumbled.

"Maybe." I sipped the lukewarm drink. "What if I am?"

"Bad business, that." He scratched his chin, sending a shower of flakes down onto the counter.

I shifted my mug to one side, away from the snow-storm. "Why?"

"The club's been trouble since it opened. Got lots of ladies taking time away from their families to go watch the punks dance." His nostrils flared open.

Angry old Felis. I glanced at his left hand. Un-married.

"Anyone hate the club enough to kill Hansa?" I took another swig of coffee.

His grey and white moustache twitched. "Lots of angry men. Lots of husbands left alone while their women 'ran errands.' Say they're going out for milk and come home two hours later smelling of sweaty men."

I held out the mug for a refill. "Care to share any names?"

His hand touched mine, the thick fingers gripping hard. I tried not to wince.

"You'd be best looking up, not down the ranks." The mug went under the counter as he refilled it.

"Thanks." I resisted the urge to shake my hand out, get the feeling back in my fingers.

He nodded and moved down the bar to chat with some regulars.

I knew he was referring to Carson and his wife. Maybe the liberal arrangement hadn't been as okay as the chief'd let on.

The bar door opened.

A man walked in and headed for the bar, strong

hard strides across the hardwood floor in work boots that had seen better days.

He slid onto the stool beside me, his Felis scent splashing everywhere. Tall, blond and about five years younger than I was.

One finger went up, getting the bartender's attention immediately. "Red Rock."

He turned toward me and smiled, deep blue eyes daring me to fall into them.

I felt like I'd been punched in the chest. Felis may not technically be cats but we sure as hell could be cougars.

"Trace Bryson." He held out his hand.

I took it, relishing the cool thrill running over my skin before reality chased it away. It wasn't a coincidence he'd walked in here and sat next to me.

"Green truck?"

He slipped his hand out of mine, the callused fingers falling away.

"Yep. That's mine."

His beer arrived just in time to let him stall for a second to sip the cool brew.

I allowed myself a scowl. "My shadow."

He took another mouthful and swirled it around, thin lips curving into a smile. "Yep."

I sipped my coffee. "If I told you to go to hell would it make a difference?"

He shook his head. His blond hair was just long enough for a woman to get a good grip.

"I hate to tell a beautiful lady like yourself 'no,' but…" He spread his hands. "You wouldn't want me to get into trouble with my uncle, right?"

My heart sank. "McCallum."

Trace smiled, showing bright white teeth. "Yep." His tongue flicked out and ran over his lower lip. "Gotta do what the Board says."

"That's really beginning to annoy me," I growled. "So what are your orders?"

He leaned back, the well-worn jean shirt tight on his frame. "Follow, watch, seduce… Oh, wait, I wasn't supposed to say that one out loud."

I didn't smile.

Trace pressed his lips together. "Tough audience." He drained the rest of the beer in a single gulp. "I'll be seeing you later, I guess."

He peeled off a handful of bills and tucked them under the empty glass before leaving.

The bartender came over and arched one eyebrow as he collected the money. "Trace ain't so bad." He nodded at the swinging front door. "Can do a lot worse."

I finished off the coffee. "It's not the player, it's the game."

It took me a few minutes to find Carson's home address with my cell phone and allow myself time to finish my coffee and slow my pulse down.

The bar was slowly filling with a mixture of blue collar workers and a slew of younger women who eyed me as the competition. I kept my eyes down and watched the mating ritual at work, noting the number of Felis hanging around. It hadn't been that long since we'd discovered Felis could impregnate and be impregnated by humans, resulting in half-breed children, but it seems the news hadn't reached this crew. Or if it did they weren't taking it too seriously. I made a mental note to mention it to the Board, as well as to Jess. The last thing I needed was a call to find another rogue half-breed.

I slipped through the crowd and out to my rental car. Trace was sitting in his truck and watched as I typed in the request on the onboard GPS. It kicked out a route easily enough and I was on my way.

The green truck stayed behind me as I wove my way through the streets, keeping a respectful distance. I wasn't sure that'd continue when he figured out where I was going.

The house sat on a good three acres of land not too far from the edge of town, a small two-story home with a yard that would have swallowed up my own house three times and then some. A small garden shed in back held at least one riding mower and a slew of tools, at least from what I could see through the open door.

The flower beds were laid out in beautiful, tasteful rows of bright reds and yellows. A handful of

ancient farm machinery spotted the lawn, continuing the rustic look.

I parked at the end of the curved driveway and
waited.

FIVE

TRACE'S TRUCK SLID in behind me. A second later he turned off the engine and got out.

I met him halfway, at where our bumpers touched.

"You can't go up there." He slid his hands into his front pockets and gave me a sad smile. "No personal visits."

I nodded. "So I've been told. But I'm going up to talk to her."

He shook his head. "Not advised."

"What are you going to do about it?" I rolled onto the balls of my feet. I might not be able to Change but I sure as heck could still fight.

Trace grinned. "Well, I could toss you over my shoulder and take you back to the bar for a drink—" he paused and dragged his eyes up and down my body, "—to start with."

I couldn't help smirking. "Aren't you full of yourself?"

He shrugged and tilted his head to one side, giving me a smoking smile.

"Is that a 'no'?" Trace drawled. "Or a 'maybe'?"

"I don't do charity." I spun on my heel and headed

up the driveway. I glanced back over my shoulder to see him leaning on the hood of his truck, waiting.

I'd dodged the bullet. For now.

The front door opened before I reached the house.

"You must be Rebecca." She held out her hand. "April Carson." Her blond hair fell over her shoulders in long, luxurious locks, unlike the limp ponytail flopping against my back.

I hated her right there.

"Dax said you might be sniffing around. I thought I was going to meet you at the farm later on today." She waved me in, swaying in purple yoga pants and matching shirt. The large glass of red wine in her hand danced to an unheard tune.

"I guess I misunderstood," I replied.

The inside of the house was decorated in various shades of brown and red, fancy paintings hanging on the walls next to dried flowers and potpourris giving off a fruity smell. Most of the furniture was a basic wood built, probably Amish from the functionality winning out over flash. A few pieces were flashy expensive ones, to be adored from afar and not actually used for anything.

It seemed to be a mixture of showing off her wealth and reassuring visitors that she was just one of them, a common woman who got lucky.

I wondered what she'd done for money before marrying the chief.

She led me to the living room and the brown

leather couch. A well-worn lounger sat in the far corner, obviously Carson's man-cave chair.

"Can I get you something to drink?" She made as if to head for the drink cart set in the far corner of the room. The red wine sloshed perilously close to the edge of the wine glass.

I held up my hand. "No, thank you."

She settled in beside me. The cushions burped their acceptance as she settled in. "So, about Mike."

"About Mike," I repeated.

I waited. I was getting used to it.

April crossed her legs and placed the glass of wine on the table in front of us. "Dax and I have a very open relationship."

I nodded.

"I'm about ten years younger than he is and I still have a lot of, ah—" she fluttered her hands in the air, "—sexual energy."

I nodded.

"We married because Dax needed to be married, to have a woman in his life. He loves being the police chief and I love being a kept woman." She paused. "Before this I worked at the diner, believe it or not. Not in the front—slinging hash in the back. Used to make a good grilled cheese sandwich."

I nodded. Wasn't hard to imagine her toasted.

She flipped the blond tresses back. "I go to the Cat's Meow a few times a week and yes, I liked

Mike. A lot. But we never did the dirty." Her petite mouth twisted into a frown. "I don't do humans."

The cold coffee taste in my mouth turned bitter.

April entwined her fingers and rested her hands on her knee. "I don't fool around on Dax. I know a divorce would embarrass him and he'd lose face with the family. Besides, I like what I have here." She gestured around at the paintings on the walls, the misshapen art pieces on redwood shelves. "I'm not going to give all this up for a piece of human tail."

"And Dax knows this."

"Dax knows." She smiled, showing off artificially whitened teeth. "Dax goes off and does what he does and I do what I do. As long as we come back here alone we're fine."

I didn't need to take notes. "How do you feel about Dax's side of this 'open' marriage? Does he like human women?"

Her lips curled into a tight smile. "He might look but he doesn't touch. He's a good boy."

I knew she was telling the truth. A number of times I'd smelled the lying on my clients before they even opened their mouths. Felis didn't take mating lightly and divorces were practically unheard of. I'd starve if I waited for jobs involving infidelity from the family.

"Tell me about Mike." I leaned back on the couch, enjoying the squeak of fresh leather. "Was he a player? Popular with the women?"

"Honey, anyone who works there is a player." April laughed. "We had fun. I stuffed dollar bills in his thong and he gave great lap dances."

"To you and a lot of other women."

She shrugged. "I never expected him to wait for my visits. He's got to make money and that's his business."

"Did he have any favorites among the rest of the women? Anyone who he spent more time with than anyone else?"

April giggled, a high tinkling sound sending me into an instant migraine. "Oh, he had them lining up for a chance to break him down, make him theirs. But we all knew his heart belonged to no one. He made that clear."

"All of them?" I gave her what I hoped was a "we women" look. "So no one had a mate getting all grumpy 'cause she was putting it in Mike's g-string?"

She shook her head. "No one that I knew of. Of course, being married to a Board member means I didn't get all the gossip." She leaned in. "Jealousy and all that. Don't want me ratting 'em out to Dax."

The throbbing behind my eyes grew. If this was what commitment was all about I didn't want any part of it.

"Tell me your thoughts on the Board."

Her eyes widened. "The Board?" she squeaked.

I nodded. "Dax is an important man. Both as chief and as a Board member. How does he get along with

the other two members?" I added another dimension.
"How do you get along with them?"

April popped her index finger into her mouth
and sucked on it. Didn't chew the nail, didn't roll it
around in any sort of sexual move. It was the reaction of a kit when faced with a difficult question.

I hated myself for enjoying her discomfort.

The finger popped out with a wet sound.
"Plussey's a nice guy. His wife has this faboo rec-
ipe for marinating deer meat, takes all the gamey
taste out. McCallum, well, he's a bit of a prick at
times. Orders Dax around to do this and that, when
they're all supposed to be equals." She pursed her
lips, nervous at revealing her thoughts. "But he's got
the best interests of the Pride in mind so Dax kinda
threads between the two of them."

I got to my feet and headed for the door. "Thanks
for your time."

She beat me to the entrance, swinging the heavy
oak door open with ease. "I'll see you this evening.
Wear good shoes."

I nodded, resisting the urge to return Penscotta's
Pig Out with interest. There might be a place for
women like this in the human world but I'd hoped
never to see one in a Pride.

Trace was inside his truck when I wove my way
down to my car, fireworks going off behind my eyes.
I kicked it in gear, praying he wouldn't call the cops
on me for drunk driving the way I meandered over

the line. I needed to get someplace nice and quiet and dark and shuffle what I had so far. With medication, if at all possible.

There was a drugstore on the way back to the hotel with an understanding pharmacist who helped me find the strongest over-the-counter painkiller before I went blind. I hadn't brought anything with me because I hadn't planned to have a major-grade headache.

Idiot me. I should have known anything to do with Jess and the Felis was migraine territory.

Trace, God bless him, kept his distance and stayed in the truck, watching from the parking lot. Either he was afraid I was buying "feminine products" or worried that I'd deck him right there in the store.

It took all I had to maneuver the car back into the parking lot and make it to my room without throwing up. I didn't look for the green pickup and didn't care if it was there or not.

I rolled onto the freshly made bed, dry-swallowing the pills I'd wrestled out of the child-proof container. As I waited for the headache to subside I went over what I had in an attempt to get my mind off the pulse-pounding pain.

It took all of a minute to figure out I had diddly. Less than diddly if that were possible.

Mike Hansa played with fire the second he stepped on that stage, playing to Felis women whose instincts were to hunt and kill in and out of the bedroom. He'd crossed the wrong woman and paid for it with his life.

I wrote April off as soon as I'd spotted her hands. Clean, manicured masterpieces. No way was she going to get her fingers dirty by digging her claws into someone. I suspected if she called them out I'd find them neatly clipped and painted a bright pink to match her fingernails. She probably hadn't hunted in years.

My eyes closed, shutting out the dim light battering my senses. I couldn't ask all the women to show me their claws and see which ones dripped blood. Any Felis worth their salt washed after a kill, cleaning up the mess. With every hour that went by it became more and more likely any women who knew Mike Hansa would share notes and compare stories, making it almost impossible to trip them up.

It might not even be intentional—one phone call, one gossiping woman and everyone would be chattering and nattering on the party line about how Mike had done this or that. It'd turn into a general gabfest and in the middle would be the murderess, putting out false information to throw an investigator off the trail or at least muddy the waters.

The truth hit me with startling clarity.

The pills must have kicked in.

I was being set up to fail. Or, if not to fail, at least put an official stamp on the death and allow the Board to put in their records that they'd attempted to find the offender, done their best by dragging me down and letting me play at being a hunter. The report would move up the ranks to the Grand Council, who would shuffle it into a file. The local Pride would send me a check and everyone looked good. Except for me for failing, but I was an outcast—who would care?

The little voice in the back of my head whispered, *Mike Hansa and his family and friends, that's who.*

Sometimes the little voices help. Sometimes they're just really, really annoying.

There was still something wrong, a niggling feeling digging at the back of my hollow skull.

How had Hansa ended up here in a dead-end town working as a stripper? With his physique he could have gone to Vegas, gone pro. What kept him in Penscotta?

The throbbing lessened, the pressure behind my eyes easing up. I held back yelps of joy and rolled over the morning's events in my mind.

His apartment was spotless. Almost like…

I forced one eye open and looked around my hotel room. Generic table, generic bed, generic toiletries in the bathroom. No pictures of family, no pictures of friends. Nothing but bare walls.

Like the rooms on each side of me.

Like it wasn't his real home. Just a way station.

A gentle rapping came at the front door. "Miss Desjardin?"

I got to my feet, thanking the pharmaceutical gods.

It was the young kit from the front desk, a wide grin on his blushing face. "Ma'am, the chief wanted me to give this to you. It's the directions to the meeting tonight." He handed me a slip of paper, the block letters laid out by an invisible ruler. "He says everything's set up for you and they look forward to seeing you there."

I gave him my cutest smile as payment. He flew back down the hallway as if I'd taken his virginity.

Ah, youth. Right now I had too many men in my life as it was—I didn't need one who had barely been potty-trained.

The headache subsided enough to allow me to grab a fast shower before re-dressing and heading out.

Every Pride kept a secure compound where their members could Change and hunt without fear. It was a sanctuary for kids to learn how to deal with their unusual skills and for adults to rest and relax away from the pressure of human society. It wasn't like everyone got furry and jumped into an orgy but it felt nice to just sit and be Felis, to act and react to the smells and scents around you. Lie in the tall grass while Changed and enjoy the bright sunbeams warming your fur. Go for a hunt and snag the slowest rabbit or squirrel just because you could. Sneak off with your lover and have a wilderness rendezvous.

I felt the heat rush to my cheeks as I thought of

Trace waiting outside for me. I was tempted and I'd be a fool to lie to myself and say I wasn't. But down that path lay madness, and not just because he was American and I was Canadian. I had no idea how to live as a Felis wife and wasn't sure if I even wanted to try to learn.

The scars on my back ached. I rolled my shoulders, the ghost memory of Brandon's soft backrubs chasing away the pain and injecting a sharp dose of guilt.

I sighed and pulled on my leather coat. Maybe a bit of fresh air would help clear my mind.

The kit didn't look at me as I strolled through the lobby.

Trace stayed behind his wheel, making it easier for me to get into my car. I didn't need another confrontation with my babysitter/would-be suitor, not before I got some work done.

The directions agreed with the GPS, pointing me to a small farm a half hour away from the hotel, the rolling fields around the scattered buildings pulling in at least one small mountain ridge and a large forest running out of sight over the hills.

Over a dozen pickup trucks and a slew of SUVs filled the gravel parking lot. I parked at the far end, giving me an easy exit. Depending on how I was received I might need it.

The green pickup parked beside me, the wheels spinning gravel projectiles into the field.

Trace got out with a smile, his work boots crunching the small stones. "Welcome to our farm." He frowned. "You look pale."

"I'm Canadian."

"No, really pale." He stepped closer and reached out, cupping my chin in one palm. "You okay?"

His touch scorched my skin. I resisted the urge to dip my head down, wallow in the warmth.

"I had a bad headache," I muttered. "Took some pills to chase it away."

"Ah." His blue eyes sought mine out, the concern on his face ripping at my barriers. "You going to be okay to work then? Or just—" the edges of his mouth twisted up, "—play?"

"I'm here to find Hansa's killer." I took a step back, retreating from his touch. "That's all."

"Right." Conceding defeat for the moment, he nodded toward the gathering. "Let's go get some food. You look like you could use a good meal."

I followed him down the well-worn path to the open field.

It looked like a lawn party with a large pavilion set up at one end of the meadow, not far from the barn. The white plastic tables under the tent groaned under aluminum foil trays of fried chicken, potato salad, cabbage rolls, pierogies and various side dishes. A bevy of women gathered at one end, fussing as they set out stacks of paper plates and napkins. Off to one side lay a stack of metal folding chairs, brothers to the ones already set around some of the empty tables sitting out in the sun.

A series of coolers stacked in the corner of the tent sweated water.

"Five types of beer and seven types of pop," Trace volunteered. "Name your poison."

"Ah…" My throat ached for a cold drink until I turned and spotted Carson. Even at a distance I could see the anger in his stride, each step ripping a divot in the grass.

My desire for a drink faded, replaced by a small kernel of fear taking root in my belly. I'd bearded the lion in his own den and he wasn't happy.

Trace cocked an eyebrow as Carson approached us. The chief's face was red and blotchy. It didn't take Felis skills to see he was pissed.

"Reaping what you sow." He glanced at me, then back at Carson.

I saw the confusion in his eyes. Carson was a Board member and his senior in the Pride. I was neither but he wanted to protect me. It wasn't just a play to get in my pants; male Felis had a natural urge to protect females.

Except I wasn't any regular female Felis.

"Go scout out the food," I said, giving him an easy out. "I'll be with you in a minute." I put on my tough guy look. "I'll be fine. Can't be any worse than telling some guy his wife left him for his sister and they're headed for Cancún with his credit cards."

Trace chuckled before accepting defeat.

"I'll see you later." He nodded before heading off toward the tables, trotting away from what we both knew was going to be trouble.

Carson shot a glance toward Trace before coming to a stop in front of me. He was visibly shaking as he wagged a finger in my face. He'd changed out of his uniform and now wore a light blue T-shirt and jeans. His cowboy boots dug into the ground in front of me, scattering dirt clumps on my running shoes.

"You went to my home. You went to my wife," he sputtered. "We told you—"

"You told me what you wanted. Then I did what I needed to do."

"You answer to the Board," he snarled. "You answer to us."

I crossed my arms. "No, I answer to the law." I paused for a second, wondering how far I could push it. "As you do. And if I'm running a murder investigation I'll do as I see fit."

"Jess said you were a bitch. I want you out of here tonight. I want you on the next fucking plane back to the tundra."

"I don't think so." I jerked my thumb back toward the nearly full parking lot. "You get the Board together and you vote on it. Then you call Jess up and explain how you're tossing my ass out before I finish my work. And then you can get your report ready for the Grand Council and repeat all the earlier bullshit."

"Get. Out," he screamed, drawing more spectators to our little discussion.

"Make me."

It was a calculated gamble. If I didn't draw the line here I'd have no chance of finding Hansa's killer with all the Pride laws and restrictions. There had already been too much lost time thanks to the bureaucracy blocking my way.

Carson Changed, his features shifting and warping into feline mode. Light brown fur covered his face as his teeth extended forward, showing me a great set of fangs. The tips of his ears grew tufts of fur as they became more pointed, his bald head disappearing under short grey fuzz blending in with the rest of his brown coloring.

I didn't move.

His claws shot out from between his knuckles, the sharp nails inches from my legs. He let out something between a hiss and a growl, slitted eyes locked with mine in a duel of wills.

I resisted the urge to yawn. There was only so far you could push a Felis before he or she snapped, and I was at a major disadvantage, being unable to Change.

"Back off, Dax." The familiar voice came from behind me. I didn't turn to look. I couldn't afford to look.

The wind shifted, sending a number of scents my way. Harris McCallum.

Trace must have sent him my way to defuse the situation. If he could.

"She spoke to April after we told her not to. She went to my house." Carson thumped his chest with one furred hand. "My house."

"I know. But giving her a beating isn't going to fix that." McCallum moved into my field of vision on my right side, unChanged. "Go get yourself a beer. Let me take care of this." His voice was a low purr, a soothing tone I suspected had wooed many women into bed.

If Trace had the same ability I was in deep, deep trouble.

I held my breath, waiting to see what Carson would do. If he attacked me there'd be no defense, no escape.

His nose twitched.

"Bitch." He spun on his heel and stomped away, growling at a pack of kits nearby who scattered to the four winds.

McCallum took his place. "I'm sorry about Dax. He takes his privacy very seriously."

"I got that impression." My voice was steady, unlike my nerves. I felt like I'd mainlined a dozen cups of strong coffee.

"You shouldn't have blown us off. We have rules for a reason," McCallum said, a touch of disapproval in his voice. He shook his head. "I know you've got your own way of doing things, but you've got to re-spect our ways."

"April's a possible suspect. I wanted to get her side of the story. Not going to get that with him standing right behind her." I looked after the retreating chief. "I didn't know it'd upset him so much. I'm sorry."

McCallum nodded, pressing his lips tightly together. "Dax lost his first wife to cancer. Married over twenty years. Happened fast. Six months and she was gone. They were high school sweethearts, inseparable. Dax mourned for a year before starting to date again. Met April a year after that and got re-married. Been together for three years now."

I felt like the mud under my running shoes.

"Since he married April he's been sensitive about people thinking he went for a young, stupid one. Anyone makes fun of her he's right there. First year they were married he fought three challenges." The older man chuckled. "It was a rough year for the kits."

I chewed on my pride for a second. "Can't blame him for being sensitive." I looked over to Carson, who sat alone at a nearby table. He hadn't Changed back. "Should I apologize?"

"Nah." McCallum shook his head. "He'll get over it." His mood lightened. "Now, let me get you settled over here at a table with some food and I'll send the women over one by one for you to talk to."

He maneuvered me over to a side table just far

enough away from the herd to give me some privacy, and waved over Trace, who had been hovering just out of earshot.

"Trace, get 'er some food." McCallum beamed, his thumbs jabbed in the waistband of his jeans. "Give her a taste of real cooking, not that pulverized crap from the city."

I settled in behind the white paper tablecloth and pulled out my notepad. A good pen and paper will never crash on you or die suddenly in the middle of a storm.

Besides, I still hadn't figured out how to use half the features on the new smartphone Bran had given me.

Trace returned a few minutes later with two plastic food trays. "I figured I'd get you a good sampling of what we've got."

I gawked at the stack of fried chicken, barbecued ribs, cabbage rolls, pierogies, potato salad, macaroni salad, coleslaw, a pair of rolls and two types of pie on my tray along with a single can of beer.

Trace sat across from me with his own tray filled with the same items. "Let's take it from the top and forget today." He cleared his throat. "So you're a private investigator, Miss Desjardin." He pronounced it the right way, day-shar-dan.

"Please, call me Reb." I studied the food tower, unsure how to attack it. The first thing I did was pop the top on the beer. It was cold and wet, meeting two of my major requirements for beer.

"You're here for the dead stripper." Trace stripped a drumstick in less time than it took for me to unfold my napkin.

"Exotic dancer."

We both grinned.

"So, you're single. I'm single. Let's get married," he said through a mouthful of coleslaw.

SIX

I CHOKED ON a thick chunk of chicken before grabbing my beer. It took half the can to wash the surprise down.

"What?"

He let out a low chuckle. "Thought I'd get that out of the way. I'm awful with the foreplay." His long slender fingers danced over a chicken thigh, pulling off the crispy skin with ease. "If you need my help with anything just ask."

I dabbed at the edge of my mouth with a napkin. "I don't need a babysitter."

"Good. I hate kids." His smile was infectious. "Don't shoot the messenger. They wanted someone watching your back and I was available."

"In more ways than one." The potato salad had chopped scallions in it and just the right amount of mayo and mustard. My stomach sang with happiness.

He shrugged. "Lost my wife five years ago to a drunk driver." His hand went up, palm-first. "Please don't say you're sorry. Everyone is. I understand. And I'm okay with it. Kid driver died in the crash and there's no one left to blame."

I worked on tearing the chicken wing apart.
"Right."

"The Pride thinks I should be ready to remarry.
And you're here and single and not a blood relation,
so…" He frowned, a hint of humor bouncing on his
lips. "I don't think you look much like a farm wife."

"I'm outcast." I never thought I'd be using the
phrase to fight off a possible suitor.

Trace nodded. "So I hear." His gaze traveled outward over the clusters of women nearby. "I'll be honest—I don't want kids and there's not a whole lot of
choice 'round here unless I go for jailbait or widows."

"You could go to another Pride."

"I could." He smiled. "But you're here and I don't
like to travel. And I don't give a shit about your status up in Canada. If you can live with it I can, and
hang the rest of them who can't."

I coughed to hide the tears building up behind
my eyelids. If nothing else Trace Bryson was a good
man. "Thank you. I'm sort of spoken for at the moment." I chewed on the non-business end of the plastic fork. "What do you know about Mike Hansa?"

"Never met the guy personally but I saw him
about town. He liked the ladies and got paid to do
it." Trace laughed. "Hell, half the men in the Pride
would be up on that stage in a second if we weren't
banned from working there."

"Banned?"

"Board says it'd be too tempting to hook up with

a human woman, grab a one-night stand every day of the week." Trace waved his fork in the air. "Avoid temptation and all that. Keeping it pure." The fork landed in the macaroni salad. "Ain't no law against marrying humans as you know. But the Board figures we should try to keep it at home as much as possible." He gave me a sly look. "Besides, it'd make the human men jealous." His hips shifted against the table. "Not a fair competition."

"And no one worries about the Felis women dating the dancers?"

Trace chuckled. "You've met April. Her attitude toward humans, especially males, isn't unique. We tend to stick to our own. Play hard, party hard, but bring it home to your Felis mate at the end of the night." His voice dropped to a low purr. "Then play hard again."

I wrestled with a fat piece of potato, hoping I wasn't blushing too loudly. "We can breed with humans, you know."

"So I've heard." He gave me a curious look. "Most interesting."

"How do the men feel about the ladies going to the club?" The tartness of the macaroni salad pulled my lips together. "Any jealousy? Anyone upset their girlfriend or mates are going to watch semi-naked men shaking it?"

"At the beginning there were a few spats here and there, especially among the younger ones. You know how couples are." He sucked on his fingers. "Got worked out. No one went to the hospital, if that's what you're asking."

"So everyone's good with the club?"

"To a degree." He loaded up his fork with potato salad. "Can I say I'd be happy if it weren't there? Sure. Not too happy 'bout the morality play going on when the license comes up for renewal from the town council. But the area needs money and we need businesses to invest in the town. They pay taxes and as long as the license gets renewed every three months they're going to be here."

"Three months?" I reached for the napkin, resisting the urge to lick my own fingers. "That's really short for a business license, isn't it?"

"Special provision of the club being allowed to open up. Every three months it comes up in front of the town council and they vote. Idea was that it'd be a good way to judge the public reaction and deal with any problems before it got too serious. Every time they've voted it's been three to two with the mayor and one other councilman casting the negative vote." He let out a soft laugh. "Langstrom may be a tough bitch but she's reliable. She's never going to vote for the club."

I wrestled with a chicken bone. "When does she come up for re-election? That might screw her out of a job if the club is successful and making money for the public."

"Another year. But people like an opposing view 'round here. Keeps things stable, balanced." He demolished a drumstick while I watched. "All 'bout keeping things level."

"Anyone ever think of running for mayor against her?" I nodded toward his uncle sitting at a nearby table. "McCallum, for example."

Trace chuckled. "He wouldn't go for that. He likes being on the Board too much to take on a major position in the outside world."

"You can do both." I dismembered a thigh with my fingers. "Carson does."

"True. But keeping the law's different than running the political gauntlet. Besides, we've already got one Felis on the town council. I don't think we need to go whole hog trying to take 'em over."

"Who's on the town council?" I resisted the urge to drop my chicken bone and scramble for my notebook and pencil.

"Lisa Darning." He looked around, getting partially to his feet as he scanned the growing crowd of Felis. "Don't see her 'round. She'll be here though—she always loves good chicken."

"What's on the schedule for today? After we stuff ourselves silly?"

Trace snapped a chicken bone in half and examined it. "We get together like this once a month. Have a big meal, chat and go for a run. Good way to keep in touch with everyone and if the Board has something to say they can tell us here without sending out emails or anything that could be intercepted."

I munched on a piece of crispy skin. "What's the vibe going 'round about Hansa's death? Deserved, not deserved, what a pain in the ass..."

His mouth twitched. "No one's really sure what to think. One of us killing a human, that's something big. Not to be done lightly if at all." He licked his fingertips again. "Unless he was a threat, and I can't see how that'd happen. I mean, a human—what could he do to threaten a Felis?" The pride in his voice was obvious.

I coughed back a comment about not underestimating humans, not taking their weaknesses for granted. True, Felis could move faster and we came with our own natural weapons, but I'd seen some pretty nasty fellows in my time who could give some Felis men a run for their money.

I spotted a woman walking toward us and opted for the easy way out of what could be a sticky conversation. "I think this is my first interview. I hate to toss you out but..."

Trace got to his feet and picked up his near-empty tray. "No problem. I'll swing by later on before the run."

I watched him walk away. He might be widowed and a bit pushy but he knew how to dress.

Those jeans were tight and showcased his ass in all the right ways.

The petite woman slid into his still-warm chair. "I'm Mandy." She didn't offer her hand, crossing her arms in front of her in a pretty obvious indication she didn't want to be there. "Got told you're looking into Mike's death. Got told to come and talk to you."

The twenty-something had short red hair, a fraction of an inch over her scalp. Well-defined muscles under her "Girlz Rule!" T-shirt told me she was a hunter and not just in the forest.

"Yep." I wiped my mouth with the napkin, hoping I didn't have greasy chicken smears all over my face. "So how well did you know Mike?"

"Well enough." She shrugged and scraped her nails across the hard plastic surface. "He danced, I paid. Nutting more d'an dat."

A whiff of alcohol brushed over me. She was a few beers ahead of me.

"Are you married?" I didn't see a wedding ring but that didn't mean anything these days.

"No. Not looking either." A glimmer of a smile appeared on her face. "Dumped my boyfriend a year ago and not racing into anything."

I nodded. "Anyone ticked off at Mike that you know of?"

Mandy frowned, her eyes focusing on the ripped-up grass under our feet. "All the women liked him. Some of the men too but he didn't swing that way. Mike was just a dancer and everyone who met him knew that straight up. He danced, you paid and everyone went home happy."

"Where were you the night he died?" It was a classic question.

"I was home after spending a few hours at the club. And yes, I was alone." She smiled. "Midnight movie marathon on one of the oldie channels. Musicals 'til I fell 'sleep." She tossed a non-existent mane of hair back. "Gotta love those moves." She put her hands in the air and gave a shimmy of her hips, rocking the plastic chair from side to side.

"Totally." I didn't see any obvious signs she was lying. "Any idea who'd want to kill him?" I nodded toward a nearby group of women, chattering away as they watched me. They glared back as one, daring me to play on their turf.

"Not really." She gave a wave to a guy walking in from the parking lot. "Like I said, he didn't have any favorites. Nice guy, easy on the eyes, but not Felis." Her attention returned to me. "Just eye candy."

"Thanks." I scribbled meaningless words on the notepad for the sake of looking professional. "I'll call you back if I can think of anything else."

She got to her feet and strutted off to rejoin the pack. Another woman walked toward me, teetering on three-inch stilettos.

The next hour ranked high among my "most useless time spent" list. All of the women had either been with mates who would vouch for their presence when Mike was killed or alone with their television/ computer/sex toy. None of them knew anyone who would want Mike Hansa dead and no idea who would want to kill such a cool, sexy guy.

A solid wall of Felis fur, fangs and claws blocking my way.

"Good luck." The last woman stood up and strode away, hooking up with a tall man under the pavilion who gave her a hug while tossing me a glare that would have disemboweled lesser Felis.

I looked at my notes. Names, impressions and how many of them told the same story. Saw Mike or didn't see Mike, didn't date humans and had no idea who would want him dead. The family had closed ranks and I was just there for show.

Carson approached me, his hands jammed into his back jean pockets. "There's one more woman on the list but she's not here yet. Got word she's running late getting out of work."

I studied his face. He had Changed back but still looked annoyed at me. Having the police chief pissed at me wasn't the way to work this case.

I took a deep breath, swallowed my pride and went back to my roots. Jess had been a hard taskmaster but she'd taught me something about when to back down.

"I apologize about going out and talking to April." I looked at the ground and slumped my shoulders, assuming a submissive position. "I shouldn't have done that. I overstepped my boundaries and I was wrong."

He scuffed the dirt with the toe of his boot. "Thank you."

There wasn't a return apology. I didn't expect one.

"They're gearing up for the run." The chief motioned toward a large group hanging off to one side. A few women stayed by the buffet table, cleaning up the remains. "You should go along. De-stress and all that."

I wasn't sure if he was talking about me or about himself.

I shook my head. "I can't Change. I can't run."

"Sure you can." Trace came up beside me. He'd lost the T-shirt, his well-defined chest and abs showing the result of years of hard work. The bronzed skin shone in the dying sunlight. He stuck out his hand. "Lose the coat and come on. I'd be a bad host if I let you stay back here while the rest of us were having fun."

"I need to wait for someone." It was a valid reason but the words sounded so lame. "There's another woman I need to interview."

"She'll be here after the run, then." His fingers wriggled. "Come on, I promise I won't bite."

His scent washed over me. Friendly, warm…and that was all. No arousal, no hot and horny male musk. Whatever his motives might be, Trace wasn't out to seduce me.

At least not right now.

The little angel on my shoulder tapped me on the ear and reminded me of Bran. The little devil waved her tail with a flourish and noted this was only a run, a fun run, a nice job in the woods with a fellow Felis.

My nose twitched as I caught the smell of the forest. Damp, fresh and wild.

I needed this. I might regret it later but I needed this.

I shucked the coat and moved around the table to take his hand.

"When was the last time you had a good run?" he murmured.

I laughed; I couldn't help myself. "That's got to be the worst pick-up line ever."

Trace chuckled as his hand went around mine, warm fingers banishing the nervous chill I felt. "You've got a dirty mind."

He Changed quickly, his blond hair shifting into shades of tawny running over his face and arms. Dark black streaks started at his nose and ran up over his head. His hand went tight around mine.

"Ready?" Trace grinned, showing off an impressive set of fangs.

I rolled my shoulders back. "Let's go."

We started off at a light jog, my leg muscles loosening up as we headed for the edge of the meadow. A small group jumped past us, a bunch of youngsters in their twenties laughing and calling to each other.

Most of them were bare-chested and in full Change, some even barefoot. No nudity, at least not yet.

Trace laughed as we leapt over a fallen log, seeming to read my mind. "I'm not that crazy. Last thing I need is to have to take time off work because I got a stick rammed through the bottom of my foot. Or any place else." He kept just ahead of me—I could tell he was holding back.

I increased my pace, pushing myself. I might not be able to Change but I wasn't going to be embarrassed in front of another Pride.

A cool sheen of sweat covered me as we veered down one trail, away from the pack of kits. The woods were thick and lush, the greenery exploding around us as I opened up all of my senses to the wilderness, let the Felis run free.

Trace grabbed a low-hanging branch from a tree and held it back for me.

I snatched the chance and let go with a burst of speed, shooting ahead of him and bounding over another fat fallen log.

His laugh followed me as I kept to the well-traveled path, my feet landing where dozens, maybe hundreds of Felis had run before me.

I drew in the fresh forest air, smelled the wildlife scattering ahead of us. Rabbits, deer, groundhogs and even a bear or two, none of which wanted to get caught by a group of Felis on the hunt. It was a thick, heady rush of power I'd forgotten about for years, the mastery over the environment. We were kings in our own little part of the world, rulers without question.

I felt a wee bit faint.

"Come on." Trace grabbed my hand. "Don't let the kids show us up."

He pulled me down the trail with a roar. I laughed and matched it as we sprinted by a couple more intent on finding a secluded place to make out than run.

I glanced back at the pair as they vanished into a field of tall, overgrown grass. A surge of heat ran up my spine, heightened by the Felis all around me. I might not be able to Change but I was pure Felis where it counted.

My free hand came up and unbuttoned the front of my blouse, letting the heat escape. I reached up and pulled the hair band out to let my blond hair fly free over my shoulders. My heartbeat spun up and settled into a rapid pace as my breathing became measured pants.

A narrow creek offered little resistance and we leapt over it together with a shared laugh. A group of kits, the oldest maybe eight years old, scrambled past us with giggles and growls, a young girl leading her pack of future suitors.

We'd gone in a long, looping circle, the thick brush and undergrowth giving way again to the trimmed-back edges of the farmland. I spotted the pavilion in the distance, people crowding around the coolers to rehydrate.

"Almost there," Trace yelled when we jumped over a small ditch.

My running shoes slipped on the well-trod mud. His grip on my hand intensified as he pulled me up out of an almost-fall and we sprinted for the tent.

My pulse hammered in my ears. I hadn't felt so alive in years. I'd gone jogging once or twice in the city in a vain attempt to recapture this freedom, this wilderness inside myself but it hadn't worked. The wilderness was where I felt the most at home, where I could be myself.

We were Felis. We were hunters and, by God, I was hungry for the kill.

Trace kicked it up until we ran full-out, my lungs sore and close to bursting as I matched him, step by step.

He glistened with sweat, his furred chest rising and falling with each deep breath. The stripes across his face became more vivid and he whistled through clenched teeth.

We skidded to a stop at the edge of the tent beside an older couple who leaned on each other, gasping and wheezing even as they kissed. The woman giggled, grey and silver streaks in her fur. Her husband put his hands on his knees and wheezed.

Her mate stood up and grabbed her in a tight embrace, kissing with a hunger I hoped I'd have at that age.

"Not too shabby," Trace said, still holding my hand.

I chuckled. "For an old broad, you mean."

"You're not that old," Trance answered. "And I bet you still have it when and where it counts."

His predatory look captured me, froze me in place like a deer in headlights. He didn't move toward me, didn't do anything but stare at me.

It was enough to begin shredding my defenses in a slow, determined attack.

The wind shifted, pulling in the scents and smells from the opposite direction.

My eyes widened as a familiar odor crashed into my lungs, tugging at my heart. It grabbed Trace's spell and strangled it, killed it and made it roadkill.

I spun around to see Bran staring at me.

He stood at the edge of the parking lot, his long leather duster flying open in the breeze. The light blue dress shirt was tucked into his jeans, the top two buttons undone and the thin black tie hanging down loose over his chest.

His deep brown eyes were wide and wild, raking over me with a fierceness I'd never seen before. Hunger mixed with anger mixed with a whole lot of testosterone.

I knew how I looked. Blouse half-open, sweaty and flushed, holding hands with a stranger.

This was not good.

Bran strode up to Trace, the toes of his running shoes brushing against Trace's work boots.

The elderly man slipped an arm around his wife's waist and pulled her close, shielding her from the crashing egos. She curled her head into his neck and watched me, her eyes wide and curious at seeing a human act so bold and daring.

The group of young kits who'd passed us earlier vanished into the forest, away from trouble.

The other Felis faded back, out of my eyesight.

Trace didn't Change back. He stared at Bran. His hand stayed tight around my fingers.

I couldn't breathe.

I couldn't move.

It was like someone had jammed an iron spike down from the top of my head through my spine and into the ground, pinning me there.

"I believe you're holding something that belongs to me," Bran growled, his voice low and menacing.

"Really," Trace replied, his voice level and calm. "Didn't know she was taken."

"You knew." It wasn't a question. "You smelled me on her jacket, on her clothing. You're not dumb."

Others moved in, forming a small circle around us. Changed and unChanged Felis watching with a mixture of curiosity and anger a human coming into their sanctuary and challenging one of their own.

"You want to fight for what's yours?" Trace tilted his head to one side, showing teeth. His tongue ran over sharp incisors, usually used for tearing meat apart.

I pulled my hand free, my mind racing as I broke away from my panicked haze. There was no way Bran could hold his own against a Changed Felis, not on his best day. I was already there investigating one murder; I didn't need to be dealing with another.

"Yeah." Bran shrugged his duster off his shoulders and threw it to the ground. He started to unbutton his shirt without breaking eye contact with Trace. "I do."

"No. Stop." I stepped between the two men, my hands raised.

I spotted Carson and McCallum on the edge of the growing crowd. Neither seemed in a rush to defuse the situation.

Bran's shirt fell open. I sucked in my breath, seeing the well-defined muscles. It was like seeing him for the first time again.

Or the last.

Trace licked his lips. "You got plenty of balls for a human."

Bran motioned downward at said parts. "Bigger than yours, kit."

Trace's eyes went wide at the slur. His claws slid out from between his knuckles, long and sharp.

The two men were looking through me as if I were a ghost. This wasn't about me now; it was about two male egos.

Bran lifted his fists in a classic boxer stance. His right foot slid back, digging into the ground as he relaxed his knees and braced himself.

Trace took a step forward. His right hand rose over his head, claws poised to strike.

"Stop." I grabbed Bran's fist with one hand and Trace's claws with the other, slipping my fingers between the razor-sharp edges. "I don't belong to either of you and don't want to."

The words burned my throat. I wasn't sure what I wanted right now but it wasn't to be a mere possession, a trophy won by brute strength.

I'd choose who I was with. At my own speed and in my own time.

Now wasn't the time or place. Not with two angry men ready to rip each other to pieces.

The cloud lifted from Bran's eyes first as he stared at me, shaking off the battle lust. He didn't drop his attack stance. He just waited.

His hand stayed closed, frozen in place with my grip.

Trace didn't move. He remained fixated on Bran, not giving an inch.

My hand began to shake, holding Trace at bay. I was exhausted from the run, from the confrontation, and if he wanted to toss me to one side and gut Bran it'd be easy.

I still couldn't breathe.

SEVEN

A WOMAN BROKE through the line and strode up to Trace. She was older than I was with long dark hair pulled into a braid, the light brown jacket hanging off her petite frame. Her dark eyes blazed as she pushed me to one side and slapped Trace across the face, hard.

I stumbled and spun, breaking away from Bran. I ended up standing beside him, facing Trace and the mysterious woman.

He turned and started to snarl at her, the threatening tone vanishing as shock turned to recognition.

"You know better than this," she whispered in a low commanding tone. "These are visitors. Is this how you welcome a member of another Pride, by mocking and attacking her friends?"

I took a step closer to Bran, who had dropped his hands by his sides. He didn't look at me, his attention still on Trace.

Trace stared at the ground as he Changed back. "Sorry, Lisa."

The tone was low and submissive, a kit to an elder. This woman might not be on the Board but she carried more weight inside the Pride than Trace did and wasn't afraid to use it.

"Sorry, indeed." She spun on her heel and faced me. "Lisa Darning. I met your man at the diner, asking if anyone knew where you were staying." One edge of her mouth twitched. "Knew he wasn't family but he said he was with you."

"I told her to call Jess if she didn't believe me," Bran mumbled under his breath.

"Which is what I did. She confirmed he was legit and able to be trusted. Figured I'd bring him up here to meet you." She glared at Trace over one shoulder. "Thought I'd show him some hospitality."

"I was just taking her on a run," he replied, a bit of a whine in his voice.

"Understood. But challenging her mate isn't acceptable." She turned back to Bran and me. "Please accept my apologies."

"Sure." I buttoned my blouse to the top button, feeling the blush on my cheeks. "Just a misunderstanding all 'round. Men."

She nodded with an understanding smile. "Men." Lisa looked over our heads at the bystanders. "Show's over folks. Get back to doing what you were doing."

The crowd wandered off at a rapid pace, the younger kids gathering to wrestle and tussle in a sand pit not far from us while the majority returned to the buffet table and beverage coolers.

Trace walked off without saying anything, kicking up grass with each heavy-booted step.

Lisa ran a hand through her loose brown strands of hair. "Damned hubris. It'll be the death of all of us." She looked at me. "I guess we need to go somewhere and talk."

"What?"

She rubbed her hands on the front of her jeans. "I'm one of the women who saw Mike Hansa before he was killed."

"I'm going to go get a beer. See you later." Bran snatched up his coat and walked away. I felt a headache start behind one eye, undoing all the good from the run. My stomach rolled.

Lisa led me back to the interview table I'd been using. "I'm sorry I wasn't here earlier. I'm on the town council and we had a meeting run late, then I had to go out to my business—I run a printing company. Then I went to the diner to drop off a box of menu specials and—" she settled in the chair opposite me, "—and that all don't mean shit 'cause you're here to do your job."

"Thanks for stepping in." The lack of trembling in my voice surprised me. "Been a long time since I caused a brawl."

"Men'll fight over a bar stool, Felis or human." She laughed. "No offense meant."

"None taken." I looked down at my notes, forcing

my pulse down to a reasonable rate. "So—" I cleared my throat, "—tell me about Mike Hansa."

"Cute, hot, human." She drummed well-manicured nails on the plastic white tabletop. "I'm single and not ashamed to say that I found him quite sexy."

"Ever jump him?" I cut to the chase.

Lisa sat back in the plastic chair and giggled. It sounded odd coming from a woman Jess's age. "I might have enjoyed seeing him shake his tight little buns up on stage but I knew I didn't have a chance in hell of taking him home. I figured he wasn't into that much...intensity." A predatory look came into her eyes. "You know we tend to be a bit rough on our men."

I silently agreed. Bran already had more scratches on his back than I could count.

"Can you think of why anyone would kill him? Upset mates, jealous women, anything?" I tossed the ball in her lap. She had to have some level of seniority in the Pride to call Trace off so quickly. She knew the scuttlebutt. "You seem to know what's going on 'round here. Anyone have a hankering to take his head off for a slight, real or imagined?" I glanced toward the clearing where we'd been only a few minutes ago. "Lose his temper over a lady?"

Lisa brooded for a minute, forehead furrowed.

I waited. At least she wasn't delivering the usual Pride mantra.

"Off the top of my head, no. It wasn't like we all

didn't know who and what he was. He never played
favorites."

"Did he know about the family?"

Her head snapped up like I'd slapped her. "Hell,
no. Rules are the same here as they are up there
in Canada. We don't tell anyone who we are." Her
eyes darted toward Bran, who sat at a nearby table
working on his second beer. "But there's always ex-
ceptions to the rule." She studied my face. "Like
yourself."

I didn't fall for the derail. "Where were you the
night Hansa died?"

She crossed her legs. "I went to the evening show,
dropped a few tens in his sweet, tight thong and then
went home. Alone."

I cocked my head to one side. "Really. No boyfriend, no husband, no lover?"

Lisa glanced at something over my right shoulder.
"My work is my life."

"Of course it is." I got to my feet and picked up
my notebook. "Thanks for the help. I'll be in touch
if I have any more questions."

"No problem." She paused for a second, biting on
her lower lip before speaking. "Regarding your man.
Might be a good idea to keep him contained. Trace
doesn't like to be taunted anywhere, much less in
public." Lisa stood up. "And I might not be around
the next time they tangle."

She didn't wait for an answer but headed for one

of the small groups hanging around the fringes of the clearing.

I slipped my coat on and tucked the notebook into one pocket. My heart was still racing and I wasn't sure what to do next.

Finding criminals was easy.

Being in a relationship was hard.

I headed for Bran's table. A handful of Felis moved out of my way as if I had rabies. I couldn't blame them—I might be a visitor from another Pride but I was definitely unwelcome.

And at least one Felis here had good reason to fear me.

The sun was setting, sending bright red lightning across the dying grey sky. A cool breeze came out of the forest carrying the scent of a dozen Felis and a hint of rabbit blood.

I sat down opposite Brandon and said nothing.

He dragged one fingernail across the wood, digging in and out of well-worn grooves.

The silence lasted for a full minute.

"I wanted to surprise you." He spread his hands with a wry twist of his lips. "Surprise."

"Where's Jazz?"

"Being spoiled rotten by Dan. Told him to check in on her once a day and give her treats. I figure in the few hours I've been gone she's wrestled a dozen treats from him."

I rubbed my eyes with the palms of my hands,

fighting back the urge to cry. "I'm sorry. I'm so fucking sorry."

Bran didn't say anything.

I intertwined my fingers, knotting my knuckles until they turned white. "Nothing happened. You have to believe me on this—nothing happened. We went for a run, nothing else." I had to repeat it—I had to. "Nothing happened."

"I know."

The two words punched me in the chest, taking away the apologies I'd lined up. "What?"

Bran smiled. "I trust you, Reb." He sucked in a breath through clenched teeth. "It's just that I show up and you're all sweaty and hot, holding hands with Mr. Furry Face. Cue machismo meltdown." He ran a hand through his short hair, a sheepish look replacing the stoic. "What they say about red hair and bad tempers—it's true."

I felt a shiver of relief crawl down my spine. "I can believe it."

"Who is he, anyway?" Bran asked, trying to sound casual but I caught the tension in his voice.

"My babysitter," I answered. "Nephew of one of the Board members. He's stuck being my shadow while I'm here."

I left out the marriage proposal.

He looked over to where Lisa Darning stood with a group of other women, all of them avoiding looking our way.

"Thank God that woman intervened before I started something I couldn't win." He shook his head.

"I don't know. I thought it was sort of sexy." I shrugged.

"Oh, really?" His lips twisted into a grin. "That I find hard to believe." He got to his feet and reached out his hand. "I think it's time for us to call it a night."

I looked around the compound. Someone had set up a bonfire and the kits sat around it with marshmallows and various types of meat stuck on sticks. Carson and McCallum had disappeared along with most of the adults. There was no sign of Plussey, if he'd even shown up.

"I won't find anything else here." I winced as I took his hand, the sharp pain flashing across my shoulders. "And I think I pulled something."

"Really." Bran couldn't hold back the sarcasm. "When was the last time you went jogging? Did you stretch out beforehand?"

"Ah…"

"Right." He nodded toward the parking lot. "Let's get back to the hotel and I'll give you a massage."

The headache behind my eyes popped like an overinflated balloon. "That sounds good."

"And then we can discuss who belongs to whom." The stoic look returned, tempered with a bit of annoyance.

The throbbing pain returned and brought friends.

I spotted Trace sitting in his green pickup as we approached the parking lot, and decided to say nothing. I had enough trouble on my plate.

He gave us a glance but didn't say anything, didn't move.

I said a quiet prayer of thanks.

Bran's rental car turned out to be a flashy light blue convertible, hardly suitable for undercover work.

"Couldn't get anything louder?" I moved toward my own ride.

"They did have an awesome Mini Cooper." Bran chuckled. "I'll follow you back to the hotel."

I spun out of the parking lot in a spew of gravel, Bran not too far behind. The cool night air rushed in through the open window. The pickup followed at a respectful distance as we drove through town, the majority of the town businesses closed and shuttered tight. The motel parking lot was nearly empty with a few stragglers hanging on for one more night.

In the rearview mirror I watched the truck settle into the far corner of the lot, a goodly distance from our two cars.

The young woman behind the counter didn't look up as Bran and I walked through the lobby.

I fumbled with the cardkey, trying three times before getting the light to turn green. Bran didn't say anything.

The room hadn't been searched again. I considered it a small victory. The scent of the two thugs was weak and almost gone, a faint shadow on my tongue.

Bran tossed his bag against the far wall. "Strip down and get in the shower. You need it." The tone wasn't threatening but definitely alpha male.

The snapback was on my tongue but I resisted. He was right. My muscles were beginning to seize up and if I didn't deal with them now I'd have a hell of a time moving tomorrow. My mind had been ready to run but my body hadn't.

Trace was lucky he hadn't ended up carrying me back to the clearing.

My cheeks felt hot at the memory. I'd walked right into that situation because I'd been so eager to be accepted again as a Felis.

I wouldn't get caught again.

Bran hung up his coat. He turned and took mine, stripping it off my shoulders with a less-than-gentle touch.

"Shower," he repeated, with a trace of a threat in his voice.

"Okay, okay." I walked into the small bathroom, hearing the squeak of the bedsprings behind me. The television came on a second later, blaring some detective drama.

I guessed I was showering alone.

The fight wasn't over, just on hiatus.

The hot water helped ease the ache out of my

bones but not out of my mind. The Pride was closing ranks to protect one of their own in proud Felis tradition. The dead man didn't matter. All that they cared about was making sure no one got tagged for his death and pulled up for punishment.

After all, it was only a human.

I angled the shower head to pound on the back of my right shoulder, letting it work on an emerging nasty knot of muscles. The sliver of hotel soap washed the last bits of the run down the drain.

Tilting my head back I filled my mouth with hot water, swishing it around before spitting it out. The headache was gone, chased away with the thoughts running through my mind.

I couldn't hold it against their Board; it was the Felis doctrine. Throw up the wall and deny everything to keep our secret.

Except now I had to break down that wall and find the killer on the other side.

I reached around with my left hand over my right shoulder to grab an itchy spot, straining as the muscles protested. Unable to get to it properly, I leaned back on the cheap plastic soap holder and shifted back and forth.

I wouldn't have this problem if Bran weren't being stubborn. All I'd have to do is ask him to reach over and scratch…

A seed of an idea blossomed at the back of my mind, cutting through the bullshit of the last hour.

A cool puff of air broke through the steam. "Jess is on the phone. Should I tell her to call back?"

"No." I turned off the hot water. "Make small talk and I'll be there in a second."

The answering snort told me how much time I had. I lunged for the hotel towel.

"Yeah, I'm here. Hold the fuck on." Bran barked into the receiver. He paused for a minute and I could imagine Jess's short, curt response. "I've about had it with the Felis, thank you very much."

I stepped out, the towel wrapped around me and my long hair stuck to my bare back.

Bran dropped the cell phone into my hand and lay down on the bed, studying the television screen with his back to me.

"Jess."

"Sounds like trouble in paradise."

"Don't screw with me right now," I snapped. "I'm in no mood for it."

"What happened?" She sounded genuinely confused. "Bran's yapping and making no sense. Tell me what's going on."

I cleared my throat. "Remember you asked me if this Pride was too integrated with the humans? I'd say they were—big time."

Bran shifted his position but didn't turn.

"Do tell," Jess said.

"Every place has Felis working there. The hotel,

the bars, everywhere. You can't swing a dead cat without hitting family."

I could imagine Jess wincing at the mental image.

"Okay, we figured that much. So what's got your buddy's panties in a bunch?"

"Bran thought he'd sneak down and surprise me. The Pride was having their monthly get-together and I went on a run and—" I stumbled, feeling like I was confessing to a priest, "—this fellow, one they assigned to me as a babysitter, he ended up holding my hand and Bran showed up and…" I glanced over to Bran who was steadfastly ignoring me. "It got sorta heated."

"Clusterfuck central," Jess replied. "Any blood?"

"Not yet. A woman stepped in and chilled the situation. Trace backed off when she called him out on his bad manners."

I left out the part where I ended up between the two alphas trying to claim me.

"Hmm," Jess said. "Bad feelings all around."

I pulled the towel off and worked at drying my hair with one hand. "Sort of worked out well in a way. Found out Lisa Darning is not only a member on the town council but also a mover and shaker inside the Pride, the way she got Trace to back right off. Good to know that." I paused for a second, deciding what to say next. "And she lied to me during our interview."

"What?" Jess's tone was guarded. "She lied."

"Her eyes. When you look up and to the left you're lying about something. Scientific tests show…"

"She's a fucking Felis, Reb. The rules don't apply to us."

"She's hiding something," I growled back. "Believe it or not, but this is what I do for a living when I'm not running errands for you. I've seen people lie and she was lying to hide something from me."

"We're all hiding something." The low rolling anger in her words attacked me, made me want to go and curl up in a corner. "Even you. Something happened on that run, didn't it?"

I glanced at Bran, who sat on the edge of the bed. "This isn't about me. It's about a dead man called Mike Hansa."

"Then ignore the politics and do your job."

"I just want…"

"I wanted a lot of things out of life, kit. I didn't get them." Jess's tone changed to a lower, reprimanding one. "Just do your job. Find the killer, take 'er down. And don't get caught holding hands with your babysitter."

My teeth ground together as I held back, staring at Bran's back. I felt like I'd just been caught making out by my mother.

Time to take charge of this conversation and put it back on track before I started asking her for mating advice.

"I think this affair story is bullshit to try and lead me in the wrong direction."

"How are you figuring that?" Jess snapped back into neutral.

Bran gave me a curious look, ignoring the television show. His eyebrows drew together as he frowned and shifted closer, almost within reach.

"Hansa's body had plenty of Felis scent all over him, plenty of women. No surprise there; the guy was a stripper. He'd get close to them, they pushed dollar bills in his thong and maybe got a kiss, a slap, whatever the situation warranted."

"I'm listening," Jess said.

So was Bran.

"The theory was he got too cuddly with one of them. I'm not just talking a slap and tickle here and there, I'm talking about between the sheets. He gets too friendly with one of the women, gets some action in bed and gets taken out either by the woman herself or her mate."

"I'm familiar with the idea," Jess droned. "Your point?"

I locked eyes with Bran. "Hansa's back was bare. Untouched. Practically pristine."

Bran frowned and turned toward me.

Time to do a little groveling. Not that I was apologizing about the run or being with Trace—I'm a big girl and my life is my own. But it wouldn't hurt to remind Bran he was still number one in my life.

Tucking my damp hair behind my ears I wedged the phone against my neck and advanced on him. I knelt on the edge of the mattress next to Bran and unbuttoned his dress shirt. "Now you tell me, how many Felis men do you know with unscarred backs?"

His eyes were wide but he didn't move to stop me. A smirk replaced the confused expression as my hands slid down his bare skin, brushing against certain spots I knew were sensitive. He closed his eyes and bent his head back, pressing his lips together.

Jess's laugh vibrated against my cheek. "None."

"Right. So how did this guy end up without a single scratch mark? No Felis woman's that gentle." I slipped the shirt off Bran's shoulders. He let it fall behind him, effectively trapping his arms in a fabric knot. He let out something between a grunt and a groan.

"What was that?" Jess asked.

"Nothing." I moved behind Bran. My hand traced the numerous small scratches on his back. Even without Felis claws I'd left my mark on him.

A trembling wave rippled across the exposed skin, his reaction to my touch.

"Pretty thin to build a theory on," Jess said.

"Very thin," I admitted. "But I find it very improbable he managed to have an ongoing affair and be unscathed."

"So he wasn't screwing with the women?" Jess said. "So who killed him? And why?"

"I don't know," I admitted. "But I don't think it was from having an affair."

Bran shivered under my touch. The smirk evolved into a contented smile.

"Hmm. Keep me updated." Jess chuckled. "And be gentle on Bran while you make up. I hear humans break easily."

She broke the connection on her end. I tossed the cell phone to one side.

"Wheels within wheels," Bran said. He opened his eyes and looked at me. A feral look, a hungry stare pinning me where I knelt. "Be worse if your claws came out, eh?"

I nodded. "Not quite needing stitches but bad enough. There's no way he was bedding a Felis woman and staying untouched."

He moved toward me, stripping the shirt from his hands with little effort. His right hand came up, touching my shoulder and pushing me off the edge of the bed. "I want to know what you meant back there."

"What?" I took another step back as he rose from the mattress.

"You don't belong to anyone." A smile tugged at his lips. "Pretty brassy statement."

"I meant it." I tucked the towel around me.

"So what's the last three months been about?" Bran stripped the shirt from his hands and moved forward again. "Just killing time?"

I felt the cool wall against my back. "You know it hasn't."

"I know." He pointed a finger at his chest. "But do you know?" He flung the shirt to the floor. "What you said out there, what was that supposed to mean?" His eyes were wide and dark. "What do you want from me? What do you want from us, from this? Where are we going?"

I started to answer him and stopped.

I couldn't. I had no idea what to say.

"Okay." Bran drew a deep breath, one hand rubbing the back of his neck. "I'm not going to press you now. We're both too fucking wired, you're working this case and it's not a good time for big decisions. But I want to talk about this later, when things calm down." His eyes locked with mine. "I told you when we started this relationship I wasn't into one-night stands. I meant it."

I nodded, my stomach twisting into knots. "I'm sorry." My fingers pulled up into fists. "I just don't—"

"Don't be. We knew this wasn't going to be easy." He took hold of my bare shoulders and stepped backward, pulling me with him. "Bed. Now. I hear makeup sex is the best."

"But we didn't—"

He kissed me, silencing any protests. "I didn't come all this way to fight." He waggled an eyebrow at me. "I just hope you have the stamina to survive a rather hungry human attack."

I urged him on with a flick of my hand. "We Felis are made of strong stuff." I grinned. "Bring it."

He pounced and I realized I'd greatly underestimated the urges of the human male.

EIGHT

AN HOUR LATER I lay on my stomach, dozing off as Bran ordered pizza in the nude. He hung up the phone and slapped my bare bottom. "No sleeping. I need some food here."

"I ate already," I mumbled. "Besides, you wore me out."

"Good." He cracked his knuckles, wearing a smug look. "Wouldn't be doing my job if you weren't."

He sprang away at my weak attempt to slap him. "Don't be a smart ass." I rolled onto my back, tugging a sheet along for the ride. "We need a plan."

Bran hovered just out of range, working on putting his underwear and jeans back on. "I thought I improvised quite well."

"Not that." I returned his satisfied smirk. "What to do with this investigation."

"You could always throw me out." He tugged his pants over his hips, giving a little hop to one side. "Have a big fight, let me go investigate on my own."

"Too cliché. They'd see through that in a second. It's a small town and everyone notices new people showing up. Two of us in two days and they'll know we're together, even before you came back here." I shook my head. "I don't want to put you out there without protection. The Pride knows you're with me and you know about the Felis. Anything happens to you they have to answer to me. And Jess."

Bran raised an eyebrow. "Jess?"

"Consider it honorary membership status, same as I have." I reached over and wrestled with my own clothing, loath to get dressed. "Screw with you, screw with me."

The lonely eyebrow joined the other, rising as high as they could go on Bran's forehead.

I winced. "Bad choice of words."

Bran put a finger to his lips, silencing me.

The knock on the door came a second later.

It was the young kit who had signed me in the night I arrived. Bran took the pizza, tipped him generously and sent him on his way.

"Think he overheard much?"

Bran looked at me. "Who cares?" He sniffed the box. "Ooh."

I sat at the small table and brought him over with a crook of my finger. "Don't be a pig. I did some work too."

"Really?" He sat opposite me and flipped the lid up, inhaling deeply. "I remember a lot of moaning and groaning. Is that what we're calling work now?"

I slapped his hand as he reached for the largest slice. "Don't make me regret not having claws."

"Your fingernails do just as well. Time to clip those, by the way." He scowled but allowed me to snatch the gooey triangle, the cheese strings stretching across the table as I maneuvered the edge into my mouth.

We ate in silence for a few minutes, enjoying the relative peace.

I knew it wouldn't last.

"Did you enjoy it?" Bran pulled another slice apart.

The casual tone should have been a warning for me to pay closer attention.

My eyes widened. "Weren't you just mentioning the moaning?"

"Not that," Bran replied. "I meant the run."

"Oh." I felt my cheeks burn but chose to ignore it, focusing on the thick pepperoni slice trying to escape by sliding off. "It was okay."

"You seemed pretty happy." The words sounded almost painful. "Being with your own kind and all that."

I rolled my shoulders back, feeling the muscles twitch. "I hadn't had one like that for a while. It was amazing."

"Hmm." The disgruntled note matched his expression.

"I wasn't talking about the run."

His eyes sparked with pride before he frowned.

"I'm not sure if that's an insult or a compliment on my past performances."

I licked the sauce off my fingers. "While you figure that out, finish getting dressed. We're going out."

Bran chewed on the doughy crust. "Where?"

I grinned.

He went pale. "No."

"Mount up, cowboy. Time to go where few men ever go."

"A day spa?"

"You'll hang out with street kids in Toronto but you're afraid of going to a club?"

"It's not my type of club." His eyes narrowed. "Is it yours? Should I be tracking where you go while I'm out of town?"

"If I do I promise you it's because of a case. And I'll take the Fifth on everything else," I mumbled through a mouthful of pepperoni.

"You're not American."

"Not the point." I snatched up a tissue and wiped my greasy fingers. "Just don't say I never take you interesting places."

Bran pouted. "I thought I took you enough interesting places tonight." He let out an exaggerated sigh as I pushed the last slice toward him. "Oh, the things I do for love."

WITHIN THE HOUR we parked in front of the Cat's Meow. The small memorial to Mike Hansa was long gone, the flashing neon lights bouncing off the hoods of over two dozen cars. Flashy red convertibles mixed with battered trucks; tan SUVs rubbing bumpers with BMWs.

Bran stepped out from the passenger side. He scratched his chest, his short nails skipping over the light blue shirt. "I can wait in the car, you know. Or even go back to the hotel. Someone could steal my rental car. I should be there to watch it."

"Now you want to be the submissive." I grabbed his coat sleeve. "Not going to happen." I spotted the green pickup truck moving into the parking lot, lights off and cruising into an empty spot. "Maybe you'll learn something." A fast spin and we were facing in the opposite direction. "Expand your repertoire, as it were."

Bran followed me in, cursing under his breath.

He hadn't seen the truck.

The inside of the club was loud and vibrant, a long bar at the side filled with excited women clapping their hands and hooting as a pair of male dancers shook and shimmied their way across a platform at the front of the converted warehouse. Swirling neon lights washed over the crowd while the women jumped and danced to the thumping rhythms of the loud music.

"I fit right in," Bran shouted in my ear as we approached the bar. "I can wait in the car, you know. No use giving these fellows unfair competition." He gave a sly wink to a pair of women nearby who giggled and dove deeper into their margaritas.

"No." I pointed a finger at a door beside the stage. "I want you to talk to the performers. You're a reporter. Find out what they thought of Mike Hansa."

"What's my cover story?" he shot back.

"Same as mine—making sure there's no upcoming paternity suit. I'd think these fellows would appreciate keeping their lineage clean of any surprises." I pulled him into an empty space at the far end of the bar, abandoned due to the distance from the dancers.

The bartender strolled over. She didn't raise an eyebrow at seeing Bran and gave me a quick once-over. She slapped down two cardboard coasters and gave us a welcoming smile. "What can I get you?"

My nostrils twitched. Felis.

"I'm investigating Mike Hansa's death." I nodded toward the stage. "Who's the manager?"

She blinked once, twice. "Sophia Martin. She's in the back."

"I'd like to talk to her." I nudged Bran away with my hip. "My friend here is going to chat to with fellows in the meantime."

I didn't ask permission.

Her eyes raked over Bran, a smile on her lips. The challenge was there if I wanted to act on it.

I did.

I reached over and pressed down on her hand, intentionally targeting the thin bones on the back of her hand. I didn't have to say anything.

She winced. "Okay, okay. Let me call her and tell her you're coming." Her free hand went to an old-style black rotary phone sitting next to a set of bottles.

The dial spun under her finger as Bran slipped away, wearing a smug grin. I made a mental note to discuss Felis challenges with him later.

Last thing I needed was some woman moving in on Bran.

Last thing I needed was Trace moving in on me.

I turned and watched the muscled blond man on stage swivel his hips, punctuating every few rotations with an outward thrust, he and his partner doing a caveman theme.

I'd never seen a rabbit pelt used to cover, well, so much.

The women screamed and roared, dollar bills held high.

He moved to the edge of the platform, just close enough for eager fingers to reach out and tuck paper into a sweaty fur band.

I didn't need to use my Felis skills to feel the arousal in the air. He could have any of these women, any of them with a twitch of his finger. The thick musk peeling off his naked, wet skin told me he was as turned on as the women and enjoying their attention.

"Sophia wants me to bring you back right away."
The bartender led me to a small door at the end of the
bar. She paused, her hand on the doorknob. "Sorry
'bout that earlier. Didn't know he was taken."

"And now you know." I swept by her.

The office was a converted storeroom bereft of
windows and good taste. Every inch of the wall was
covered with flyers for the Cat's Meow, a virtual
chorus line of half-naked men staring and smiling
wherever you looked.

A metal folding chair sat in front of the matching
desk, office surplus. Whatever extra money she'd
been making from the club didn't go into redecorat-
ing. Her long red hair was pulled up into a bun so
tight you could bounce a quarter off her head.

Sophia Martin didn't get up from behind her desk,
watching me approach her with narrow, suspicious
eyes. She looked exactly like she did in the flyer
photograph, give or take ten pounds.

She drew a deep drag on a cigarette and blew
smoke in my direction. She had to have ten years on
me, maybe twenty depending on how you counted
the age rings around her eyes. Her fingernails were
short and jagged from nervous chewing, one digit
scabbed over with fresh blood. She popped it into
her mouth and sucked as she juggled the cigarette
to the other side.

"Before we start…" She tapped the papers to her
left. "I got all my paperwork up to date. Local taxes,

state taxes, business licenses, whatever you want to see."

"Not why I'm here." I shook my head, helping myself to the lone chair. A thousand eyes watched my every move. "Rebecca Desjardin. Private investigator. Insurance company wanted me to run the numbers on Hansa before closing the file and paying out to the family."

Her eyes narrowed as she studied me. "Yeah. Right." The tip of her cigarette burned bright orange as she inhaled. "He had good insurance?"

"Better than most." I didn't flinch under her stare. She had nothing on Jess.

She leaned back in the chair. "Town council's been bitching for months about making it mandatory to lock up the garbage bin; keep the animals from digging in the trash. I told them I'd put locks on the fucker when they put the law in. I don't have time to worry about losing keys and all that shit. I was a damned idiot and I feel like shit 'bout it." She stubbed out the half-smoked cigarette in an overflowing ashtray and lit another. "I'm thinking about putting a bounty out on that bear."

Sophia paused, waiting for a response.

I shrugged. "Wouldn't hurt. Don't know about the laws down here but if you'd feel better doing it…"

"Damned hunters should be out there looking for the fucking bear." Sophia took a deep drag on the death stick. "Damned animals," she repeated. "I'll start it at two hundred dollars. That'll get 'em out." A glint came into her eyes. "Insurance company want to get in on it?"

"No," I said. "But thanks for asking."

"I bought the locks today." She glanced down to one side. "Better late than never." There was regret in her voice, honest remorse at Hansa's death. Whether it was from losing a good dancer or a good human being I couldn't tell.

Another white cloud of smoke drifted into my face. "I understand you weren't welcomed by the town when you opened up the club, even though you're way out here in the wild." I tried not to cough.

"We jumped through the hoops, filled out the paperwork to get our business license. Every three months we get recertified by the town council." She leaned forward, the oversized purple blouse barely able to hold in her ample breasts. "I don't like that but I tolerate it. I could get a lawyer to scream and file papers but I don't. I don't because I want the public, via their elected representatives, to have a say."

"How democratic."

She laughed. "Everyone hates us until they make money. The hotels, the restaurants—they all make money off my business, off the customers we pull into the area. Then they all love us." Her bright red lips split apart in a smile. "Especially when tax time rolls around and we pay our fat share."

"Wouldn't a dead stripper put a damper on all this fun?"

"For a day or two." She studied my face for a minute before continuing. "Miss Desjardin, I grew up in this town. I saw the mills shut down and the unemployment rate rocket. I saw most of my generation move away to try and get jobs, move anywhere for a chance at a good life. My father worked in a mill and retired a broken man with nothing but a ghost of a pension despite being a loyal union worker for decades." The fresh cigarette bobbled on her lips. "When I got the chance to open this place up I jumped at it. Better than busting my hump at some dollar store for minimum wage." She leaned back and plucked the cigarette out with two fingers, waving it in the air as she wrote invisible numbers. "Believe it or not I went to college for business administration. I can show you my diploma if you'd like."

"I'm good." I looked at the man-paper surrounding us. "Who put the money up to start this show?"

"Consortium out of Philly." She sucked on the filter. "They've got their fingers in all the local pies. Casinos, clubs, whatever makes them money. Don't worry, they're clean, they're clean. Honest men looking to make honest profits."

I put up my hand, stopping her. "I'm not working for anyone but the family."

That much was true.

"Anyone have a grudge against Hansa? Unpaid debts, anything?"

"He was a straight player. Never hit on the staff and never begged free drinks. Never cried for an advance on his next paycheck. Not that he ever needed it; these boys make enough on tips." She shook her head. "Hansa was a nice guy but he's easily replaced. Look at the ladies out there tonight. They can't tell one from the other. As long as they've got tight buns and a good smile, that's all they want."

"All wrapped up in a sweet little package with a bow attached."

She looked at me. "I'm not going to apologize for what I do, Miss Desjardin. I know Cassie Prosser and the mayor aren't happy with me being here, but I'm providing employment and paying taxes, which is more than they can say for their own efforts to revitalize the area."

"Hey, I'm not looking to close you down. I just want the truth."

Sophia tilted her head to one side and sighed. "Truth is rarer than true love these days, sister. But good luck with that."

I got to my feet. "I'd like to send someone to talk with the men. Just to make sure there's not going to be any surprise paternity suits for the family to deal within a few months. His family's got enough to deal with; they don't need any legal beagles racing around to make money."

"You mean that cutie you sent back there before you stepped in?" She shifted her chair to the left and waved at the line of tiny screens that appeared. "I got security cameras for a reason." The cigarette bounced around her lips. "No problem as long as they hit the stage on time." Her eyes drifted to a bottom screen where Bran was talking to a pair of dancers.

"Don't suppose you have one out back by the garbage bin." I tried to sound casual while my blood pressure shot into the danger zone. If she had a recording of a Felis attacking and killing Hansa...

"Nope," she said. "Never figured I'd have to worry 'bout getting my crap stolen. Just paid to get one installed today. If that bear comes back I want to get him on tape so they can make sure they kill the right bastard."

I tried not to let out a sigh of relief. The last thing I needed was more complications.

She let out a giggle as she watched Bran slide from one screen to the next. "I can slip your boy into the schedule if he's looking for the whole experience. Be nice to have some fresh blood on stage." One edge of her mouth went up into a smile, holding the cigarette in place. "Like to see his moves."

"I'll let him know." I slipped my business card onto the desk. "I'm staying at the Super 6 if you think of anything."

Her long slender fingers traced my name, running over the embossed letters. The bloodied index finger drew the card toward her as she licked her ruby lips and nodded.

The blinding noise swamped my senses as I came out beside the bar. A fog machine was running full blast, sending wave after wave of white smoke across the stage and flowing down onto the dance floor. The current dancer wore a cape and a pair of fake fangs—and not much else.

The blood-red banana hammock gyrated toward the front line of women, homing in on the waving dollar bills.

I turned and leaned on the bar, catching the attention of the bartender.

She trotted over, eager to please. "Beer?"

"Sure. Surprise me." I spun and rested my elbows on the bar, eyes on the stage.

Never let it be said these men didn't work for their money.

The vampire put his hands behind his head, lowering himself down to his knees and vibrating muscles I didn't know existed. I wondered how much he spent on chiropractic bills.

"Where are you from?" The bartender interrupted my medical observations.

"Toronto, Canada." There was no way anyone could bend that way. I made a mental note to ask Bran about certain parts of the male anatomy. Or maybe check it out myself.

"Heard there was a Pride up there. Never met

anyone from Canada before." She tapped her chest. "Patty Mills."

I turned away with regret from the well-oiled muscles and picked up the cold beer, trying to place the woman's unfamiliar face. "Rebecca Desjardin. Weren't you at the farm earlier tonight?"

"I'm on shift from six until close," she said, a trace of regret in her voice. "Usually I can trade off but couldn't get it this time."

My throat welcomed the cool brew. It'd been a long day and a rather annoying one. "Lisa Darning come here often?"

Her eyes narrowed. "She comes in. Why?"

"Just wondering. She smacked down a kit tonight. Fun to watch." I sipped the dark beer and waited to see if this bartender lived up to her brethren's rep about chatting and delivering information.

"Lisa doesn't tolerate shit on her watch." A bowl of popcorn appeared from under the counter and slid next to my drink. "She's a good woman."

"Seemed like that to me." I took a handful and began popping the puffed kernels into my mouth one at a time. "How come she's not on the Board?"

Patty let out a snort. "She's next in line, been in line for years. But no openings."

I frowned. "Can't she just challenge for it?"

She picked up a black plastic stir stick and began chewing on it. "She could but it'd be a hell of a fight."

"McCallum and Plussey aren't that young." I

nudged the conversation forward. "Wouldn't be that hard to put either of them down."

"Give me a second." She strode down to deliver a tray of refills to a waiting server. As the cold beers slopped over the edges of the frosted glasses I spotted Bran at the side of the stage, fully clothed. He was deep in conversation with the next dancer about to strut his stuff, a young man wearing a too-small firefighter's coat and carrying a plastic ax.

He laughed as the dancer bent his knees and thrust outward, showing off a move. Bran mimicked him, adding a twist of his hips to the action. As the two men laughed I glared at him, hoping our psychic link would tell him of my annoyance.

Bran didn't twitch.

So much for mental connections.

Patty returned, glancing around at the nearby customers. They ignored us, focused on the stage. It was a perfect time to talk about family business.

"Don't know how they do it up there in Canada but we allow proxy fights." The swizzle stick bounced around in her mouth. "When you get too old to fight but you're wise beyond your years and all that. Brain over brawn."

"For everything?" I shook my head. "Sounds like there'd be a lot of scratched-up kits."

She laughed softly. "Usually by the time we hit puberty we've figured out what's worth fighting over and who's going to back you up on it. If you're going to pick a fight it'll be over something big, and you better be ready to deal with whatever comes your way."

"Brutal but fair. So if Lisa challenged either of the men she'd have to face a younger fighter."

"And they're not ready to retire just yet." She grabbed a rag from under the counter and swiped at an invisible stain. "Lisa's a damned good leader but she won't get a chance if she challenges. They'll set some strongman on her and that'll be done."

"She doesn't have any fellows willing to fight for her?" I sipped the beer, wondering how Jess would fare under this system.

I suspected there'd be ambulances at the farm day and night.

"She's had her fair share of suitors," Patty said, "but no one was able to handle her. If they can't handle her they're not going to fight for her and end up being the Board's boy toy."

I bit back a number of sexual comments.

Her eyes darted around the bar. "No offense, but I'm getting a bit uncomfortable the way this chat is going." She let out a sniff. "Nothing personal but we ain't blood kin and you're looking to put one of our own down."

I sipped the beer. "I hear you. I'm not here to cause trouble, just to help figure things out."

"Yeah, well…" She folded the damp towel into a

tight little square. "I'm sorry he'd dead. Mike was a nice guy."

"I'm hearing that a lot." I lifted my glass and tipped it toward the stage in salute. "Any of the usual crowd ever think about getting some private dancing with Mike?" I tilted my head and gave her a knowing look. "Humans included. I know we're not the only ones who like some beefcake."

"Not a chance. Mike never let any of the women get too close, anyone." She nodded to someone in the crowd. "He kept mostly to himself when he was here, which was a lot of the time. Came early to practice his moves, took extra shifts when asked and stayed late to walk me to my car when we locked up." A sad smile touched her lips. "Sort of wasted but I appreciated the intent. A real gentleman."

I sensed Bran coming up behind me, his distinctive scent cutting through the perfume and foggy air. "You got any idea who killed Hansa?"

"No idea." She smiled at Bran over my shoulder. "Can I get you anything?"

"Not right now," he purred in a low, heavy tone. I'd heard that tone recently, within the last hour.

I fought back a growl starting at the back of my throat and finished off the beer. "I'm at the Super 6 if you think of anything else." I put another business card down.

"Sure." Her eyes stayed on Bran. "I'll call."

I turned to see Bran wearing a wide, friendly smile.

"Let's go." I scowled at the grinning man before leading him out of the club. I might have deserved it but I sure as hell didn't have to like it.

"That was interesting," he mused as we walked through the parking lot. "Do you know how much those guys make a night?"

"More than I do. You considering changing professions?" I resisted the urge to look over at the green pickup.

Bran chortled. "Well, they do look like they're having fun."

I wanted to slap the smile off his face. Instead I tossed him the keys. "I had a beer. Last thing I need is a conviction for drunk driving. I'm willing to bet Carson's boys have this place on their radar every night."

The headlights shot bright beams across the darkened parking lot as we maneuvered our way out of the maze of parked cars. "Learn anything about Hansa's death?"

"Maybe. I learned he wasn't doing any of the girls here." I looked in the rearview mirror and spotted a set of headlights far behind us.

"Still got our ghost. If he's smart he'll keep that distance." Bran drove along the darkened road.

I didn't say anything.

"Guy I spoke to said the performers tend to keep

away from the women. Don't need a catfight in the parking lot." He looked over at me and I spotted a smirk in the dim light. "So to speak."

"Smart ass." I blew a raspberry at him. "Owner's tough as nails with bigger balls than most of her dancers."

"Sort of have to be." Bran blinked. "Was that just a deer?"

I twisted around and spotted the shadowy figure behind us, fleeing across the road. "Yep. Thanks for not hitting it."

He let out a wheeze of relief.

"Bartender says Mike didn't have any favorites among the women." I peered ahead into the night. "Which pokes another hole into the angry-jilted-lover theory."

Bran tapped on the brake, keeping us well within the speed limit. "Doesn't mean he didn't have something quiet on the side and wasn't meeting her elsewhere. The last place you want to have an affair is someplace obvious like the club. Go elsewhere to do the dirty."

"There's no scent in his apartment. It's practically sanitized. His truck, well—it was a mess. Not the place to get in the mood unless you were desperate." I glanced in the side mirror. Trace was still a goodly distance behind us, keeping pace. "If he was doing any of the women it had to be at her place or in a hotel."

"A lot of work for sex." Brandon slowed down to take a turn. "And how do you keep that a secret in this small a town? Especially, like you told Jess, there's Felis all over the place. He books into a hotel with a Felis, you can bet the Board would know tout de suite." His fingers drummed on the steering wheel. "Maybe they were connecting through email, making arrangements that way. Go to another town, maybe use her car."

I shook my head as we parked at the hotel. "I didn't find a computer in his apartment. If it was there Carson's boys took it, and since I'm still here it's obvious Hansa didn't have his girlfriend info on it. If he had a cell phone it was taken by the killer, and I don't have the ability to get to his phone records. Carson could ask for a warrant but without due cause it'd be refused."

"Because it's a bear attack," Bran said.

"Exactly. Great cover story but it kills a lot of options for us to explore legally," I grumbled. "I can't be sure about the legitimacy of anything at Hansa's apartment. The place was searched before I got there."

Bran cut the engine. "What?"

I got out of the car and stretched, letting the brisk breeze wash over me. "Pride had his place tossed before I got there. While I was there they tossed the hotel room here." I nodded toward the lobby. "Clumsy oafs."

I could hear his teeth grinding as he locked the car. "They went through your stuff?"

"Don't worry; I didn't bring down any sex toys." The joke fell flat as I saw his face. "It's what they do, Bran."

"It's not what we do." He headed toward the front door. "I'm going to talk to the manager."

"Don't." A few quick steps and I was at his side. "I don't want them to know that I know. They're assuming I'm as slow as most humans." I lowered my voice. "Let me play this out my way."

He paused with his hand on one of the two stainless steel doorknobs. "I hate this."

"Me too. But until I figure out who's friend and who's foe I can't risk alienating anyone." I took his hand, squeezed it. "Let's just go back to the room."

I saw the anger in the way he strode past the night clerk, his eyes darting toward the woman as if he expected her to Change and challenge him.

I fumbled for the cardkey in my pocket and unlocked the door in silence.

Bran walked in and tossed his coat on the far chair. "So aside from being spied on do you have any more clues?"

I toed off my shoes and hung my coat up, grateful for the chance to do something simple and menial. "I've got some solid facts that can't be disputed. Mike Hansa was slashed up by a Felis. Those claw marks weren't from a bear."

Bran opened the minibar and helped himself to a water bottle. "Right." He perched himself on the edge of the bed. "And Carson thinks he was killed 'cause of a jealous feud."

"Which I can't deny or confirm." I hopped up on the bed and wriggled my socked toes at him. "But it seems to be what everyone's thinking."

"But you can't find any evidence he was seeing anyone. And the guys at the club say he was happily single." Bran drained half the bottle in two gulps. "So someone's not telling the truth."

"Either he was having a relationship and kept it very, very well hidden..." I picked up the file folder containing the crime scene photos and handed it to Bran. "Or there was no relationship and he was killed because of something else."

"Like what?" Bran opened the file. "False advertising?"

"Smart ass."

"And all the rest of me, baby."

Bran stared at the gory autopsy photographs, showing no emotion. I figured he'd seen worse working as a journalist. He flipped through the clinical shots of the mutilated torso, pausing for only a few seconds on each one.

His eyes narrowed as he studied the promotional body shot provided by the Cat's Meow at the back of the file. "Who is this guy?"

"Mike Hansa." Even as I said the words my pulse doubled. "What?"

Bran tapped the photograph. "I know this guy."

NINE

I RAISED ONE eyebrow. "Want to tell me something about your illicit past?"

"I mean, I've seen him somewhere else." He closed his eyes, forehead furrowed with concentration. "I've seen him before. With his clothing on." Bran reached over and plucked his laptop from the travel bag. "Let's see what I can find."

As it booted up Brandon shook his head, deep furrows appearing on his forehead. "Maybe it was an article. A photo op." He chewed on his lower lip. "I don't remember, damn it."

I glared at the small screen, mentally speeding the process up. "Maybe you did an article on male dancers already? Small towns going under?" I let out a sigh as the familiar generic desktop image appeared. "Maybe his last place of employment let him go on a grudge; maybe he ticked someone off in his last job and wrote a letter to the editor that got published. Maybe he got into a fight and made it on YouTube."

"Nothing rings a bell." He took the laptop and balanced it on his thighs. "Let me see what I can find out."

I helped myself to a soda. "I did a search on Hansa. Nothing much out there other than a few promo shots for the club."

"So who was he before he became an exotic dancer," Bran murmured. "He didn't go to school, never graduated, no cyber trail behind him."

"What, he was an international spy?" I drained the can in two gulps. The caffeine rush went straight to my head along with the carbonation. I burped loudly.

"Such a lady." He didn't look up as his fingers banged out a rhythm on the keyboard. "Let me surf around for a bit. Do a search on his promo pic and see if it jogs my memory."

I spotted a candy bar in the side pocket of his bag. A sideways swipe had it in my hand.

"That's stealing." He moved to the desk. "I'll expect you to pay for that later." He wagged his finger.

"I thought I already did." I shot him one of my come-hither looks. "And credit."

The low chuckle sent a hot rush up and down my spine. "We'll discuss a payment plan later."

His fingers danced on the worn keyboard, the white lettering almost rubbed off with prolonged use.

I sniffed the candy bar. Nougat and caramel wrapped in a chocolate coat of delight. Sweet, sweet sugar rush.

"Ah." Bran leaned forward, his nose almost touching the screen. "Oh. Wow."

"What?" I scrambled over to the desk, my mouth full of chocolate gooeyness.

"A man of many talents." Bran grinned. "He's not only a male stripper—" he swung the screen around so I could see it, "—he's also a shit-disturbing investigative reporter."

I stared at the full-sized color image on the screen. A long line of tuxedo-clad men stood in a line, holding some sort of award between them all. It was an ugly varnished piece of wood with a silver quill sticking out of one end.

"Mike Hancock, among others, receiving the Silver Quill for his story on government corruption," Bran droned. "Give me a second and I'll pull up the esteemed tome."

"Sounding a bit bitter there." I took another bite of the chocolate bar as he spun the laptop back to face him.

"Me? Pshaw." He tapped on the keyboard. "Glory hound. Wins one award and thinks he's God's gift to journalism."

"He's dead. I don't think he's going to be winning any more awards." I glanced back at Bran's laptop. "So he was running undercover as a stripper."

"Won the award for a series detailing massive abuse in the waste management services for three counties in Pennsylvania. In other words, he dug up the garbage on the garbage." Bran smacked his lips. "Good report. Clean kill. Got a lot of dirt stirred up and investigations started on all levels of government."

"Was anyone powerful fired? Could be a revenge killing. Depending on how high he went with his crusade it's pretty plausible." I moved to stand behind him, trying to make sense of the images on the screen. "Let me see if the hotel here has a printer. I want to get a hard copy of that award ceremony picture."

It took only a few minutes to call up the front desk and confirm they had a printer we'd be able to use. I motioned at Bran to send it through and headed for the door.

I peeked out into the parking lot as the clerk waited for the printer to finish. Sure enough Trace was there, napping behind the wheel.

I resisted the urge to go over and thump on the window. Then thump on him until he'd just go away. I didn't need the distraction and sure as hell didn't need to worry about Bran running into him again.

Bran looked up as I re-entered. I gave him a thumbs-up and passed him the photograph.

I looked at the screen. "Any idea what he was working on here?"

"None," he admitted. "If he's like the rest of us he doesn't kiss and tell." Bran smacked his lips at me. "Competition's the name of the game. Your story can become someone else's byline in a minute."

"You're kidding me."

"Not on this." He pointed at the laptop screen. "It's not uncommon for reporters to be working on the same story but different angles. It's a matter of who gets to market first. You may have the better article but if it's on page eight because the headline went to Jane Smith who got a juicier twist…" Bran blew a raspberry. "Done like dinner. You don't get any prizes for second place."

"But he didn't have any notes?" I asked. "I've seen your journals, your notebooks."

"Not everyone puts their findings down on paper. Too easy to lose or have stolen by the competition, especially if you're running under an alias." Bran tapped the table with one finger. "There's something, somewhere."

"His cell phone's missing. There was nothing at his place. No laptop." I rubbed my forehead with the palm of my hand. "But I wasn't the first one there, damn it."

"Did the Board know he was a reporter?" Bran asked. "Might have made a difference in the way they searched the apartment. It's one thing to be looking for evidence of a mad mistress, another to be digging for a reporter's notes."

"I doubt it." I shook my head. "Carson would have let me know that from the start. If Hancock was working on a story about the Pride there'd be no reason to have me investigate."

Bran looked up. "Why not?"

The words stuck in my throat. "He'd be a threat to the Pride and to the family. If a Felis killed him there'd be no questions as long as the death was to protect our secret. They'd have filed a report with the Grand Council and been done with it."

A shadow drew across his face. "Right. I'd forgotten the first time you took me to the farm."

I winced inside. I'd taken Bran there to keep an eye on him while we worked the same case, albeit from different angles. The Board misinterpreted it and I'd had to do some fast talking to get Bran out from under their claws.

I scowled at the laptop screen. "No, they ran with the adultery angle, ran the story to ground. Damned cleaners might not even know what they destroyed as they plowed through Hancock's place looking for evidence of an affair."

Bran rubbed his chin, swiveling the chair around to face me. "Everyone assumed and is assuming he was killed because he was in a relationship with one of the women. Killed by either her or her mate."

"Except for the murderer," I interrupted.

"Except for the murderer." Bran rested his elbows on his knees. "Who should have tossed his apartment as well." He shrugged. "I would have. Get rid of all the evidence."

I wriggled my nose. "I didn't smell anyone other than the two Felis and Hancock. She or he either didn't get a chance to get inside the apartment or they're in cahoots with the two enforcers."

"Cahoots?" He rolled his eyes. "No more late-night film noir for you." His expression turned serious. "Who do the enforcers answer to?"

"The Board. But that doesn't mean they wouldn't cover for anyone else if asked." I sucked on my bottom lip. "If the Pride was at risk you could get any of them to cover for anyone."

"But then they wouldn't call you in and the entire thing's moot. So we're back to the angry lover and/or her mate. Who we don't know even exists." Bran frowned. "This doesn't make sense."

"I know." The fog grew in my mind, threatening to shut it down. "What the hell was he doing down here?"

"We need his notes," Bran said. "They're out there somewhere."

"His cell phone," I answered. "The killer took Hancock's phone. Could he have put his notes on that?"

"Possible. It'd be a good place for his raw data, photographs, the bare bones."

"The killer never went to the apartment because she figured she had it all. She couldn't risk it, risk having her scent found there." The fog lifted for a second. "She took the phone and figured the enforcers would take the laptop. Or something like that."

Bran brooded, his lips pressed tightly together.

"It doesn't make sense. Why even leave him out to be found? In an area like this she could have hidden the body easily."

"She wanted him found," I said. "If Hancock just disappeared it'd be a bigger story—more so if and when he was exposed as a reporter. But if he's killed by a Felis and left out in public, Carson has to make it look like an animal attack instead of conducting a proper murder investigation. Cuts down on outside interference—the less people looking into Hancock's death the better." I looked down at the empty candy wrapper. A small line of melted chocolate ran along the inside, tempting me. "Whatever he was investigating, it was enough to kill him and keep the real reason for his murder from the Board."

"We need to find out what Hancock was writing about," Bran said. "Whatever it was, it was enough to get the Felis involved."

I shook my head. "But why? If Hancock wasn't trying to expose the Pride then there'd be no reason for him to be killed."

"You're thinking like a Felis." Brandon reached forward and tapped me on the forehead with his index finger. "Think like an investigator."

I tossed the wrapper in the garbage and rubbed my aching eyes. "Right killer, wrong reasons. Still Pride business. Still my case."

"I can't think clearly. Let's go to bed. We'll think

better in the morning." Bran shook his head. "It's been a long day."

I watched as he got to his feet and undressed. The shirt went over the back of the chair, joined swiftly by his jeans. Damn man had gotten better looking in the past few months, if that were possible.

I let my eyes wander southward. Whatever was in the future between us was in the future—right now there was only he and I and a whole lot of want. "Learn any new moves at the club?"

His wide smile sent my heart racing. "Maybe. Want me to put some songs on?"

I yawned and rolled over. "Meh. I don't feel like listening to more loud music."

"I can be quiet," Bran said from behind. I could hear the smirk in his voice.

Time to call his bluff.

"Show me."

He did.

WE ATE BREAKFAST the next morning at the same diner I'd been to before, settling ourselves at the opposite end of the restaurant from the already-present Board members. I wasn't sure if there was any place to eat without running into the family and having them report back—so I didn't even bother trying.

Besides, the food was faboo.

Carson was on his third cup of coffee in less than ten minutes. I hoped it was decaf.

Plussey kept doodling on a napkin, filling three of them with notes he tucked into a side pocket.

McCallum focused on his steak. He didn't look toward the parking lot where nephew Trace waited, still trapped on guard duty in his pickup. I almost felt sorry for the poor man—obviously when they set a babysitter on someone they were darned serious about it.

I didn't feel sorry enough to take him breakfast.

I repeated my earlier meal of steak and eggs, watching Bran work on pancakes the size of manhole covers.

"That should be illegal," I mumbled through my teeth as he poured maple syrup over the stack.

"Gives me ideas." He winked.

I focused on the bloody slab of meat. "Behave."

"Tease." He pointed his fork at the ceiling. "I'm innocent, I tell you. Innocent."

"Keep it down." I glanced toward the other end of the restaurant. "I'm hoping they can't hear us this far away. I'd rather keep some things private."

"Can you hear them?" he asked. "Vice versa and all that stuff."

"No. But I'm out of practice." I cleared my throat. "Okay, I'm putting you to work." I sighed when Bran raised an eyebrow, a playful grin spreading across his face. "No, not taking a job at the club. We sort of shot that one down with you showing up at the farm."

He let out a dramatic sigh. "Damn. Not really an option with everyone knowing I'm with you."

"Let me handle the Felis side. I need you to run the human angle. I want you to dig around and talk to the local press. Hancock wasn't here on a whim—he had something or someone he was investigating. We need to know who and what." I wrestled with a tough bit of gristle. "Newspaper's run by Cassie Prosser, rabidly anti-club. If there's anyone looking for local corruption it'd be her. I don't see how Hancock would be running undercover and not on her radar. She might have been the one to bring him in since any of her local boys would be easily identified." I sliced off another mouthful of steak. "When we met at the crime scene she didn't seem to want to buy the animal attack story. And when we spoke at the bar she wasn't too accepting of my cover story 'bout the insurance."

"Corruption." Bran pushed a blueberry the size of a marble around in the syrup. "That points to local politics and that gets really nasty, really quickly." He popped the berry into his mouth and spoke around it. "What do you think he was digging up?"

"The easy answer is payoffs to the town council to keep the club around. But that doesn't explain how the Felis got involved. They don't own the club. The men aren't even allowed to work there. Whether the Cat's Meow goes or stays doesn't affect them. There's no reason why a Felis would kill Hancock or get involved with the cover-up unless they had something to gain. Lisa Darning is on the radar, being both Felis and on the council, but I'm not seeing her as a killer." I added more hot sauce to a forkful of scrambled eggs. "But it could be anything using the club as a front. Drugs, prostitution, rigging local elections. I can't just go by the venue. I need to know what Hancock was digging up."

Bran looked down the diner to the three Board members. They studiously ignored us. "How much do you think they know?"

"I'm not sure," I admitted. "Problem is, I need their help. I can't barge around here like a bull in a china shop and get answers. If I were back in Toronto—no problem digging up the bodies and cutting through the bullshit. Here, everyone's connected either through blood or through family. I need the family connection." I tried not to look outside. "Tempers flare quickly 'round here. Carson blew up at me yesterday; I can't say I won't be challenged as I dig deeper."

He hacked away at the mound. "Could always call Jess. Get some backup from your own kind. Bring down your own enforcers, bodyguards, whatever you want to call 'em." His eyes flashed to the window and the parking lot outside. "Could always quit the job."

I shook my head. "Jess'll just tell me to do what I need to do to get to the truth. She's not going to send down any help. It'll raise the Board's hackles and make it even more difficult to find the truth." I met his eyes. "And I know who I can trust. I can trust you."

He gave me a sly wink. "And this Grand Council? Can't they do something? Don't they have, like, a strike force? Felis Special Forces?"

I chuckled and shook my head. "It's complicated. They oversee all the Boards and Prides but it's more of an honorary thing. They don't like getting involved with the day-to-day running. They make recommendations and establish policy. If the Prides don't follow there's no actual penalty but it's harder to do business and make friends—that sort of quiet intimidation."

Bran beamed as the waitress refilled his cup and dropped a half dozen creamers by the mug. "Thank you." He waited until she moved away. "But they're scary enough to make this group call Jess to ask for your talented ass." His hand moved down under the table to stroke my thigh. "Very talented."

I wriggled on the thick, red leather cushions. "Thanks." I sipped my own coffee. "It's because no one wants a Felis to get away with killing a human for no good reason. Once it becomes acceptable it'll happen again."

"Once you've tasted blood?" Bran quipped.

"More or less. It'll start as a trickle, a killing over an implied slight or a drunken fight, and turn into a flood and the family won't know what to do about it. Do you tell the world about us and deal with the consequences or start killing our own to keep the secret?" I watched the three men mumble to each other, casting glances at us. "No Pride wants to be the first to have that on their record."

The trio got to their feet and headed toward our table.

"And here we go." I sighed.

Bran wiped his mouth with a napkin. "Good. I hate too much foreplay." His hand gave a last squeeze before retreating to hold his coffee cup.

I tried not to twitch. Carson was the first to speak, stopping in front of the table.

"May we join you for a minute?" He held his uniform cap in both hands as if he was begging for an audience. I didn't miss the significance.

"Sure." I slid closer to Bran. McCallum and Plussey moved in next to me, Carson next to Bran. The discomfort was evident in all three men, their eyes darting from Bran to me and back again. They might be living and working beside humans, but these Felis didn't embrace them as equals.

It didn't escape me that they'd effectively trapped us between them.

"We'd like to start by apologizing for the misunderstanding last night." McCallum spoke first, twisting his fingers into a knot. "If we'd have known your—" he stumbled over the word, "—boyfriend was coming down we wouldn't have ended up in that situation."

"No problem." I smiled, ratcheting up their stress level another notch with my calmness. "It was good of Lisa to bring Brandon up."

"Yes." McCallum's nostrils twitched. "Trace sends his apologies as well. He was a bit wound up after the run and didn't understand what he was getting into. He was overenthusiastic, as young men tend to get." He switched from Board member to the friendly uncle in a flash. "He's a good fellow. Works hard, plays hard and takes care of his own."

I resisted the urge to look out into the parking lot. Either he didn't think I'd picked up Trace tailing us or he was trying to put in a good argument for me dumping Bran for his nephew.

Bran gave McCallum a wide grin. "Hey, we're cool. I'd have taken him out anyway." He paused for a single beat. "Nah…"

The three men gave a group chuckle. I could see they were still trying to figure out what to make of Bran. The number of humans privy to the inner workings of the Felis had to be less than a handful, and here was one right in their collective faces.

I held back a smile at their discomfort.

"Have you made any progress on the investigation?" Carson said. He dragged his finger through a bit of spilled salt.

"As a matter of fact, yes." I watched him brush his

hand off on his sharply pressed trousers. "It seems that Mike Hansa wasn't who he appeared to be."

"What?" McCallum pressed. There was a thin line of sweat on his forehead, threatening to break free. "Who was he?"

"His real name was Michael Hancock." I studied their faces, looking for a flicker of recognition at the revelation. "He's…he was an investigative reporter."

A wave of fear splashed over me. These three were lousy poker players.

"What was he doing at the club?" Carson whispered. His pale skin had gone even whiter.

"Trying to uncover our secrets," Plussey said before I could answer. His fingers drew up into fists, the wrinkled skin tense and shaking. "It would make sense. He tries to find out about us and gets the wrong woman mad."

"Or man," Bran added. "If I recall correctly you've all got claws." His eyes went down to Carson's hands and back up to the chief's face. There was no joking here, just straight-up undiluted Bran.

My left leg pushed up against Brandon's. "I'm keeping an open mind as to what he was looking for."

McCallum shook his head. "If a reporter was actively seeking information about the family, the murder could be justifiable." He glanced at the other two members. "I would have no problem ruling it self-defense under those circumstances."

Plussey let out something akin to a hum, studying his fingernails. Carson shifted from side to side, reminding me of a child needing to find the bathroom and fast.

Bran's left eye twitched. "Wait a minute. You'd condone and cover up the murder of a human just to keep your little secret?"

I dropped my hand down onto his knee and squeezed. Hard.

"Are you asking me to terminate the investigation if I find out that was what he was working on?" I phrased it as officially as possible. If they wanted me gone I needed it as clear as possible without any wriggle room.

It'd make it easier to disobey.

McCallum started to speak and then stopped. He glanced at the other two men. "I think we should discuss this revelation privately before handing down any decision."

Plussey nodded. "We need to assess the pluses and minuses of keeping this investigation going."

Carson looked at me. His tongue darted out to wet his lips. "It's complicated."

"Welcome to life," I said. Bran's leg began to bounce under my touch, despite my best attempt to hold him at bay. "I do want to tell you that with or without your blessing I'm going to continue to investigate this. A man is dead and he deserves justice."

McCallum's jaw tensed. "Without our blessing you'll have a hell of a time getting around town."

"I'll manage," I said, letting the frigid tone speak for itself. "If you spoke to Jess you know what I'm like. You're not going to call me off like a trained dog because it's inconvenient for you to deal with." I threw down my invisible hand of cards. "If he was killed because he knew about the family, why hasn't she or he come forward? Why aren't they claiming credit if they think it was a justified and honorable kill?"

The three men exchanged glances as I maintained a killer hold on Bran's leg.

Carson was the first to break ranks. "Someone's hiding something—that much is true." He didn't look at the other two men. "I want you to see this through. What can I do to help?"

I felt the leg muscles go limp. "You had men search Hancock's apartment, looking for evidence of a Felis lover. I need whatever they removed from the apartment." I didn't mention the intrusion into my hotel room. "Whatever they took, even the smallest thing, I need to know."

Carson frowned. "They didn't take anything." His voice edged on a whine.

"I think they did." I held up a hand, stopping him. "It was probably something they didn't even think mattered, something not connected to looking for a woman. I'm not out to blame them, I just want to know what they took and get it back. No harm, no foul." I looked at the other Board members. "We've got enough on our plate as it is. I'm not interested in your internal discipline. Do what you want, I don't give a damn."

Carson rubbed his right ear for a second, kneading the earlobe between two fingers. He glanced at the other two members, his expression hovering between embarrassed and annoyed. A minute later he nodded. "Dang fools. Let me get hold of them and we'll all meet you at the hotel."

"No," McCallum interrupted. "Call them and have them come here." He looked at me. "I want to see them as well, let them know we're not happy."

Carson's nostrils flared. "We had the right to do that. We had the right to investigate and search his home." He narrowed his eyes. "We did what we needed to."

McCallum pursed his lips. "That you did. But if they took anything, the smallest thing, they need to know it's not acceptable." He glared back at Carson. "We know about it this time. What about the future? What about the past?"

"My boys aren't thieves," Carson said in a low, measured voice.

I watched the power play with as stoic an expression as I could manage. It was plain that McCallum was topping Carson and the chief didn't like it.

Carson wrestled with his cap for a minute before throwing it down on the seat beside him and digging out his cell phone. I didn't hear what he growled into the phone but it was short and fast and not friendly.

The waitress reappeared, coffee pot in hand. She refilled our mugs with a smile before placing three fresh empty ones in front of the Board. On McCallum's nod she filled them and strolled away—but not before giving Plussey a flirty wink. He responded with a low chuckle and shake of his head.

We sat in silence and sipped good coffee.

It took all of ten minutes before a large grey pickup truck roared into the parking lot, digging deep ruts in the gravel as it settled down beside my rental.

Trace looked over from where he sat. He didn't move.

I sucked in my breath as two men exited the vehicle.

The middle-aged blond men wore identical T-shirts and jeans, their short-cropped hair at exactly the same length as far as I could tell. The only distinguishing marks were tattoos on their necks, long flowing scripts of their names. The twins were tall, at least six feet and a whisper each.

They strode into the diner and headed for our booth—a pair of dominant males who filled the role of Felis enforcers easily.

The pair snapped to attention in front of us and waited.

Their blue eyes drilled into mine. They knew who they answered to and it wasn't me.

I felt Bran's muscle twitch under my hand.

McCallum glanced at me and nodded, giving permission to start the conversation.

"Thank you for coming." I started short and simple. "Chief Carson told me you were the ones who searched Hancock's residence."

"Who?" The twins said in unison.

"Mike Hansa's place," I said. "You two were asked to search his apartment."

Mike spoke first. "We did."

They fell silent. I wondered which one had peed in my toilet.

"What did you find?" I prompted.

"Nothing at all." Dave answered. His tattooed name rose and fell on his skin as he spoke. "We were told to search for evidence of a woman, someone who would have reason to kill the stripper."

I noted their depersonalization of Mike Hancock. Standard practice for Felis.

"How long have you been working for the chief?"

The pair shifted as one. Mike spoke first. "Since we were teenagers. He's a crib brother." His eyes snapped over to Carson's and back again, re-establishing the battle for control with mine.

I flinched inside. I'd seen firsthand what crib brothers would do for each other, how far they would go to keep secrets.

"Okay. Did you find anything?"

"Nothing," Dave answered. "It was like no woman had ever even entered the place. Couldn't sniff out anyone, couldn't find nothing." He glanced at his twin. "Kinda strange. Maybe he was a faggot pretending he liked women?" His face scrunched up as if he'd drunk skunky beer.

I resisted the temptation to roll my eyes. Backwoods, redneck Felis. Wonderful.

"He was actually a reporter." The blank look threatened my patience. "An investigative reporter."

The twins stood up straighter, a bemused expression on both faces. Between the two of them you might have a sniff of a brain cell.

"A reporter," Mike repeated. "Who'd have thunk that?" He turned and grinned at his brother. "Goddamn tabloid trash."

Bran's leg jumped against my palm. I pressed down with all my strength.

"You took something from his apartment." I held up my free hand before either twin could respond. "I'm not your mother and I'm not your priest so I don't care that you took it. All I want is to get it back."

Dave's eyes snapped to Carson's face, searching for permission.

I slammed my hand down on the table, pulling all attention back to me. "Don't look at him. You're not helping him any by stealing like a common criminal."

Mike's nostrils widened.

I was about two seconds from a challenge.

I stood up and leaned forward, pressing both palms down on the table. "You answer to this Board. But right now you answer to me."

Carson moved back out of my vision, pushing himself into the cushions.

McCallum and Plussey said nothing. I knew this was another damned test.

I didn't intend to fail.

I glanced toward the truck. "Guess I'll have to find it myself. Starting with searching that truck and then going to your homes and searching there."

TEN

THE TWO MEN spoke at once.

"You can't—"

"We won't—"

"It's not your choice." I remained standing. "What did you take?"

"Nothing." The two replied as one.

I resisted the urge to go over the table.

"Rebecca," McCallum interrupted, "it's possible they didn't find anything."

"Was it his laptop?" I pressed forward, ignoring the Board member. "Did you take his laptop? Did you take his flash drives, his file folders? His journals, his notebooks?"

Mike didn't look at me, keeping his eyes pinned to the wall behind us. Dave did the same in classic military style.

"What did you take?" I repeated.

Carson tugged at my sleeve. "They didn't find anything. Let it go."

I pulled away, continuing to glare at the twins. "What did you take? Who are you covering for?"

My voice rose, pulling attention from the other diners.

"We didn't take nothing," Mike said, the low, measured words carrying an air of menace. "You better not be calling us liars."

"Double negative," Bran murmured.

"What?" Dave cocked his head to one side. "What?"

"Double negative. Cancels each other out to be a positive." He examined his syrup-covered fork. "You're saying you did take something."

Mike took a step forward, breaking the solidarity. His eyes flashed from Carson's to Bran's, searching for a weakness.

Bran maintained the link, not blinking.

"We. Didn't. Take. Anything." Mike ground the words out between clenched teeth. "You calling us liars?"

I moved my leg against Bran, trying to warn him. He could only push his luck so far.

McCallum broke into the would-be challenge. "Mike, Dave, go back out to your truck while we talk this over. Please."

Mike and Dave shuffled from side to side as they waited for direction.

Carson nodded at the pair. "Dismissed."

The twins fell over each other to retreat from the diner. They tumbled into the truck and waited. Trace stayed inside his own vehicle but I saw him watching the twins.

They didn't look at him.

McCallum cleared his throat. "I don't think they took anything."

"I think they did," I replied. "I think they snatched a laptop. If not to help cover up the crime, then to re-sell and make some extra cash. They may not even know the importance of what they stole."

Carson's lips curled back from his teeth. "I don't think I like you calling my boys thieves."

"Bet it makes you wonder what I'd call their keeper." The words were out before I'd had a chance to mentally edit them.

It was a mistake.

Plussey picked up the paper napkin and dabbed at his lips. The other two members sat in silence as he finished his preening.

"You are here as a guest." He pounced on the last word. "A guest. While I understand you have a job to do, I don't think planting seeds of distrust with our people is the way to go."

The smug look on Carson's face made me want to slap it off.

"If you have any proof of these accusations I will back you going to their homes and searching for this item." Plussey folded the napkin into a neat, perfect square. "But I won't have you going on a wild-goose chase and messing up our lives, our routines." He pushed the paper square into the center of the table. "We'll use our resources to see if either of the twins tries to dump a laptop or any other electronic device—and we'll call you if it happens. Until then I repeat that you're not to go banging on doors and making a nuisance of yourself."

I flashed back to a lunch date with my police contact, Hank Attersley. He'd been scorching mad about being denied a search warrant because he hadn't had enough evidence.

"I know he's dirty, Reb," he barked, "but I can't get the warrant until I have the dirt and I can't get the dirt unless I have the warrant."

We'd decided to wash the afternoon away with a bottle of tequila and enough salt to empty the Flats. In the end he'd gotten the warrant due to an informant giving the right story to the right officer and justice had been served.

I wasn't sure I'd get that lucky.

"I think it's a good time for us to go and leave you to your work." McCallum shuffled out of the booth, Plussey following close behind.

Carson joined the pair with a slower, more calculated retreat. His lips were still curled up in a half snarl. It didn't take a genius to see I'd showed him up in front of the Board and would pay the price eventually.

"I'll keep you updated as the investigation progresses." I nodded to the Board, letting my shoulders slump barely enough to be submissive. "Thank you for your help."

The three men walked away.

Bran let out a hiss as he rubbed his thigh. "That hurt."

Now it was time for me to bare my teeth. "Do you know how close you came to getting in another fight? Are you just looking to get killed?"

He popped another forkful of syrup-soaked pancake into his mouth and winked.

"You are not taking this seriously," I snapped.

"I take this very seriously." Bran dipped his index finger into the syrup and tapped the edge of my nose. "What you don't get is that I don't have to play by your rules. And that's what I want them to know."

I resisted the urge to try to lick the syrup off. "What?"

"I'm the damned wild card in the deck. They may think they know you but they sure as hell don't know me." He slid out from the booth. "Let's go to the hotel and pick up my car."

"You think Prosser is going to be up to talking?"

"She's going to want to talk about Mike's death to somebody, anyone. Especially another reporter." He tapped his chest. "Consider it our own type of family."

"How are you going to handle it?" I asked, scowling as I thumbed through my wallet. Damned American money, all the same color. How everyone didn't get constantly overpaid was beyond me. "You can't call it a murder."

"I can say it's a suspicious death." Bran grinned. "I've got official credentials. I'm a fellow journalist."

"You can't call it a murder," I repeated. "Whatever Hancock was into probably caused his death but you can't say that. If she calls in the outside cops it's going to get really messy."

"Messy" was an understatement.

"Murders have been hidden as accidents before," Bran answered. "She's already suspicious—you said so yourself."

I resisted the urge to slap my forehead. "Suspicious, yes. But if you give her reason to go higher and demand further investigation…"

Bran put up his hands. "It's an animal attack. That's what the coroner ruled. It might look odd but stranger things have happened. She can't stir up shit if there isn't anything to back it up."

I sucked in air over clenched teeth.

He continued. "I'll behave myself. I can tell her I'm looking to pick up the story, whatever it is, and slap Hancock's name on it as a memorial. If she's as dedicated to the truth as she thinks she is she'll want the story over the mysterious death, consider it a living memorial to Hancock's memory."

I shook my head. "Just try to keep her clear of Carson. If she goes in guns ablazing and screaming that they're trying to cover up a murder…"

"She'll be next. I got it." Bran jerked a thumb to one side as we walked to the car. "Ghost is still here."

I ignored the pickup truck waiting in the parking lot and jammed the key in the ignition.

I wasn't in any mood for this.

We traveled in silence back to the hotel, me worried about Bran getting himself and/or Cassie Prosser killed and Bran probably worried about the same thing if he was smart.

Or he was trying to figure out how to kill Trace and hide the body. I figured it was a 50/50 split.

We pulled into the parking lot beside the loud blue rental. Trace stayed on the side of the road, just in eyesight range.

"Is it possible there is no laptop?" I mused.

"Possible. Not probable but possible." Bran fished in his pocket for the second set of keys. "Hancock might have kept all the evidence on his cell phone or committed it to memory. When you're in enemy territory you have to consider your equipment being confiscated or destroyed."

"If there was a laptop and they took it, it'd be to protect Carson." I put my head back. "Which implicates either him or his wife."

"In what? The affair or the cover-up?"

"I don't know." I rubbed my eyes with the palms of my hands. "I just don't know at this point. But the clock is ticking."

Bran got out, watching me exit from the other side. "What are you going to do?"

"What I should have done yesterday." I jabbed a thumb back toward the hotel. "Basic research. I can't believe anything I've been told up to this point."

He nodded. "I'll be back as soon as I can. Just play it safe."

I resisted the urge to snort. "Just see what you can get from Prosser and get back here. No side trips and watch your back."

"Aw," Bran replied with a grin. "I feel so loved."

He headed for his rental before I could respond, and turned out of the lot onto the small street.

The green pickup cruised into the parking lot as soon as Bran moved out of sight. Guess Bran wasn't worth his own babysitter.

I scowled at Trace and headed toward my hotel room. This might be a good thing. If I kept Trace here he couldn't "accidentally" run into Bran. There was enough testosterone flying around to choke a herd of horses. Zebras, even.

I drowned my worries by searching Bran's bag for any more chocolate bars.

He had plenty. Emphasis on "had."

I spent the next hour devouring nougat and doing computer searches on some of the more notable personalities I'd met. Sophia Martin. Trace Bryson. Lisa Darning. Dale Langstrom. Cassie Prosser.

There wouldn't be much there about Lisa or Trace,

other than what was given out for public consumption—a bit more fluff for Councilwoman Darning, the politician, than Farmer Bryson. The Felis kept their private lives private.

I studied the news articles I'd pulled up via a search engine. The Cat's Meow had been a major event for Penscotta, hiring a lot of locals for the construction and renovation of the old warehouse. The local unions were thrilled and it'd been built without any accidents or labor unrest. The mayor had actually been at the ribbon-cutting ceremony, wrangling oversized scissors to maul the bright red ribbon while hiding her annoyance under a flat smile. Prosser was there to one side, scowling while Darning beamed and engaged in a mock tug of war with the two dancers holding the ribbon.

After the opening they'd opted to bring in male dancers from other cities, keeping away from local talent. That was understandable. Add in the boycott from the Felis for men working there and it pretty well demanded outside entertainers.

A smile tweaked my lips as I remembered the dancers from the previous evening. Good money if you can stay in shape and take the abuse from the women. I wasn't foolish enough not to admit I'd been pretty turned on by the time we'd left.

The quarterly votes on the town council to keep the club were public records. Boring reading filled with long words and fractured phrasing to try to keep the words "stripper" out of the transcript. Every meeting had a few community activists standing up and ranting about destroying the town with this immoral business but it seemed to be more of a ceremony than a serious protest at this point.

Dale Langstrom might be the mayor and anti-club but she kept being outvoted by three other members, including Lisa Darning, the lone Felis on the council. The other negative vote came from a woman who'd been on the council for decades and phoned in her vote via telephone, being homebound with crippling arthritis. Every few months the same routine—rinse and repeat.

A twinge of pain shot down my spine, alerting me that I'd spent too much time hunched over the laptop.

I got to my feet and winced at the muscle spasms rolling over my back. A walk out to the lobby would accomplish two things—stretch out my body and allow me to see if my shadow had moved on to greener pastures.

The lobby was empty except for the young kit working the front desk. He buried himself in paperwork after glancing over at me.

My attention moved to the green pickup at the far end of the parking lot. Trace didn't look at me directly but I knew he was watching.

I rolled my shoulders back and strolled toward the truck. I'd had enough of this crap.

It was time to dump the babysitter.

Trace didn't flinch as I rapped on the window. He rolled it down slowly, wrestling with the well-worn mechanism.

"Hey."

"Hey yourself." I jerked a thumb back toward the hotel. "I'm tired of this. Go home and tell your uncle I'm not going to stop until I find out who killed Hancock, with or without his approval."

He looked at me, a smile tugging at the edge of his lips. "I can't do that."

"Can't or won't?" I snarled. "Didn't know the men down here had no balls."

A flash of anger in his eyes almost sent me back a step. "I got them." His left hand slipped down from the steering wheel. "Want to see?"

"Nothing I'd be interested in," I deadpanned back. It took all my mental strength not to look down into his lap.

"You sure 'bout that?" Trace replied. "This fellow of yours, he doesn't seem very tough."

"He's tough enough for me," I snapped. "At least he's helping me find a murderer instead of sitting in a parking lot jerking off when no one's looking."

The door flew open. I jumped back, barely clearing the metal.

Trace stepped out and advanced on me, his hands on his hips. "You do your job and I'll do mine. I don't care who killed him but I do care about the family."

He paused. A sudden softness replaced the anger on his face. "Including you."

I resisted the urge to step back. I felt my cheeks go warm as my pulse shot up into the danger zone, responding to Trace's musk. A surge of heat crept down my spine, pooling between my legs.

I may not have wanted him in my mind but my body was betraying me fast and furiously.

"What do you see in him?" Trace asked with a jerk of his head toward the hotel. "I mean, a human?"

"I…" My throat went dry. "I've always dated humans."

I couldn't have sounded lamer if I'd tried.

"Well then," Trace drawled, "how do you know you'd be happier with him than with me?"

The directness took me aback, robbing me of speech for a second.

Trace dragged his eyes over my body, any attempt at subtlety gone. "I know you can't Change. I don't care." His blue eyes found mine. "I'm not proposing marriage here. I'm just making an offer. Come with me for a bit and see what happens."

"I think I can guess what'll happen." I tried to sound flippant but it fell flat.

"Come on. Don't you want to cut loose?" Trace leaned in, his voice now a seductive whisper. "I know you've got to hold back with him, you can't let yourself go. Don't you want to know what it's like to let it all out, Changed or not?"

I swallowed, feeling the tension grow between us.

I'd left the farm when I was still too young to understand all the urges and needs of Felis women. I'd run with the youngsters, giggling and snickering when we saw the teenagers dash into the barn for a quick tryst, wondering what the fuss was all about.

Ruth had been in charge of what passed for sex education back then, and grateful parents sent their kits over for the Talk. We'd sat in a circle, just the girls, with the boys off in the forest until it was their turn.

I didn't remember much of the speech due to embarrassment and a shared case of the giggles with the others, but one point came through loud and clear, breaking through the bashfulness.

Felis love was fierce and possessive, a crash of emotions drowning out everything else. Scratching our mates was only the visible sign of love. The emotional and physical dedication was intoxicating, almost overwhelming for some. We scratched and bit, owned and were owned inside and out.

There was a reason we tended to mate for life.

Like the others I'd covered my mouth and tittered, relieved when Ruth had released us with a wave of her hand, pointing to the freshly baked apple pies as payment for our attention.

I'd never really explored the depths of my passion with any of my human lovers. True, they'd all been one-night stands before Bran came along, but

even now I held back. I always held back part of myself with him because I was afraid of hurting him.
Even without claws I'd already marked Bran more
than once and I didn't know what would happen if
I lost complete control and surrendered to my inner
emotions.

Felis didn't kill Felis.

I could kill Bran. Changed or unChanged, I didn't
know what would happen if I let myself go, let my
feelings run rampant and dragged my body along
for the ride.

I just didn't know.

I couldn't risk it.

"I see you thinking," Trace said. "I'm offering you
a chance to see what it'd be like. No commitment,
no questions." He extended his hand, letting it hang
between us. "Let me take you for a ride." His lips
tweaked into a smile. "I won't tell."

I bit down on my bottom lip, chasing the sharp
pain to keep my mind clear. "I don't cheat."

Trace chuckled. "He's only a human, Reb. He's
not one of us. Think about it, what can a mere human
offer you?" he sneered.

I drew back, pulling myself out of danger. The
simmer in my blood settled down to a dull whine
and then to nothing.

"Himself." A burning spread over my back, the
scarred tissue heating up under my shirt. "And all I
can offer him is myself."

I drew a deep breath, trying to cleanse my system of Trace's approach.

I needed to get this investigation back on track now before I lost any hope of keeping sane.

"Did you know Hansa was a reporter working undercover at the club?"

Trace's expression went from angry and aroused to confused and curious. The seductive tone fell away. "What?"

"His real name was Michael Hancock. He was working as a stripper to get information on something or someone at the club."

"On what?" Trace frowned. "The family?"

I shrugged. "We don't know yet. Bran's getting what information he can."

"Cassie Prosser," Trace said. "You think she brought him in to run undercover."

"It's likely," I confessed. "Bran'll know as soon as he starts talking to her if she's part of this or not."

"And if she knows about us and called this fellow to dig up the story..." He shook his head. "This just keeps getting worse, doesn't it?"

"By leaps and bounds." I hesitated, caught between what I needed to do and what I didn't want to do.

"I need your help." I was running into the middle of a minefield wearing clown shoes.

A devilish smile appeared. "You need me?" He

tilted his head to one side, bright blue eyes catching mine. "You need me," he said proudly.

The grinding sound spun me around in time to see Brandon's car stab into a parking spot, pebbles flying in all directions.

I stepped back from Trace, wincing inside.

Bran stepped out and advanced on the two of us. The leather duster whipped around his legs as he strode right up to Trace. He didn't body-check me out of the way but he might as well have, sliding between the two of us with obvious intent.

"Is this punk bothering you again?" Bran didn't look at me, eyes locked with Trace's.

"Stop." I sighed, wishing men weren't so...well, men. "I need to talk to both of you." I took a step back. "Let's go inside."

Bran didn't move.

Trace's nostrils flared open. His eyes went wide and I spotted the first flush of Change, the irises beginning to narrow.

"We are not going to do this here." My mouth felt like it was filled with sand. "You can't Change out here in the open. And you—" I directed this to Bran, "—should know better."

Neither man moved or looked at me.

"I have a murderer to catch. So you can either whip out your dicks and measure them here or come back to the hotel room and help me figure this out. Both of you."

Two sets of eyes flashed toward me before returning to their standoff.

"I need Bran to help figure out the journalist angle. And I need you, Trace, to give me the inside track." My throat felt as if it were on fire. "I've got no one inside the Pride I can trust. I can't trust Carson."

Trace's attention flickered to me. "Why not?"

"He had enforcers take something out of Hansa's house and he won't tell me what. The same thugs who searched my hotel room," I said. "They're helping him hide something under the guise that Hancock was endangering the Pride."

Trace's left eyebrow rose.

"I don't know if he was or not," I admitted, "but I'm not leaving until I figure out who killed him and why. I sure as hell can't trust your uncle—he's a Board member and has to do what's right for the Pride." I sucked in my breath, praying I was making the right call. "I hope I can trust you to want justice for a dead man."

He pressed his lips together into a tight line. I could see the gears and wheels spinning in his mind.

Follow me and possibly betray his family. Don't help me and risk allowing a killer to go free, Felis or not.

It didn't escape me that he could also be looking at a way to get into my pants.

"She wants both of us." Trace addressed Bran, ignoring me. "Guess you're not enough on your own."

"I've had no complaints," Bran replied. "At least I don't slink around with my tail between my legs, playing with what's not mine."

Trace's nostrils flared again. He turned to me, pointedly ignoring Bran. "My first priority is to protect the family. That includes finding out who killed this guy and keeping our secret. If it's one of our own he needs to be disciplined, at the very least. If there's corruption…" He chewed on his bottom lip. "My uncle's an honest man. I don't like to think he's involved but I won't let something taint the family. Board members come and go but the family's eternal."

He eyed Bran. "How about a truce until this is done?"

Bran waited ten heartbeats before responding, giving me a near heart attack. "Done." He offered his hand. "Then we'll take this up again."

I didn't have to ask what "this" was.

I spun on my heel and headed for the hotel, cursing all men, Felis and human, under my breath.

ELEVEN

THE HOTEL CLERK raised an eyebrow as I strode by, the two men in tow. He didn't say anything but I knew the rumor mill would be running overtime.

I could do worse.

I turned when I reached the door. "Ground rules. No fighting, no sparring, no spitting. Either of you break them and I'll toss your ass out onto the street." I glared at Bran. "Either of you."

"Does she bite much?" Trace asked as I fumbled with the door key.

"Enough," Bran answered with a note of pride in his voice.

"Stop." I pointed through to the empty room. "Just. Stop."

The two sprinted inside—Trace sat at the table while Bran took the edge of the bed. The territory grab didn't surprise me.

"You." I gestured at Bran. "Talk." I knelt down by the minifridge and dug inside for a bottle of cold water.

"Mike Hancock was contacted by Cassie Prosser six months ago. She wanted an undercover reporter to come in and investigate the club." There was smugness in his voice as he glanced at Trace. "Bribery concerns. How the club kept getting the votes to keep going."

A knot in my stomach untangled. He hadn't been seeking out the family. It didn't explain how the Felis got involved but he hadn't been actively digging us out.

"She didn't say anything to me." I frowned. "I met her when I was checking out the club with Carson, right after I arrived."

"Why would she?" Bran tilted his head to one side. "She met you hanging out at the crime scene with the chief. Automatically on the other side."

"Other side of what?"

Bran looked at Trace for a second before replying. "Carson is officially neutral on the decision to have the club, as far as his public statements go. He has to be neutral. He's the police chief. But he's been a quiet supporter from the start."

I emptied the water bottle. "But shouldn't she have told him she was running someone undercover at the club? When he's found dead, supposedly from a bear attack?"

"When it's well known that the chief's wife is one of their best customers? And Hancock's sliced up like deli meat?" He looked at me sideways. "She's buying the bear attack story but she sure thinks someone smeared Hancock with honey beforehand."

"Ouch." I chewed on the water bottle mouth before speaking. "How did Prosser hook up with Hancock?"

"Online. Offered him the chance to find a juicy exposé on corruption in Penscotta. Come on down, go undercover and dig where she can't go." Bran plucked the bottle from my fingers and tossed it in the garbage. "Going to save the world. Or at least this small pocket of it."

"Why did she talk to you?" I asked. A long thin strand of blond hair had worked its way free of my ponytail and I now wrapped it around my finger. "She could have come out to the state troopers, gone over Carson's head. Why you?"

"She's still confused on what to do. Call the troopers in, get the media exposure she and the town don't want for what's supposed to be a simple animal attack. Sort of the same reason why Carson's kept it quiet, flipped 'round. Add in the simple fact that she's got no proof of these accusations other than Hancock's dead body, and she's stopped dead in her tracks." He grinned. "I, I have professional credentials." He puffed his chest out so far I was afraid he'd pop. "In case you've forgotten I do have some standing in the journalism area."

"And you didn't tell her you were with me." I allowed myself a smirk.

"And I didn't feel the need to volunteer that information," he added dryly.

"What did Hancock tell her before he was killed?"

"Nothing. They met about a week ago as part of their routine." Bran let out a sigh. "He told her he was working on it and not to bother him. She got all pissy about it but let him ride. Temperamental artist and all that crap."

"Is that standard for this sort of work?"

"Depends on the situation." He spread his hands. "Sometimes you don't want to show your hand until you've got all the ducks in a row and there's nothing left to find. Hancock looks like that type of guy."

"Where's the proof?" Trace interrupted.

"Either on the cell phone that mysteriously vanished from the body or in the twins' hands. Which means probably destroyed or at the least, well hidden." I shook my head. "Laptop, netbook, handwritten notes, whatever he was digging up went with the twins. And to whoever they're answering to—could be Carson, could be another Board member."

"Hmm." Trace rubbed his chin. "Lots of places to dump stuff 'round here. If they took anything it's long gone."

"Not a chance they'd keep it as a souvenir, something to sell later on?" Bran asked.

"Not if they're smart," Trace said. "Those two, they've been Pride enforcers for years. Plenty of dirt under their nails if you get what I'm saying."

"Great." I rubbed my eyes. "So any evidence of corruption at the club is long gone. Bet they were copies of financial records showing payoffs. It'd be the best evidence to put forward." I looked at Trace. "Any chance you can get the boys to fess up?"

Trace snorted. "Not in this lifetime. They're loyal to the end." He looked over at Bran. "I'd stay clear of those two if you can."

"Too late," Bran replied.

I grabbed another bottle of water. "Okay so there's no chance of retrieving the evidence." The white plastic cap gave me a hard time as I twisted it. "But we're not trying to build a court case. It's an animal attack, remember."

Both men reached out, offering to open the bottle for me.

I snarled and wrestled the top off with a violent yank. The shuddering pangs up my arm reminded me I was still recovering from the run. "Someone on the town council's taking bribes. That's from Cassie Prosser herself and I don't see any reason to doubt her."

Trace spoke from his seat at the table. "There's only five people on the council." His eyes narrowed. "And only one Felis."

"Lisa Darning." I completed the thought. "But why the hell would she get involved with this and why kill Hancock?"

"Isn't it obvious?" Bran looked up from the screen. "She was involved with the payoffs and didn't want to be exposed. She's already voting to keep the club open."

"And she's visited it as well as knowing Hancock." I shook my head. "She could have dumped the body anywhere out here—it'd never be found. Why leave him there? Right behind the club where he worked? It may not send up red flags for humans but it sure as heck set off the air raid sirens for the Pride."

"Why kill him in the first place?" Trace broke in. "No offense, but this ain't Felis business. It's between the humans and we don't have anything to do with it. If that club stays open or closed it don't make a difference to us financially." His tone took on a steely resolve. "We take care of our own. No one in the Pride ever goes hungry, no matter what's happening in the world." He shook his head. "I've known Lisa for years. She's not a killer. She's tough and one hell of a woman but she's not a murderer."

"Evidence would say otherwise," Bran said smoothly, the invisible slap ringing loud in the room.

I placed myself between the two men. "What's the worst that could happen if the news broke that she was taking bribes? She might lose her place on the town council and that's it—maybe a fine for corruption but I don't see any serious jail time happening. Is that enough to murder Hancock for?"

"I'd say no. And I don't know why she'd be taking payoffs," Trace drawled. "Her business is one of the few successful ones in the area. Maybe she's got some sort of gambling problem or something that'd justify all this but…" He gave me a wistful look. "We don't usually kill for nothing. You know that."

I sat down on the edge of the bed. This was turning into something far more complicated than just an angry woman killing a wandering lover. We were getting into local politics and going much further afield than I was comfortable with.

"I'm going to go talk to Lisa Darning," I said.

"Is that wise?" Bran replied. "If she's guilty of the murder you're putting yourself in a dangerous spot." He glanced at Trace before continuing. "She didn't have a problem killing Hancock—she'd have no problem killing again."

"If she's guilty she'll answer to the Board and to the Pride," Trace said.

"Not to the courts?" Bran threw out the bait. "What sort of justice is that?"

"Let's leave that for the moment." I jumped in before the truce shattered in front of me. "She was lying to me in our first interview. Let's see how she reacts now."

Trace stood up, his back ramrod straight. "If she did kill him it was not to protect the family. That would make it outside of the family's rules. We've had Felis arrested before for criminal offenses. You don't get a pass just because you're part of the Pride." His eyes were hard and unforgiving. "You answer for your crimes."

It was a compromise, an olive twig.

I stood up and crooked a finger at Trace. "I'm going out."

Bran looked at me, hard brown eyes unwilling to concede an inch of possession. "You taking him along?"

"He's family." It was impossible to put my emotions in words.

Bran got to his feet and took my arm. "May I talk to you in private?"

I let him lead me to the bathroom. As he closed the door I saw Trace grinning, a smug look begging to be smacked off.

"Are you sure about this? His uncle is a Board member," Bran asked. "What makes you think he's not working both sides here? What if he drags you into the woods and kills you to keep their little secret?"

"You don't think I can take care of myself?" I crossed my arms in front of me. "Hate to break it to you but I was doing fine before you rode into my life."

"That's not what I mean," he growled, his face turning scarlet. "I just don't want to see you getting hurt 'cause he can get all furry."

I tamped down my rising annoyance. "I'll be fine. Look, I have to trust someone local down here." I waved at the wall. "He's not going anywhere and I might as well put him to work. Besides, I need his help."

"You need his help or you want his help?" Bran moved inside my personal space, his voice dropping to a whisper. "You want to be with him?"

I resisted the urge to break away from the close scrutiny. "This isn't about you and me or Trace. It's about giving me the best odds to find out who killed Hancock."

"Is it?" Bran's dark eyes searched mine. "Because I'm not keen on sharing."

"I wasn't asking your permission." I held back on the snarl building in my throat. "Save the personal crisis for later." I reached for the doorknob. "Sulk if you want or you help me find a killer. Your choice."

Before he could answer I was out of the room.

I picked up my leather duster and slipped it on. Bran came out of the washroom and settled himself at the table while Trace moved to stand by me.

"I'll be back as soon as I can." The words sounded odd to my ears as I prepared to hunt a killer. I might as well be going out for bread and milk.

Bran let out a snort. "And what am I supposed to do? Knit booties while you're gone?"

"I need you to get online and use those journalistic connections to find out something, anything about the club and Hancock. If you can find out what he uses to collect his notes it'd be great. Cell phone, whatever."

Bran moved to the table, entwining his fingers and cracking his knuckles. "I do have mad finger skills, as you know." He leered at me.

I winced at the loud popping noise. "Down boy. Put that energy into finding out what Hancock dug up. He must have at least had an email account— maybe he was emailing files to someone else, back-ups. See if you can sneak in."

"You mean, hack?" Bran's eyebrows rose. "I am shocked, shocked that you would suggest such a thing."

I rolled my eyes. "Just do that voodoo you do. You're a reporter—get me something to report."

I strode from the room, Trace close behind.

"We'll take my car." I ignored the curious smirk from the hotel clerk. "You, you keep your eyes open for any trouble."

"Like?" He scrambled to open the front door for me, following close behind as we headed for the parked cars.

"Like someone trying to stop me." I jammed the car key in the lock. "Bran isn't the only one who'll be pissed if I get hurt or killed."

Trace's directions to Lisa Darning's business were as convoluted as a skein of twisted wool, taking us over the same bridge at least three times. He chuckled as I pulled into the parking lot, lightheaded from the curved and hilly roads.

"Lord, how did your people settle this area?" I shook my head, fighting back the nausea.

"It's a gift," he answered with a sly grin. "I can think of better ways to make you dizzy, though."

I put up my hand. "Save it, Romeo. Just stay here and behave." I got out of the car before he could toss another snappy retort my way. Between him and Bran I could seriously consider giving up driving stick.

The street looked like a child's building kit, the bricks laid out in perfect lines with painted wooden signs designating each different store. The narrow lanes were lined with cobblestones, showing the original horse-and-buggy roads and the age of the town. I could imagine tourists scuttling along the sidewalk, snapping pictures of the rustic buildings and nattering to themselves about historical sites.

At least before the recession hit, killing off any tourist trade. Add in the mills and mines closing and I could understand the appeal of a business, any business, which brought in money.

Darning Print was wedged between a second-hand antique store and a skateboard shop, neither of which seemed to be bulging with customers.

The smells hit me as I walked in. Ink, sweat, different types of paper running through greased machines and gears, flushed out on the other side with images and words. Peppermint gum, a barbecued brisket sandwich and cigar smoke made up part of the rest of the odors.

I walked up to the counter and rang the small desk bell. A young woman scurried over to me, her long dark hair snapped back into a tight bun.

"Can I help you?"

"I'm here to see Lisa."

"Just a minute." She headed down a narrow path between stacks of boxed paper and vanished from sight.

I studied the samples spread out under the transparent plastic counter cover. Flyers for local yard sales, pages from the high school yearbook and one for the Cat's Meow in blinding neon colors.

Lisa flew toward me, her eyes blazing. She looked as if she was about to jump over the counter but veered toward the door at the last minute.

"I didn't expect you to come here," she hissed. "What is it?"

"I wanted to talk to you again." I held my ground. "I didn't realize I'd have to call and make an appointment."

Her upper lip twitched, dangerously close to a scowl. "I told you all I know. What's there to talk about?"

"More." I nodded toward the door. "Either you take me to your office or we go for a walk. Unless you want your employees to listen in as we discuss this right here at the counter."

A machine nearby went into a loud, grinding scream, throttling my threat. Lisa winced as the grinding moved down into a tolerable crunching noise.

"That piece of shit's been falling apart for years." She held the swinging door open for me. "My office."

The corner office held a single dying fern in the far corner, almost hidden behind the stacks of paperwork on the old wooden desk. Lisa gestured at the empty chair, moving a pile of folders to see me from behind the desk.

"As you can see, we're pretty busy. Got a few big contracts and they're all due at once. Usually you can hear a mouse around here." She smiled. "But I'm not going to complain."

"Your current contracts include the Cat's Meow?"

"We do work for them." She didn't flinch from the question. "Last one was a set of lottery tickets for a slave auction a month ago. Steady money and they pay on time."

"Good customers?"

She returned my steady stare with interest. "I've got better ones. But they're up there in the top five."

"How well did you know Mike Hansa?" I shifted gears. "I know you said you liked him but not enough to sleep with him." I shot her a girls-are-girls grin. "Were you being truthful about that?"

She shifted in the chair, eyes darting around the room and settling on the fern. "I told you, I don't do humans." Her fingernails drummed on the desktop. "They're disgusting." Her upper lip curled up.

I raised an eyebrow. "Disgusting enough for you to stuff money in his g-string?"

Another nervous shift. "It was something different. Something out of the usual."

"I know there aren't any Felis men allowed to work at the club." I studied my own ragged attempts at fingernails. "I saw a lot of handsome humans when I was visiting the club. Not family, but…" I grinned. "Pretty darned tasty-looking. You telling me you never thought about walking on the wild side, not even once?" I tilted my head to one side. "Going for the other white meat?"

Lisa blushed, a deep scarlet tickling every inch of visible skin. "I…I considered it." Her eyes moved off the plant and came back to mine. "I asked him out, once. Thought I'd see what it was like."

"And?"

She let her breath out in a disappointed sigh. "Not what I expected. A bit of a letdown." Lisa rubbed her burning cheeks with both hands. "God, you must think I'm a damned, lying fool. Here I am all mouthy about not doing humans and you come here to hear me confess bagging a dead man."

"Well he wasn't dead when you 'bagged' him." I gave her what I hoped was an understanding smile. "Although I've had some dates where I did have to check for a pulse."

This brought a smile to her face, fighting back the embarrassment.

"All show and no go?" I prodded.

"We just, ah, didn't mesh." She straightened a pile of folders to her left. "It was quick and it wasn't much fun for either one of us."

"Weren't you afraid of what the other women would think? From what I've heard Mike didn't date anyone, much less sleep with them." I watched her continue to fondle the files.

"It was a few months ago when he first arrived at the club," she offered as she tapped the edges of the tower. "He hadn't made up his mind then about keeping away from the locals, I guess. And we decided to keep it quiet in order to keep everyone happy. Guess we were both too embarrassed to put it on our résumés."

I studied her face. She stared at me directly, not the elusive eye dance I'd seen at the farm.

"Where did you go for your one-time liaison?"

"My car. Toyota Tercel. The club's parking lot, believe it or not." She wrinkled her nose. "It was a bit awkward."

"Tight squeeze." I held back a chuckle, imagining the two adults wrestling inside the small car. "Should have sprung for a hotel room."

She giggled, the relief of telling her dark secret showing in the high-pitched sound. "Thought I was going to sprain something. I think he did—he was dancing odd for a few days afterwards."

I put on my sisterhood face. "I wish you had told me this before."

Lisa gave me a tight smile. "I knew I'd be the top suspect. You're looking for a Felis who slashed him to death, a disgruntled lover or her mate. I'm an ex-lover in the technical sense but hardly disgruntled." She surveyed her nails. "I had no reason to kill him. No angry husband or boyfriend in the wings waiting to take revenge. It was a one-time mistake and I didn't want that spread around the Pride." She let out a low, nervous breath. "I hope you'll consider keeping this between us."

"Of course." I sat back, trying to get comfortable in the wooden chair. "Did you ever talk to Mike about how he ended up in Penscotta, Pennsylvania, dancing in a small club?"

She shrugged, crossing her legs under the generic sheet metal desk. "We didn't talk much." Her cheeks stayed scarlet at the memory. "Better things to do with his mouth, you know?"

We both chuckled.

I studied her face, looking for any sort of sign she was lying. A twitch of a lip, avoiding eye contact, arms crossed in front of her.

Nothing. Either she was a darned good liar on the level of your average sociopath or she was telling the truth.

"Did he ever ask you about your job on the town council? About how you kept voting to keep the club open?"

Lisa frowned. "He asked me something about why I kept working when my business was doing so well, especially in today's economy. I told him I wanted to serve the community—my council salary is a fraction of what I pull in from here." She shook her head. "My political stance isn't a big secret. Everyone sees me going to the club." Her eyes narrowed. "Is that why he was killed? Something about the club?"

"I'm exploring all possibilities." It wasn't a total lie.

"I hope you find out who killed him," Lisa said, and the tone in her voice was genuine. "It's wrong to kill without good cause."

"You don't think Mike's killer had good cause?" I stared at her.

She traced a circle on the scratched metal with one long finger. "I think killing over a woman or a man is wrong. We've got divorce laws, we've got equal rights—women are fully empowered in our society." A smile tugged at the edges of her mouth. "Even before the rest of the world, if I recall my Felis history right."

I nodded. It'd been much harder back then to keep the family secret when you had strong women like Jess either running Prides or asserting their authority. Meek, mild women weren't our forte.

"And Mike might have been good in the sack or whatever, but you know we don't kill without cause." She repeated it as if convincing herself. "Kill without cause." Lisa put her hands together, fingernails tapping against each other. "Do you still think I killed him?"

"Someone did," I responded, finding my voice.

Lisa nodded. "But it wasn't me. I have nothing to gain."

"You're on the town council. There's power there." I stepped as lightly as I could through the minefield.

Her lips split apart, reshaping into a wide grin. "Did someone put this into your head? Some whack-adoodle theory about me taking bribes for votes? Do you know how often that gets tossed into my face for everything from garbage pickup days to library funding?" She answered her own question before I could reply. "I keep voting for the club because it's good for the area. People may whine about the morality of male stripping and all that but the club's parking lot is full every night." She studied me for a minute before continuing. "I didn't kill Mike Hansa. I have no reason to."

I shifted gears. "Why aren't you on the Board? You're pretty tough and you can handle the men. Saw that out on the farm."

She flushed again at the direct praise. "I'm busy here with my business and being on the town council."

"Doesn't say you can't be on the Board." I drew my fingertips together in what I hoped was a sign of support. "Have you considered it?"

"Sure." She rolled her shoulders back, a note of pride in her voice. "Just waiting until one of the members retires or dies."

"You could challenge." I gave her the sisterly eye again. "Jess didn't get her spot by sitting back."

Her fingers began rattling out a different rhythm. "I'd have to be strong enough to beat down their yes-man." She tilted her head toward the street. "McCallum has your babysitter Trace. Plussey could call up any number of strong men to stand for him. I'd be a fool to challenge and lose."

"Could challenge the chief," I said.

"Could but he'd call up the twins. I may be good but I can't take either one of them on my best day." She gave me a weary smile. "Believe me, I'm working on it. Takes a bit of work to convince someone to take on a challenge for you. Debts to be paid and all that." Her eyes narrowed. "Carson's racked up a lot of favors over the years from humans and Felis."

"Doing what sort of favors?"

She gave me a knowing look. "I think you know the answer to that."

I stood up. There was no point in showing my hand about Mike's real occupation, and she wasn't giving off any more signals. "If you think of anything else please call."

She watched me from her office door as I threaded the maze back to the front door. A handful of employees gave me a fast look before turning back to the copying machines. I smelled a few Felis among them.

I stopped and peered at the Cat's Meow flyer under the plastic sheet again before going to my car. Sophia Martin posing with Mike Hancock and both smiling like they'd eaten fat canaries.

"Find out anything?" Trace asked as I got in.

"That she's a lousy liar." I dialed Bran's cell. "I don't think she killed Hancock."

Bran answered the phone on the first ring. "You okay? Need any help?"

"I'm fine. You got anything yet?"

"I got everything," he smugly replied. "Mike used SafeHaven to back up his files."

"And that is…" I tapped the speakerphone function, balancing the phone on my thigh. No way I was going to try to wrestle the phone and drive at the same time.

"An online site where you can store files. If you lose your flash drive or your laptop your files are still safe and stored." I could hear his fingers banging on the keyboard. "It's very useful overseas where your luggage can be 'accidentally' lost for hours and what you get back isn't what you started out with."

I pulled out into traffic, the cell phone in my lap and Trace sitting beside me. "So he stored his information off-site. How did you get in? Wasn't it passworded?"

"Yeah, and Mike wasn't that creative. Let's just say that password1 still holds the record for easiest hack ever." He chuckled. "I went and changed my password just now."

"So we've got the files." That earned me a sharp glance from Trace. "What was Mike digging up?"

"He doesn't say who on the town council was taking the bribes. All he says is that bribes were being handed out for certain favors. Still haven't found that info yet."

"Damn it." I ignored Trace's smirk at my cursing. "I just left Darning. She admitted to having a quickie with Hancock but nothing more. I need those notes."

"I'm working as fast as I can to pick these apart," he growled. "He wasn't exactly writing these to go up on public display. A lot of bastardized shorthand and whatnot."

"Don't you all use the same secret decoder ring?"

I never heard the smart-ass answer because a copper-colored SUV jumped in front of me, cutting me off.

TWELVE

I YELPED, JERKING the steering wheel to one side. The cell phone slid off my lap and down by my feet as we jumped onto the sidewalk.

I stood up on the brake pedal, locking my right knee and narrowly missing a parking meter as we skidded to a stop. I threw the car into park, my pulse pounding loud in my ears.

Trace threw his door open and advanced on the car, his teeth bared.

"What the fu…" His curse trailed off as Cassie Prosser jumped out. The wild-eyed brunette ignored him and headed straight for me, dismissing the growing line of cars building behind our little meeting.

"Reb? Reb?" Bran frantically yelled from the car floor. "Are you okay?"

I snatched up the phone. "Call you right back." I cut the connection and pocketed the cell.

I leapt out and strode toward her, meeting her in the middle. Trace, thankfully, kept his distance. I guessed he knew when to stay out of a catfight. He drifted out of eyesight as I zeroed in on the enraged woman.

"You." The challenge behind the single word had the hairs on the back of my neck standing up. "You lied to me when we met in the bar. You knew who Mike was."

"Not as much as I do now." I nodded toward her vehicle. "If you'd like to talk I'm open to it." My nostrils twitched at the scent of fresh gun oil rolling off her, mixed with nervous sweat. "But not at the point of a gun."

She took a step back, her mouth half-open. The anger deflated, just enough for her to realize where she was and what she was doing.

Trace stepped up behind her and waited, eyes locked on me. I had no doubt if I'd asked him to snap her neck and dump her in the trunk he'd do it without question.

A woman could get drunk with that sort of power over a man.

"Park your car and we'll talk." I looked around and saw a green spot, the handful of trees hemming in a war memorial and a handful of benches. "There."

Trace got back in as I edged the rental car back onto the road and into a proper parking spot. The scowl on his face spoke volumes.

"Got to deal with her sometime." I launched the preliminary strike.

He shook his head. "Rather not."

"What does she know about the family?" I watched Cassie maneuver the copper SUV against the curb. The backup behind her straightened out and traffic began to flow down the narrow street. Good thing too—I didn't need Carson or his boys showing up and demanding answers.

"Nothing. And we'd like to keep it that way." He scratched his thigh. "She's usually just plain old boring news, the local bingos and garage sales. Then the club started up and she got all antsy, put the paper against it. Long-winded editorials, digging up statistics about the moral decay, all that crap." He let out a snort. "Do-gooder on a crusade. Nothing more dangerous."

A little parkette burst onto the scene, fighting for breath between the brick buildings on the street. The small stone bench sat in front of the war memorial and waited for visitors.

"Stay here until I call." I got out of the car and headed for the small park, not waiting for Trace's response. The small stone headstone showed names from both World Wars and a handful of more recent additions from Afghanistan and Iraq.

I stood by the memorial and waited. A fresh flower display lay propped up against the cool marble, no card or note attached.

"You're no insurance paper pusher." Prosser stepped up beside me. "I checked you out. You're a private investigator."

I spotted the pistol on her hip, the leather holster pushed around to almost be out of sight. Almost.

"Got that from Bran?" I smiled. "Darned man doesn't know when to keep his mouth shut."

The casual tone brought a frown in response. She'd expected me to come out guns a-blazing, as she did.

In another time and another place I would be.

This wasn't it.

"Doesn't take too many strangers popping into town at once to trigger my bullshit sensors." She licked her lips. "I expect Hanover told you Mike Hancock came to town at my request to go underground at the club." She dug at the edge of the grass with the toe of her cowboy boot. "I didn't expect him to die."

"I've found most people don't expect to die," I replied. "And yet it still happens."

"A goddamn animal attack." Cassie shook her head. "Doesn't sound right to me. Doesn't smell right to me."

I didn't look for Trace but felt his presence, just out of sight. Cassie had no idea how close she was to her own death. If Trace felt she was getting close to the family he'd be forced to do something about it.

"Something" being another mysterious death. Two in a week in a small town might be suspicious but it'd vanish in time into the odd files next to Mothmen and Chupacabras.

But I needed information and I couldn't get without giving.

I started my dance on the razor's edge.

"Mike was killed by an animal, according to the police and verified by the coroner. I saw the body myself," I said slowly and carefully. "But I think he might have been assaulted beforehand, making him vulnerable to the attack."

Cassie formed an *O* with her lips, the thin red bars pressed so tightly together I thought she was about to whistle. Her facial expressions shifted and I spotted the hardcore journalist come out.

"Who attacked him?" she asked.

"I'm not sure yet," I admitted. "But I can tell you honestly and without a shadow of a doubt that in the end Mike Hancock was killed by a vicious animal."

I felt Trace's glare. It was the truth, covered in a wee bit of honey.

"But—" I paused, letting the natural pacing carry my words, "—there's no doubt in my mind the assault was connected to his working for you. Did he tell you what he'd uncovered? Give you any information?" I watched her face as she shook her head.

"Mike told me that when he goes undercover he goes deep. We never spoke; he'd send me text messages once a week just to let me know he was still alive. Short ones just saying he was getting the data he needed to bust the story wide open." She sniffled. "I never thought it was dangerous. I mean, people would be pissed off. But enough to kill? For God's sake, it's only money."

I watched one of the rose petals break free in a soft wind and drift down to the ground. "You thought the town council was being bought off. Who specifically?"

She shook her head. "I don't know. There's only five of them and they're all local folks who've been here for decades, got their roots sunk deep. But you know how money can change a person—wave enough in front of someone's face and eventually they're going to give in." Her hand worked free of her leather jacket pocket to brush through her short brown hair. "I didn't want to think any of them were taking bribes."

"But you suspected."

Cassie nodded. "When the club came to town we were told there'd be polls, surveys, and whatever the majority of the townsfolk wanted would happen. Everybody, they were all for the club at the beginning—until the club opened and people found their girlfriends and wives, mothers and daughters running over for a night of hot man dancing."

I couldn't hide a smile. "What's good for the goose and all that. Bet there's a few strip clubs around the men like to frequent."

Cassie chuckled, a bit of the tension easing out of her face. "Sure there are—but not locally. At least the men have to drive a bit and it tends to keep the trouble out of town and away from the locals."

"Trouble?"

"Domestic disputes, drunk driving, underage drinking. It's different when it's in your backyard." Her voice dropped to a whisper. "I suspected drug trafficking. And I'm not just talking dope."

"Right at the club?" I hadn't picked up on anything on my previous visit.

"No." She sighed. "They do this outside in the parking lot, supposedly. Carson's been picking them up here and there, but for every one dealer you put away two come out. Helicopter in with the goods, grab the money and get out, leaving the mess behind for us to clean up. He's a dedicated cop but there's only so much he and his department can do."

I couldn't deny her logic. I'd seen too many attempts to clean up rough neighborhoods end in despair as new scum moved in to replace the old.

"So the residents started to change their minds about the club," I prompted.

Cassie nodded. "I saw a story about Hancock busting some government official; dropped him a line. Told him I thought the club was paying off someone to keep the votes going the right way."

"And he leapt at the chance to get another award."

She let out a rough laugh. "Yeah, well—that's Mike for you. Was, I mean. He got here with a fake identity and made it into the club without even trying hard. They were desperate for dancers and he was easy on the eyes."

The loose rose petal blew along the grass.

"Did he say anything about who was getting paid off?" I didn't want to dwell too long on Mike's death.

She shook her head, her arms now wrapped around herself. "No. He just told me it was going well and it'd be a blockbuster when it broke." A light sob broke free. "I didn't think it was gonna kill him. I mean, I knew there'd be hurt feelings and a whole lot of name-calling and finger-pointing and maybe a bit of shoving when it came down to it, but…"

Cassie looked up at me, her eyes brimming with tears. "You said he was beaten up before, ah, before…" Her hands formed curved claws, fingers shaking in the cool breeze. "They set him up for that thing, that bear, to find him and kill him."

I put on my best lying face. "Possibly. It might have been attracted by the blood or just been passing on by and took advantage. But I think it was a quick death, personally." The truth would be even more horrific. I'd seen what Felis claws could do, had suffered under their attack.

"Mike has—had family," Cassie whispered. "The body's been shipped home. What do I tell them? They're already leaving messages, wanting to know what he was doing here. They know he was working on a story. What do I tell them, how much do I tell them?"

I nudged the petal back onto the grass and away from the sidewalk. "You tell them he was doing his job."

"Are you going to finish it?" she asked. She tugged at a dark lock of hair at the side of her face. "I'm not being mercenary here. I just don't want his death to be in vain. If I could just get hold of whatever he'd dug up, what led to his death…"

A whisper of the journalist sparked in her eyes.

I shrugged. "I don't know what he found." It was a half lie. Until Bran deciphered those notes I truly didn't know.

"Just promise me you'll give me the headline if you do find something, anything I can put in the paper," Cassie said, a touch of pleading in her words. "Let me do the right thing by Mike."

"If anything turns up I'll let you get first bite before the big boys." I turned to see Trace waiting by the car. He shifted his weight from side to side, his hands in his pockets. "Best I can offer."

"I'll take it. Better than just printing his obit." She pulled out a business card and passed it to me. "Any time, day or night—call me. Please." She gave me a curt nod and walked away.

Trace moved up beside me.

"She's tough," I said.

"As nails. Her dad was a miner. Busted his hump to get her to college."

I turned and studied his face. "Would you kill her if I asked? Or if the Board did?"

Trace's stoic look told me everything. "You know I can't answer that."

"You just did." I walked toward the car.

Bran answered on the first ring. "Are you okay? Do you want me to come out there?"

"You don't even know where 'there' is." I smiled. "I'm fine. How are the files coming?"

"I'm still working on it," he answered. "Give me a little time."

"I just met Cassie Prosser," I said. "You could have told me she carries a pistol."

"Didn't know she did." The surprise in his voice was tinged with worry. "You okay?"

"Yeah. She wanted to talk about Mike." I wrestled with the seat belt, cell phone propped against my shoulder.

"Well, there's a surprise," Bran replied. "How's she holding up?"

"About as well as can be expected. She feels guilty for Hancock's death."

I imagined him nodding back in the hotel room. "Can't blame her. It's sort of hard to push this bear attack angle after a certain point."

"But we have to," I snapped.

"I know," he murmured. "I don't want anyone else dying."

I pulled out onto the road. Trace sat beside me, the window rolled down and enjoying the wind in his face. I risked a glance at his well-tanned profile, feeling a chill enter my bones.

If I'd asked him to kill Cassie Prosser he would

have. A clean, fast kill, and found a way to hide the body to keep our secret. He might have a few rough nights, a handful of nightmares but he'd justify it away as part of the price we paid to be part of human society. Be close but not too close to the humans— and be ready to kill to protect the Felis.

He was family.

I wasn't sure what the hell I was but I sure wasn't that.

Bran cleared his throat over the open phone line. "I've managed to make some sense out of the notes. Looks like it was small and local, only one person at the club making the payoffs. No mob connections, no one outside of the town bringing in money and doing the dirty."

"Sophia Martin?"

"Her name's not here but I'd say it's a good bet. She's got the power to cook the books and keep it secret. But we need to know who was getting the payoffs—where it all ended up. I should have it all deciphered within the next hour. Where are you going to now?"

"We're heading for the club. I want to take another look at the spot where Hancock died."

Bran gave an affirmative grunt. "Think you missed something?"

"I could have." I swerved around a half-flattened squirrel on the road. "First time I was there Carson was talking in riddles so Darning and Prosser didn't clue in, and I was looking for signs of a pissed-off lover. Now things are different and I just have a feeling I missed something."

"Be careful. I don't trust anyone in this town. Anyone," Bran said, biting down on the last word. He disconnected before I could answer.

Trace scratched his thigh. His fingers twitched and I knew he wanted to scratch elsewhere but was holding off for courtesy's sake.

I enjoyed his discomfort.

A handful of cars sat in the Cat's Meow parking lot. I guessed cleaning staff and maybe a dancer or two working on a new routine before the doors officially opened in a few hours.

Trace hopped out of the car, shaking one leg after the other. "Too early for the shows to start." He brushed invisible dust from the front of his jeans. "It's only three in the afternoon."

I rubbed my forehead. My inner clock was all types of screwed up. "I need a cup of tea. A proper cup of tea."

Trace chuckled. "Canadian."

"Yes." I led him around to the back where the garbage Dumpster stood. "Here's where it happened. Let's go back and take it from the top without anyone watching over my shoulder."

Trace moved to stand by the curb, instinctively finding the dried blood. "He died over here."

I nodded, walking around the large dark green container.

"What was he doing out here?" I put my hands on my hips and slowly did a circle, surveying the area anew. "Not exactly a scenic spot."

"Maybe he came out here for a smoke?" Trace pointed at a handful of cigarette butts spread across the concrete. "Impromptu smoking area."

"Mike didn't smoke. I would have smelled it on him or in his truck. Nothing at his apartment either." I knelt down and inspected the half-smoked cigarettes.

"Lisa doesn't smoke," Trace said.

I felt the light verbal slap.

"True," I admitted. There'd been plenty of smokers working in the shop but she hadn't been one of them.

He scuffed the tip of his shoe on the edge of the curb. "He bled out pretty good."

"No blood trail leading to or from the scene." I pushed one butt around with the edge of my fingernail. "Could have been a body dump to try and throw us off the track."

Trace shook his head. "Look at the amount of blood. No way he bled that much anyplace else."

I went over to him and leaned over the stained grass. The thick soil still reeked of blood, the coppery scent sticking to the back of my throat. If Mike Hancock had been killed elsewhere and dumped here, the killer had carried a bag of blood with him or her.

"He doesn't smoke. So he comes out here to… what?" I stood up and spread my hands. "Meet someone? His contact giving him info about the club's finances? Practice new dance moves?"

Trace shuffled to one side. I recognized the moves—standard tracking practice. He sniffed the air and grimaced.

"You wouldn't think a nightclub would generate so much garbage." His nose wriggled as he fought with the ugly smells contaminating his senses.

"And yet they do." I moved away from the darkened grass, trying to pick my way through the competing scents. It was like maneuvering inside a kaleidoscope.

"Must be picked up once a week." Trace waved a hand toward the Dumpster. "Damned thing's probably full of used hair gel bottles and body wash." He gave a visible shudder.

I paused. It'd been technically part of the crime scene but I'd ignored it, pursuing the original theory that Hancock'd been killed by a jealous lover.

I'd also assumed Carson had checked it out already.

Insert "ass-u-me" joke here.

I approached the box, swearing under my breath. Dumpster diving was one of the things I hated about this job—you never knew what you'd land in. One time I'd had to jump in to retrieve a receipt to prove a false insurance claim and ended up ankle-deep in rancid wonton soup.

My stomach flipped at the memory.

Trace grinned. "I know what you're thinking."

"Not a chance." I flung the thin sheet metal flap open and peered inside, trying not to inhale. "No pain, no gain."

Trace knelt down and linked his hands together. "I'd offer to go but I'm not a trained investigator."

"And your work boots are too pretty." I stepped onto his intertwined fingers, using the makeshift step to swing my leg up and over the rusted metal top.

I winced as my shoes crushed something glass, the tinkling loud in my ears. "Come on in, the water's fine."

"I'm good," Trace said. "I've got your back."

I coughed, trying to sort out the various smells. "Thanks." I knelt down on a flattened cardboard box. "Wish I had a pair of gloves. I'm afeared of what I'll find in here."

Trace appeared at the edge of the Dumpster. He leaned in and took a deep whiff. "Not much rotting food."

"Probably just from the bar and fast food lunches." I turned over a plastic bag to reveal a stack of shredded coffee-stained napkins. "Lemons, cherries and the like from those fancy drinks with the umbrellas. I don't remember them having a full menu." I shuffled the ragged streams with one foot. "Hello. What's this?"

The folded bloody napkin lay at the bottom of the stack, the dark stain almost blending in with the coffee.

Almost.

I pulled it out with care, easing the dried, brittle paper edges over.

The long, slender half circles lay in the middle of the napkins, edges touched with crimson.

I leaned in and sniffed.

Blood.

Mike Hancock's blood.

It wouldn't stand up in a court of law but I was hell and gone from anything resembling a courtroom.

"What are those?" Trace stared at the scattered light blue crescent moons littering the area. Half of them were bloodstained in some way or other. The edges were curved up into sharp points, artificial claws.

"The murder weapon. Or weapons, depending on how you look at it." I leaned in and sniffed again, trying to pick up the owner's scent.

"Whose are they?" Trace studied the small pile.

I drew in another deep breath, holding back a cough. "It's a mess. I got Hancock clean and clear but this, this is a mess."

"Can I see?" Trace sounded like a little kid eager to see a fresh gash on someone's arm.

I used the remnants of a half-shredded page to push them together on another sheet. "Let me just get out here first." The whiff of something dead and decaying spurted up when I shifted my foot to one side.

I resisted the urge to gag and took small puffs.

"Don't you need an evidence bag or something like that?" Trace asked.

"Fuck, yeah." I carefully folded the page again and again, trapping the thin wafers inside. "But I'm a master at improvising. Now help me get out of here before I puke."

I moved to the side of the container, keeping a firm grip on the evidence. It took an effort to swing my foot up and over the thin wall. A sharp pain ran up my back, reminding me yet again that I wasn't as young as I used to be.

At least when it came to straddling iron bars.

Trace grunted and helped me out of the Dumpster, pulling me over the rough metal edge as gently as he could. His hands tightened on my waist, tucking under my duster with an unsettling familiarity.

I let out a short meep as he set me on my feet, holding onto the packet as tightly as I dared.

Trace chuckled, his voice low and seductive. "Cute sound."

"Don't get used to it. I need to call Carson." I dug my phone out of my coat pocket with one hand, not daring to relinquish my death hold on the paper.

"Here." Trace took the phone from me and tapped

in a number. He looked up at me, seeing my curious glance. "We don't use 911 out here. Not for that, anyway. Pride's got a private number for him."

I hefted the small package in my hand, wondering what else we had missed.

"Chief? Yep, I'm out here at the club with Rebecca. She wants you to come here pronto." Trace said. "Girl's a damned good tracker."

I plucked the phone from his hand, giving the alpha male a scowl. "Chief Carson?"

"What do you have?" Carson spoke quickly, his tone somewhere between a yell and a whine. "What do you have?"

"I think I've got the murder weapon." I hefted the paper in my hand.

"Is Trace working with you now?" There was a note of confusion in his voice.

I glanced at Trace. "Yes, yes he is. We agreed to disagree on the method of him babysitting me."

"Your man let you hang out with Trace?" Carson let out a hoarse laugh. "What's he doing, pouting back at the hotel as he knits you a sweater?"

"He's following a lead, working online from our room." I tried to take command back of the conversation back and pull it away from my love life. "Look, why don't you meet me at the hospital. I'd like Henry to get what he can off this evidence. If you've got DNA on any of the family..." I hoped that between

Henry, Carson and Trace we'd be able to scent the
real killer. My nose just wasn't that good.

"No, no. You stay right there. I'm coming over,"
Carson barked. "Have you spoken to anyone else
yet about this?"

I shook my head, forgetting I wasn't using one
of those newfangled video phones. "We just found
it and the club isn't open yet. A few people hanging
around but no one's seen us yet."

"Good. I don't want this getting around. You
know these small towns—rumors travel faster than
deer in hunting season." He chuckled. "Best we keep
this as quiet as possible until it's time to move."

"I hear you." I felt the hairs on the back of my
neck twitch. "Meet me in the parking lot. We're traveling in my car."

"I'm on my way." The line went dead.

"Hey." Trace touched my arm. "What you just
said 'bout no one seeing us yet? Look up and smile."

I followed his outstretched finger to see a mini-
camera mounted on the edge of the building, pointed
squarely down at the smoking area.

At us.

THIRTEEN

"DAMN," I SWORE, holding back on more colorful language in case the camera had audio. "Didn't even think about it."

"What?" Trace asked.

"Sophia Martin." I peered at the small lens. It wasn't mounted on a swivel base, meaning it couldn't follow us. I gestured for Trace to follow me just out of range, back around the corner of the building. "She's got a set of monitors in her office. She told me she just installed that one after the murder."

"Think she's in her office and saw us?"

"Only one way to find out."

I'd taken only a handful of steps toward the front door when it flew open.

Sophia Martin strode out, leveling a shotgun at the two of us. Her long red hair stuck to her sweaty face and shoulders, covering the scrap of a T-shirt she wore.

The long dark-steel double barrels pointed at my chest. I knew my leather duster could take a few smacks, but it wasn't body armor.

Trace made as if to move in front of me.

"Don't even think about it," she shrieked. Her eyes were bloodshot and wide. "I can get you both at this range."

Trace let out a low growl. Out of the corner of my eye I saw him tense up, ready to Change. At his age with his experience he could do it within a minute.

If Sophia didn't blow him away first.

I could distract her, make a move to separate from Trace. She'd follow me. I was her main target. I could buy time for Trace to complete his Change.

There was a chance he could wrestle the shotgun from Sophia before it went off.

A small, minuscule chance. Felis reflexes were good, but with her finger on the trigger and in her emotional state it'd be too close to call.

I gave him an almost imperceptible shake of my head. The last thing I needed right now was a shoot-out.

He hissed between clenched teeth but remained human.

"You know what happened to Mike. You know how he ended up dead." I spoke slowly, letting each word take up optimum air space.

A thick tear washed out of Sophia's right eye, dribbling through the thick makeup to land on her chin.

"Was it an accident?" I held up the small packet in my hand. "Is that why you cut your nails?"

Trace looked from me to the folded paper, the

revelation dawning on his face. I saw his right hand
flex, his claws ready to come out if needed.

Sophia's eyes darted down to her own mangled
nails. The one I'd spotted at our first interview bled
freely now, the blood oozing over her finger. She
licked her lips and I knew she wanted to pop it back
in her mouth and continue her painful penance.

"In your flyer you've got long, beautiful nails." I
advanced a step. "Now they're short and mangled.
You must have hated to clip them. A lot of time and
work there."

She took a strangled breath. "He shouldn't have
been here. He shouldn't have been poking around."
Her voice rose a notch. "I work hard for my money.
Everyone here, they work damned hard for their
money."

Trace held his ground as I shuffled closer.

"You smoke. Mike doesn't. You were out here,
having a smoke." I started to lay out my scenario,
hoping and praying Carson would arrive soon.
Maybe if she saw a lawman she'd be less likely to
blow a hole in my midsection.

"I smoke in my office but sometimes I come out
for a bit of fresh air." She puffed at a wet strand of
hair stuck to her cheek.

I tried not to smile at the oxymoron.

Another tear dripped off her chin. "I suspected
he'd been poking around my office. Papers shuffled,
little things like that." Her eyes darted toward Trace's

before returning to mine. "I set up a camera in my office, caught him red-handed going through my drawers after his last shift." One side of her mouth twisted upward. "So to speak."

I grinned at the weak joke. "So you knew he was messing with your stuff. You come out here, try and get your thoughts together about what to do. Have a smoke, relax for a minute and figure things out. Think about how to deal with him, how to keep your secrets."

She nodded. The shotgun barrel wavered a bit but stayed trained on me. "It's the end of the night; no one's left but me and the bar staff. Mike comes out, heads for his car. I call the shithead over and tell him I know about his stunt. I know he's digging for dirt and I don't want him around. I'm not going to have a good deal screwed up 'cause some punk wants to get his name in the papers."

Inwardly I cursed Mike Hancock for responding to Sophia's challenge. His pride had gotten the best of him—he'd walked back here without fear, thinking he could take anything the short old woman could hand out. He had the files, he had his story. All he needed to do was walk away and write his little heart out.

I didn't want to speak ill of the dead but Hancock had been an idiot.

"You got pissed 'cause he was acting like a smart

ass." I shuffled forward at a snail's pace. The shot-gun was almost within reach.

Where the fuck was Carson?

"He bragged about it. The bastard bragged about how he was going to take the club down, take me down." The tears now flowed freely, drawing tiger stripes of mascara down her cheeks. "We're impor-tant to the town. We can't be shut down. It'd ruin this area."

"I hear you." A short lunge could put the shotgun in my hands. Or have me farting pellets for the rest of my short, painful life. "He made fun of you. He shouldn't have done that."

Sophia blinked away more tears. "He was a prick. I thought he was a nice guy, a decent man just trying to make some cash. The ladies loved him and he was one of my best money-makers." She sniffled. "Son of a bitch was playing me. Played me for a fool. Took advantage of my generosity in giving him the job in the first place."

I heard the pain in her voice. She'd cared for him—too much.

"He mouthed off. He was being an ass." I filled in the details. "You got mad. You got pissed. Who could blame you?"

"It was an accident," she sniffled. "He laughed at me, told me to go back inside and get ready to lose the club." Her hands tightened on the shotgun, fingers resting on the trigger. "Bastard grabbed my arm and shoved me, shoved me hard."

"And you fought back. Who could blame you?" I nodded, hoping the sympathetic tone would cool things down. "You get back up and show him you're not one of the girls, you're not someone he can mess with."

She nodded.

"You lash out at him, mess up that pretty little face." I continued the scenario. "Make him not so hot, not so pretty."

"Show him not to fuck with me," Sophia whispered.

"And you cut deep." I lifted the paper packet. "Your long nails hit just the right spot at the wrong time."

Trace looked at me, the shock evident in his eyes.

Sophia's eyes went blank and I knew she was reliving the moment she became a killer. "He started to bleed and bleed and bleed," she stammered. "He sat down on the curb and put his hands to his throat. The gurgling..." She gulped for air. "He couldn't speak. I didn't know what to do." Sophia shook her head, the disbelief showing in her eyes. "How can that much blood come from a cut?"

I heard a noise from Trace, something between a cough and a laugh despite the desperate situation. We knew how fast a seemingly innocent cut could bleed out.

"Sophia, put the gun down. We're not the bad guys here." I nodded toward Trace. "We're here to help you. It was a mistake, a horrible accident. Let's work on finding the right way to deal with this."

She shook her head, the shotgun barrel bouncing up and down. "I can't fix it. A man's dead and it's my fault. I can't ever fix it."

I opened my mouth to say something witty and deep when the front door opened behind her.

Sophia spun around with a gasp, weapon at the ready.

I sprang at her back, sensing Trace right behind me. The nausea ball exploding in my stomach told me that I wasn't fast enough; there was no way I'd ever be fast enough to stop her from shooting that weapon and someone innocent was going to die.

I felt Trace's hand on my shoulder, either to push me aside or pull me back. I twisted my body to one side and shook off the grip, still charging.

Everything went off in a smeared blur as if a mammoth hand had brushed over a fresh watercolor print of the scene.

I'd forgotten how fast Felis could be. How fast I could be.

Hands reached out and closed on the double barrel. The metal tubes shifted upward and to the right. Sophia's fingers twitched on the trigger.

The shotgun pellets cleared the top of the building by inches and shot into the sky, hopefully falling to earth without hitting anyone.

Patty Mills stared at the shotgun in her hands for a second before snatching it all the way from her boss.

"You shouldn't be playing with this," Patty said in a nonchalant tone as if chastising a child. "Be bad for business if you start killing off the customers." She looked upward. "Hope you didn't hit any birds."

Sophia looked down at her empty hands before falling to her knees, sobbing uncontrollably.

"Where the hell is Carson?" I spun around, searching the parking lot. "Where the fuck could he be?" I crumpled the packet in my hand. "Where is he?"

There was a squeak in my voice, a mixture of fear and relief. I didn't like guns before I arrived in Penscotta and I liked them even less now.

Sophia looked up at me, her tear-stained cheeks a Picasso of makeup. "Carson? How did you know it was Carson?"

The world whirled around for a second. I staggered to the side and would have fallen if Trace hadn't grabbed me.

"Oh, fuck." Patty cradled the shotgun in her arms, still perched over the hysterical woman. "Carson killed Mike?"

Sophia wiped her nose with one long flowery sleeve. "He sat there. Mike sat there with his hands over his throat. His eyes were so wide…" She balled her hands into fists. "I called Carson. I asked him what I should do."

"Instead of 911," Trace said in a low voice. I threw him a warning glance.

"I didn't want anyone to find out it was me," Sophia babbled. "I called Carson. Told him I didn't mean to do it, I didn't mean to hurt anyone."

"Was Mike still alive when he arrived?" I had to ask.

Sophia looked off to the side, her eyes focused on a distant, unseen target. "He fell over onto his back and gasped a bit. He didn't look at me." Her breaths were shallow and strained. "Carson pulled in 'bout then. He got out of the car and leaned over Mike, said something to him."

Patty, Trace and I exchanged glances. If she had seen Carson's claws…

"What did he say to you?" I knelt down by the broken woman. "What did he do?"

She looked down at her own jagged fingernails. "Told me to go inside and get a drink, forget the whole thing ever happened. He pulled out a knife, told me he'd make it look like an animal attack, take care of everything. Be our own little secret." She popped the bloody finger into her mouth, talking around the injured flesh. "I went to the bar and didn't come outside until the cop showed up saying he found a body in the back."

"How did you make sure no one else found him?" I asked.

Patty interrupted the trembling manager. "She told us there was a problem with the Dumpster—it was overflowing and she didn't want anyone getting hurt if they slipped on garbage." She let out an annoyed huff. "There's so few of us at the end of the night and no one smokes. It was just easier to head out." She glanced at Sophia. "I balanced my till and left."

Sophia nodded. "Carson told me he'd fix it all up. All I had to do was play along."

The reality slapped me across the face like a cold northern wind. Carson knew everything, had known everything all along. We'd been played from the minute I got on the plane in Toronto.

"So where is Carson?" Patty tilted her head to one side, keeping a wary eye on the broken woman.

My breath caught in my throat.

A Felis is a hunter. And like all hunters, we go for the weakest in the herd. Cut him out, get him alone and then kill him.

"Oh God." I pushed Trace away and stumbled toward my car, fishing in my long coat for my keys. "He's going for Bran. He's going for the easy kill."

The keys fell out of my numb fingers and bounced along the gravel.

Trace's hand landed on my shoulder. "You can't drive." He picked up the keys. "Patty, keep 'er safe until we clear this up." He hustled me into the passenger seat, taking precious seconds to do up my seat belt. "I've got to call my uncle."

Patty nodded, keeping guard over the hysterical woman. "They'll want an update."

They being the Board. The Board being the people who hired me. One of which was as corrupt as you could get.

I gripped the dashboard with both hands, trying to slow my breathing. It'd been right in front of me and I'd failed to see it, failed to see the obvious.

"Carson's the one taking the bribes from the club and funneling them to the corrupt politicians, using his position to avoid questions." I wheezed as the tires skittered over the small stones before leaping onto the highway. "It wouldn't be odd to see him at the club, see him talking to Sophia. Same when he paid visits to the councilors to give them their cut. Goddamn bastard was probably taking payoffs from everyone for everything."

Trace tapped on his cell phone as we bounced over a railroad crossing. "Keep talking. Keep breathing." He glanced at me. "And for fuck's sake, don't Change."

I started to curse him back but snarled instead. "He's going to kill Bran. He's going to kill Bran and take the laptop and we'll never be able to find Hancock's notes again."

"I meant it," he roared, spinning the car around a corner. "Stop it."

I growled again, about to remind him I couldn't Change until I spotted my hands on the dashboard.

The long Felis claws dug into the dark blue plastic, scarring the blank surface. I clenched my teeth and tried to slow my breathing, take command back. It was one of the first things we learned as kits— to control our Changing and do it when and where we wanted.

I wanted.

But I couldn't. I held my breath, working through old exercises like a feeble boxer trying to remember how to work the bag.

The claws retracted through the punctured skin slowly and painfully, the only evidence I'd ever manifested my Felis heritage the small wounds between my knuckles. Blood oozed from the cuts but I knew that'd heal quickly enough.

"It's Carson. He's the killer," Trace snapped into the cell phone. He glanced at me as we fishtailed around a corner. "Martin killed Hancock by accident but Carson fixed it to look like a Felis did it." Another sideways look. "Carson's been running bribe money to the town council to keep the club open."

"Good work. We'll take it from here." The gruff voice did nothing to cool my temper. "We're calling a hunt. Won't take long to find him."

"You'll fucking get Bran killed," I shouted.

Any answer McCallum gave was cut off by the tires squealing as we hit the hotel parking lot, bouncing over the curb and skidding sideways toward the entrance.

I undid the seat belt, flung the door open and threw myself out, tucking and rolling like I'd done this all my life. The leather duster took the worst of the abuse and my left shoulder throbbed from even more abuse, but I was up on my feet and running for the hotel door.

"Reb!" Trace's voice came from behind me but I didn't stop. I couldn't.

The hotel clerk's eyes went wide as I raced past him, the same young kit from earlier. If there was anyone else in the lobby I didn't see them, my tunnel vision aiming only for my hotel room, our hotel room.

The door was open when I hit it with my shoulder, slamming through into the bedroom.

It was empty.

The overturned table rocked from side to side. A water bottle lay on the floor, the clear liquid rocking back and forth at my approach. Cracks spread out to the edges of the television set from something or someone hitting it dead center.

I smelled Carson.

I smelled Bran.

I smelled Bran's blood.

The dark smear on the carpet screamed at my senses as I knelt down and touched the damp fibers.

"Kit at the front desk says Carson told him he was here to bust a drug dealer." Trace appeared in the doorway. "He said he had a warrant for Hanover's arrest. That's why no one challenged him." He shook his head. "Man's still the police chief."

"He'll need more than a title when I get hold of him." I stood up, ignoring the throbbing in my shoulder. "What's McCallum say?"

Trace shook the cell phone in his hand. "Everyone's gone on high alert all over the town and throughout the county." He locked eyes with me. "If he pokes his head up we'll have him."

"He's gone to ground with a hostage. He's not going home to wait for us to visit." I pushed by him back into the hallway. "He's going to negotiate Bran's life for his own. For immunity for covering up Hancock's murder and for taking bribe money."

"Shit." Trace's voice followed me back down the corridor. "This isn't going to end well."

I stopped in the lobby. The kit was nowhere in sight and a handful of black pickups were pulling into the parking lot.

"This is going to end in blood," I rasped.

FOURTEEN

McCallum got out of the first truck as I approached the truck posse. He looked greyer and older than the last time I'd seen him.

"We've got Sophia sequestered in her office under guard. Patty's closed the club down—story's that there's electrical problems, too dangerous to open 'er up for the public."

Plussey got out of another truck. Mike and Dave, the twins, out of a third. They didn't look at me or Trace, moving as one to stand behind Plussey.

"I've called Carl Stanford," Plussey said to us. "He's on his way."

I glanced at Trace.

"State trooper," he offered. "He can move in here and take care of the situation without anyone poking around more than they have to."

Translation: another Felis who could help cover the tracks.

"He'll be here in a few hours." Plussey turned toward the twins. "Where is Carson?"

Dave answered first, sputtering as he rocked from side to side. "He didn't tell us nothing."

Mike nodded. "Nothing, boss. We ain't seen him since the diner."

I stepped up in front of the pair, moving far within their personal space.

"If I smell Bran's blood on you," I snarled, "there is nothing in this world that's going to stop me from taking you both apart." I curled my fingers into a fist. "Claws or no claws I'll flay the skin right off your miserable hides if you're lying."

Dave flinched under my gaze. Mike stared straight ahead as if I wasn't even there.

I closed my eyes, leaned in and inhaled. Sweat and a faint whiff of beer—but no Bran.

"We ain't seen Carson," Mike repeated as I stepped back.

McCallum moved up beside Trace. "Think he went to his hunting camp?"

Trace shrugged. "If he's going to ground it'd be a place to check." He moved toward his truck, still in the parking lot. "Might want to talk to April first."

"Already got some women with her," McCallum said. "She ain't going nowhere."

"I'll take the camp," Trace replied. His shoulders drew back, the predator in him taking control. "Creep in from the side, take the trails."

"I'm going with you." I turned my back on the twins. "Where's this camp?"

Trace froze.

McCallum opened his mouth a fraction before

clamping his lips shut. He glanced at Plussey, the sharp look sending the second Board member at me like a bullet.

I let him move in front of me, paying respect to my elders. "You wanted me to find Hancock's killer and I did."

"And we're grateful for that. Now we'll take care of it." Plussey put as much authority as he could into his voice. "It's our problem now."

"No." I sliced the air with one hand. "I'm the one who let Bran get into this situation and I'm going to be the one to get him out."

Dead or alive, the small voice in my mind said.

A smile tugged at Plussey's thin lips. "Jess said you were a handful."

"She understated the obvious." I headed for my rental car, watching what the other men did. I didn't want to fight my way out of the parking lot but I would if I had to.

McCallum gave Trace a nod, sending him after me.

He intercepted me before I opened the door. "This could get messy."

"Tell me something I don't know." I clasped the handle tight. "You're either going to help me or stop me. If you're going to stop me you're going to have to knock me out." I nodded toward the twins. "And I'm not above ball-busting to get what I want."

Trace's right eyebrow rose. "Tempting. Very

tempting but I'm not into that much kink." He reached over and plucked the keys from my hand. "I'll drive. We can get to the camp faster than me giving you directions."

I slid into the passenger seat. Trace jammed the key into the ignition and we were off.

Trace said nothing until we were well clear of the parking lot, speeding along the narrow road far above the posted limit. The trees sprang up on each side of us, splitting the sunbeams into narrow daggers stretching across the road.

"We should have figured it out earlier," he said so softly I wasn't sure I'd heard him. "Damned idiots."

I wasn't sure who he was referring to. I didn't care.

Trace's phone squawked. He looked down at his lap where it lay and gave a snort.

"Roadblocks already set up by the troopers. Told them Carson took a hostage. He's not getting away from us." He slipped it back into the holder on his belt.

I bit down on my lower lip, holding back my response. I might be a city girl now but I knew how easy it was to disappear in the wilderness.

"How many back roads are there out of the county?" I asked.

A low growl answered me. "Enough. But he's going to want to stick to the highways for the first bit to gain ground on us. He can drive faster than he can jog, especially dragging a hostage with him."

He smacked the steering wheel with the heel of one hand. "Why did the bastard run? If he'd brought it to the Board, fessed up, it wouldn't be so bad."

"He killed a man," I stated. "He killed Hancock to keep his bribery secret. There's no excuse for that."

"We could have fixed it," Trace said. "We could have done it right." He gritted his teeth together. "No reason we couldn't have."

I tamped down the anger bubbling up near the surface.

A blast of music came from the cell phone, some trite pop tune. Trace looked down.

I turned my attention from the dense trees back to the road.

"Trace!" I shouted, grabbing at the dashboard.

He glanced up from the small screen and slammed on the brakes. His knuckles went white as he wrestled for control of the steering wheel, gripping it with all his strength.

The car twisted and lurched from side to side with the smell and scream of burning rubber filling the air.

We fishtailed for a good fifty feet before coming to a stop. Pain pulsed through my shoulder as I leaned back in the seat, the pressure of the seat belt grinding against my skin.

"You okay?" Trace unsnapped his belt. "Fuck."

"Yeah," I gasped, undoing my own seat belt. "I wasn't using those lungs anyway."

The police cruiser lay on the shoulder of the narrow road, the front end smashed in. A dump truck sat before it with an elderly man sitting on one crushed bumper, shaking his head. He seemed unharmed and confused.

We both bolted from the car. Trace headed for the old man, I for the police car.

I stopped at the open driver's door. Blood on the windshield, blood on the steering wheel. Airbag deflated and hanging limp from the dashboard.

Carson.

Blood on the back seat. A few drops smeared across the hard plastic seat shells.

Bran.

"I swear I didn't do anything wrong," the driver stuttered to Trace, his cigarette trembling in one hand. "I put out the flares like I was supposed to."

I glanced behind the cruiser. The safety flares continued to spark and smoke where they lay scattered in the brush.

"Saw the lights flashing and he come right down the road, fast as blazes. I thought he was gonna pull over and help me. Instead he goes all wild, jerking back and forth across the road." The man's hands flew back and forth as he illustrated the car's frantic movement. "Then he smacks into the back of my truck." The cigarette bobbed up and down. "I was broke down before—now I'm crashed as well. Boss is gonna be pissed."

"What happened then?" Trace continued the interrogation, his hands flying over the minute keyboard on his phone.

"I goes over to see if he's okay, you know?" The well-worn Pittsburgh Steelers baseball cap bounced as his hands continued their pantomime. "I sees the officer slumped over the wheel. Fella wasn't buckled in or nothing—I thought they was supposed to follow the law same as us."

"Then what?" Trace demanded. He wasn't going to be sidetracked.

I walked around the other side of the car, edging into the deep brush. The trail was there, easy for any half-assed tracker to find.

One man on the run, one following.

"Officer wakes up, starts screaming about getting away. I open the door and pull him out onto the road." He rubbed the bristles on his chin. "Thought car was gonna blow up."

"A good decision." Trace nodded, encouraging him on. "Then what?"

"The guy in the back, he's pounding on the window. I figure he's hurt or something and I see he's handcuffed so I let him out." The trucker turned his head and let loose a stream of liquid tobacco into the dirt.

I whirled around. "Pounding on the window? His hands were in front of him?"

Trace shot me a curious look. "Carson is a pro. He would have cuffed him in the back."

"Bran must have gotten them down around his

feet and up in front." My pulse increased at the mental image of him wrestling in the back seat. "Then he must have attacked Carson somehow, made him crash."

The trucker looked from Trace to me to Trace again, licking his lips. "Is he a murderer or somethin'? I didn't do nothing wrong, right?"

Trace patted his shoulder. "You were checking to see if they needed medical attention. That was a wise decision."

The older man's forehead furrowed as he continued. "The guy from the back, he starts wrestling with the cop's belt. I figure he wants to get the gun so I grab him and tell him to back off." He looked at me, trying to judge my reaction. "He grabs something off the cop's belt and runs into the woods."

"What did he take?" Trace prompted.

"I dunno." He shrugged. "It wasn't the gun. I wouldn't have let him go off with that, no siree." The baseball cap shook back and forth. "So suddenly the cop wakes up and he's all shaky. I tell him what happened and he draws his pistol and stumbles off into the brush. Don't even thank me for keeping the fella away from his gun." The driver wiped sweat from his forehead with a filthy dingy-grey handkerchief. "I called after him, said I was gonna call 911 but he didn't say nothing back."

Trace stepped back, fingers dancing as he frantically texted the information to the hunters.

I patted the older man on the shoulder. "Thank

you for your help. Someone's going to be here in a few minutes and give you a hand." My pulse pounded in my ears as I muttered something else about the weather.

"They're coming in from the north and east." Trace touched my arm. He looked at the trucker, raising his voice. "There's going to be some state troopers coming here to help out."

The old man nodded and lit up a cigarette, leaning on the hood of the wrecked police car. "I ain't got nowhere to be."

"Thanks." Trace caught my eye and nodded toward the brush. "We're going to check on those flares, make sure they're not setting fire to the woods. Please stay here with the cars and make sure nothing else happens."

His tone was so gentle and polite it took me a second to remember who and what he was.

We were Felis.

We were about to go on a hunt.

We walked over the ditch and into the deep brush as quietly and quickly as possible. Trace dropped to one knee as soon as we were out of sight of the road. He shed his jacket and unbuttoned his shirt, a handful of resistant buttons popping free to roll in the dirt. The clothing flew to one side as he closed his eyes and snarled.

I barely held back my gasp as he Changed in a flash of fur, dark streaks contrasting with the tawny fur now covering his skin. He smiled, showing off white feral teeth.

"I can't," I whispered, on the edge of tears.

"You don't have to," he replied in a low, measured tone. "He's out there, your mate. All you have to do is tune into him. You know him, you know his scent and you know how he moves." His words became shorter, clipped as he moved into hunt mode. "Carson's hurt. He's on Bran's trail. We're on his. We're going to push him toward the rest of the Pride. They'll take him."

"Before he catches Bran?" I pulled the elastic out of my hair, releasing my long blond hair. The duster slid from my arms as I drew deep breaths and forced myself to listen, to sense, to feel.

"I hope. But that's out of our hands." He stood up and reached out for me. "Ready to run?"

I grinned. "Hope you can keep up."

A low growl started in his chest, rolling out to a chuckle. "Let's see what you can find."

I closed my eyes and inhaled, filling my lungs with the smells around me. Oil from the nearby crash, sweat, fear…and there it was.

Bran.

Carson.

And a whole lot of blood.

I sprinted forward, ignoring Trace as I pushed through the branches. The jagged edges pulled at my shirt, snagging and ripping small tears. My running shoes sank into the damp soil.

"There." Trace grabbed my arm. He moved up beside me and pointed at an almost invisible dent ahead of us. "Boot. Police-issue."

I held back a snarl and moved forward.

The wind shifted and I caught a whisper of a gasp, maybe a cry.

Trace heard it too and stopped. One arm shot out and pulled me close to him. "Don't."

A curse bubbled up before I realized I'd been on the balls of my feet, ready to spring toward the source.

"I know you want to." Trace's iron grip on my arm didn't ease up. "Let's go together."

We moved through the forest, careful to stay upwind.

Trace released my arm, taking the chance I wasn't going to leap out ahead of him and into trouble. It took all my willpower not to clock him and rush off on my own.

I sucked at being a team player.

A shout came from our right. A pained, angry shout.

It wasn't Bran's.

I sucked in my breath through clenched teeth, trying to force myself to Change. Just my claws, that'd be enough. Enough to take care of Carson.

Trace caught my eye and nodded to the left. Circle around, survey the scene.

I crept along, pulling the scents and sounds into my mind's eye to create a picture.

Blood.

Sweat.

Fear.

From both men.

I frowned as we stepped over a fallen tree much like the one we'd leapt over on the farm. I could understand Bran's fear, his trepidation at being hunted by one of the family and his probable death. But I couldn't fathom why Carson would be so afraid.

Trace crouched down and pulled a thick clump of branches to the side. He put his hand on my shoulder, fingers digging in to draw me down and keep me in place.

Carson stood there in the clearing, Changed. He threw his head back and roared an angry yell that would bring any hunters running—human and Felis. His uniform shirt was torn open, his furred chest a stark contrast to the sharply pressed fabric. A wide gash on his forehead bled openly, the blood running down through the fur on one side of his nose and dripping off his chin. He shook his head every few seconds, keeping his vision clear and spraying blood everywhere.

He wrestled to hold his pistol steady, his extended claws making it hard to grip the weapon. Another angry toss of his head sent more blood flying as he rocked back and forth.

At best he was having trouble seeing his target. At worst he was concussed and dealing with possible brain injury.

I'd take both.

A few seconds later he threw the automatic down at his feet with a loud curse. Positioning himself over the discarded gun he gestured with one hand, a "bring it on" move, followed by another angry shake of his head.

I shifted to one side and saw Bran standing less than ten feet from the chief.

His red hair was streaked with blood from a cut on the top of his head. The blue dress shirt had been yanked free and busted open, showing bare skin. Blood splatter across the front could have been his or Carson's, I couldn't tell.

His wrists were swollen and striped red from the cuffs. Mottled black and blue bruises crisscrossed his chest from both Carson's rough treatment and the crash.

He held the unlocked handcuffs in his right hand like brass knuckles, weighing them as he glared at Carson. There was something in his eyes, something familiar.

A hunter's stare.

Trace grabbed my arm as I started to move forward to break up the fight. Carson might not want to or be able to shoot Bran but there was no guarantee that'd last past the next few minutes.

"Don't," he whispered. "You'll distract him."

I opened my mouth to say something snarky when Carson sprang forward, teeth bared. His hands reached out in a classic Felis attack, claws aiming for the face and torso.

If you were lucky you'd only be blinded. If you weren't you'd be holding your intestines in for the last few agonizing minutes of your life.

Bran crouched as if he'd practiced for this fight all his life, muscles tensed and ready to spring.

He slipped to the side at the last possible moment and landed a vicious kick to Carson's right shin, following up with a punch to the shoulder with the cuffs. Another kick sent the automatic out of sight, bouncing into the surrounding underbrush.

The claws skittered across Bran's right arm, shredding the fabric and lightly slicing the skin. They weren't deep but I knew they'd be painful.

I'd had enough of my own.

The Felis snarled as he spun around and prepared for another charge.

The blood smell screamed at my senses.

Carson feinted once, twice, staying well clear of Bran's armored fist.

I squinted, studying Carson.

He was slow, slower than I'd ever seen a Felis move. He was still faster than most humans but something was holding him down, holding him back from his full potential.

"Concussion," Trace murmured in my ear as if he'd been reading my mind. "And the bastard hasn't kept in shape."

I bit down on my lower lip, muscles tensing under

Trace's grip. Every nerve, every muscle screamed for me to get out there, get out there and save Bran.

Problem was he was doing a fine job of that himself.

Carson leapt forward again, swiping across Bran's exposed midsection with a force that would have disemboweled a deer with ease.

Bran threw his hips back and brought down the cuffs hard on the extended right forearm. I wasn't sure if I'd heard the bone break but from the way Carson yelped and withdrew, cradling the injured arm, it was a definite hit.

The smell of fresh blood stung my nose. The gouges across Bran's torso weren't deep, but enough to bleed. The only sign of the burning pain was a twitch of his left cheek.

The wind shifted and a dozen different scents flew into my mind, Felis men and women nearby.

I scanned the underbrush around the two men as they continued their lethal dance.

"They're there," Trace said to my unasked question.

"What are they waiting for?"

He looked at me, a puzzled expression on his face. "For the challenge to finish."

"This isn't a challenge," I snapped. "He's not Felis."

"He's enough of one to hold his ground with Carson." Trace gestured toward the clearing where Bran had just scored another hit on Carson's injured arm at the cost of another scoring, this time across Bran's left arm. The tattered remains of the shirt sleeve hung limply from the bloody wounds.

"You've never had a human fight a Felis before?" I barked.

"No," Trace replied. There was a tone of wonder in the word. "Why would we?"

I had nothing to say.

I'd never seen one either. In the few years I'd been with the Pride, I hadn't ever seen a human stand up to a Felis, not to the point of physical contact. Usually the Felis gave in and backed down, even in drunken bar fights, knowing we had the advantage and not wanting to exploit it at the risk of being discovered.

Carson shook the blood out of his eyes and let out a low grumble, the sound rolling up from his belly.

Bran turned his head to one side and spat on the ground, the scarlet saliva sucked up within seconds by the soil. He grinned and tilted his head to one side, motioning Carson on. There was a glazed look in his eyes, the look of an angry man that would not be denied.

Carson stiffened for a second, his nostrils twitching.

He knew we were here.

He knew there was no way out.

His eyes darted around the clearing, seeking us out.

"Don't move." Trace's grip on my arm intensified.

Carson looked at Bran, a scornful look on his face.

"Fucking human. I'm going to kill you in front of her," he declared. "Damned nosy bitch."

"Maybe." Bran smiled. "But she's my damned nosy bitch." Bran shifted his feet further apart. "Now shut up and bring it."

Carson roared and charged again, his head low like a bull. His claws aimed for Bran's torso.

Bran waited until the last minute to react, leaning forward and grabbing him around the waist as if they were sumo wrestlers battling in the ring. His left hand locked Carson's arm in place as his armored right hand shot up and over, slamming into the back of the chief's head in a single, sharp strike.

Carson's left hand and claws were nowhere in sight. I prayed they weren't imbedded in Bran's stomach.

The pair dropped to their knees as one, the dust rising around them in a long, spinning vortex.

I couldn't breathe.

FIFTEEN

TRACE RELEASED MY arm, letting out a low whistle. "Don't see that too often."

I couldn't move.

A rustling came from my right and McCallum emerged from the bushes, unChanged. He wheezed as he crouched down beside me.

"Damn. Gotta start eating more salads." He pulled a handkerchief from one pocket and wiped the sweat from his face. He spat on the ground and drew a deep, stuttering breath. "What a fight."

I pushed Trace aside and sprinted for the clearing. The thorny branches caught my torn shirt, my jeans, my face—drawing minute scratches over my chin and cheeks.

Bran gave a heaving sigh as I dropped to my knees beside him. His arms were still wrapped around Carson's body. The two of them wove from side to side in a slow, agonizing rhythm.

I waited a long, horrible minute for him to do something, anything.

Bran coughed and turned his head to the side, spitting out blood. I saw the split lip clearly, the fresh blood invading my senses. His blank eyes came into focus as he stared at me, the recognition chasing away the tunnel vision. A weak smile replaced the bloodlust I'd seen earlier.

"Damned fool." He scowled and pushed the unconscious man away. The handcuffs fell off his hands into the dirt and grass.

Carson fell onto his side, wheezing heavily. Both his hands were tucked into his own torso, claws retracted. He'd pulled back just in time but they'd still left wounds deep enough for stitches. Whatever his attack plan had been it didn't hold up under a concussion and Bran's final punch.

The gouges on Bran's stomach were superficial and they'd mend. I brushed my fingers over the angry red trails. They'd leave scars, a permanent reminder of this fight.

Like mine.

Still on his knees Bran reached out and grabbed me, his hand wrapping around the back of my neck.

He pulled me toward him, hard, and kissed me.

I tasted his blood and his anger and his rage and his lust.

This wasn't just an "I'm glad to be alive" kiss.

This was a kiss of domination, of possession.

He pulled back and rested his forehead on mine, pulling in deep breaths. Drops of blood fell from both our lips as I waited for his next move.

"Mine," he growled, sounding more Felis than human.

I nodded, afraid to speak.

I wasn't sure what had just happened here but I knew we were bound by blood, tied together as surely as if we'd just uttered wedding vows.

He released me and we stood up together.

I looked around. A circle of Felis formed around us, men and women, Changed and unChanged. They waited in silence, watching us.

Plussey walked out. He stood by Carson and sniffed the air, his nose wrinkling with disgust.

"Someone get this piece of shit out of here. He's spoiling a good camping spot."

Carson moaned as the twins stepped up and dragged him to his feet. Mike's and Dave's faces were expressionless as they held up their crib brother.

"You don't understand," Carson murmured as he Changed back. "It was just business."

I moved in front of the beaten man. A string of bloody saliva dripped from one side of his mouth down to the ground. The gash on his forehead continued to bleed, smeared blood mingling with fresh as Carson weakly struggled against the iron grip of his former enforcers.

"A man is dead. And even if you didn't kill him yourself you sure as hell didn't help save him." I looked at Plussey. "I don't know if Hancock could have been saved if he'd gotten proper medical attention in time—we'll never know that. But it was his duty as a police officer to try."

Plussey nodded. "Well put." One edge of his mouth twisted up into a sneer. "A disgrace to your profession and to this Pride."

McCallum came out of the brush, still wiping his face, to stand beside Plussey. Trace followed close behind.

"You can't do this to me. I'm on the Board." Carson ground the words out. "I'm the police chief."

"You were all of the above." McCallum waved the twins away. "Now you're just a problem."

The two men marched out of the clearing, dragging the semi-conscious Carson between them.

"What are you going to do with him?" Bran spoke, his tone quiet but firm.

McCallum looked at him. "We're not going to kill him if that's what you're asking." He smiled. "We're not animals."

"Question is—" Plussey raised his voice, "—who will take his place on the Board?" He let out a chuckle. "Usually the replacement would be the one who beat 'im, but..." He nodded toward Bran. "I doubt you want the job."

Bran shook his head.

I cleared my throat. "Seems to me that the best man for the job is a woman." This earned me a handful of smiles and a few chuckles, mostly from the female contingent. "I'd nominate Lisa Darning for

the job if I had a say." I spotted her at the edge of
the crowd. "She's got good business sense and she's
already integrated with the town council. When this
story breaks you're going to need someone steady
to ride it through." I paused, letting the reality sink
in for the Pride. "And the story will break. This one
isn't going away."

Plussey cleared his throat.

I spun around. "This is not up for discussion. Hancock was murdered by a human but he was mutilated
by a Felis." I kicked a stone over the dragged tracks
Carson had left behind. "Carson set down a false
trail hoping we'd follow it to the end."

"Why do that?" Lisa asked. She'd made her way
to the front and now shifted closer to the other two
Board members in a less-than-subtle announcement
of her intentions. "Why make it look like a jilted
lover?"

"Because if the body disappeared, dropped into
the bush or a wood chipper, then Prosser would know
Hancock was onto something and start kicking up
a fuss—you'd be up to your necks in reporters and
journalists looking for the truth. If he's killed by an
'animal'—" I made air quotes with my hands, wincing at the phrasing, "—then she doesn't have any
legal recourse. Suspicious, yes. But she can't prove
anything. She can't call in the authorities and claim
a trained bear clawed him to death."

I jerked a thumb in the direction the twins had

gone. "Martin calls Carson for help. Carson arrives and either finishes the job or just lets Hancock bleed out. Either way Hancock dies. Carson slashes the body and leaves it for one of his patrolmen to find. Then he supports the decision to bring me down, a neutral party to look for this mystery lover. I can't find the phantom lady because there isn't one—I run around in circles."

"Then you go home in disgrace," Bran added. "And the murder just goes away 'cause it's a Felis killing a human." The distaste in his voice came through loud and clear. "After all, what's a dead human here or there?"

McCallum stepped in front of Bran. "I know we've been at odds over most of this but—" he extended his right hand, "—I'd like to thank you for your help. We were…" He swallowed loudly. "We were wrong about the situation."

Bran stared at the thick callused fingers for a long, heart-stopping minute before grasping his fist in a tight grip. "Guess we can all learn something from this." He drew a ragged breath. "My laptop's in the trunk—he threw it in there. We've got Hancock's notes and I'm sure it'll lead to Carson at the end of it all. Along with the members of the town council taking the bribes."

"I'll send it to the hotel. If you could send us your notes we'd appreciate it." The Board member's eyes flickered to the trail Carson had left in the dirt. "We'll use it to build the case against him."

Bran's cynical look was brassy and challenge-worthy but McCallum let it pass.

McCallum glanced at me. "I can't promise you we'll mend our ways and all that but I can tell you that you've given us a lot to think about."

"And a lot to clean up," I added. "I don't want anything to happen to Sophia. She might have killed Hancock but it was an honest accident." I looked down at my own nails, chipped and ragged. "I think we can all understand the rage she must have felt at being betrayed by someone she trusted."

McCallum nodded. "We'll arrange a plea deal; get her a good lawyer. Do right by Hancock's family as best we can." A heavy sigh escaped the older man. "We'll make it right." He looked at Bran and me. "What can we do for you?"

"Call Cassie Prosser." I spoke first. "Give her the story and let her run with it. She deserves as much of the truth as we can give her. Let her break the news about Carson and about the corrupt councilmen."

McCallum paused for a minute before nodding. "Agreed." His lips curved into a smile. "We can control what gets out that way. Good idea."

I held back a stinging retort, taking what little success I could get.

"We need a ride back to the hotel," Bran said. His hand moved over the razor thin cuts on his stomach.

I saw him start to wince and then hold back, not wanting to show weakness in front of the Pride.

Plussey gestured to one young kit. "He'll take you home." He paused. "Both of you."

It was a question, not a statement.

I looked around the circle, recognizing some faces from my visit to the farm. Instead of suspicious looks I saw respect—for both of us.

"Let's go." I moved closer to Bran, close enough to grab his arm if he faltered.

Bran moved away from me and stood up as straight as he could. He strode up to Trace and stared at him, way inside the Felis's personal space. His scuffed running shoes brushed against the toes of the well-worn work boots as he leaned in, almost touching noses.

Trace smiled, a knowing smile, and lowered his eyes. His shoulders slumped, giving him a submissive position.

Bran nodded and reached back for my hand without blinking or looking away.

I slipped my hand into his and he led me out of the clearing, brushing through the crowd without hesitating.

WE RODE BACK to the hotel in silence, the kit sweating buckets as he maneuvered his pickup truck through traffic. He didn't look at Bran and only gave me a curious glance as we exited the vehicle.

The hotel clerk was out from behind the desk before we got halfway through the front doors, her distress showing.

"We've arranged another room for you." She waved down the hallway. "Your luggage has already been moved." Her fingers trembled. "We're so sorry." Eyes wide with panic, she waited for our response.

Bran smiled and shook her hand. "It's okay." He calmed the nervous kit, patting her shoulder. "We're okay."

I chewed on my lower lip, not too sure of the truth of that statement.

"We've placed some supplies in your suite," the clerk said. "Please call me if you need anything else." She offered the new cardkey. "Room 111. Just around the corner."

Bran nodded and took the room key from her.

He strode down the hall at a furious clip, pushing me into a trot just to keep up with him. As soon as we rounded the corner and were out of sight of the main lobby, Bran slumped against the wall. He drew short, harsh breaths, one hand pressed over his midsection. The raw skin shone through the tattered remains of his shirt even though the bleeding had stopped.

"Are we clear?"

I nodded.

"Take this fucking key and help me get inside," he rasped, dropping one arm across my shoulders.

I felt him collapse against me as we shuffled down to the last door.

The suite wasn't exactly Las Vegas-worthy but it beat the small room we'd been in before. The living room table was covered with various bandages and first-aid ointments, the Felis having intimate knowledge of how to deal with claw wounds.

Bran grunted as I lowered him into the straight-backed wooden chair. "Son of a bitch."

"Yes, he was." I carefully tugged at the remains of his blue shirt. "He skated offside around us while we were at the club waiting for him."

"Sophia killed Hancock?" He grunted as the fabric fell away, revealing a series of bruises running across his shoulders. "Don't panic. It looks worse than it feels."

"Sure." I let the lie alone and poured the bottled water into the empty bowl. "She nicked his throat with her nails. He bled out and Carson tore him up to cover her attack."

"Hell of a risk to take." Bran gasped as I touched the wet gauze pad to the first of the thin scratches across his ribs. "He must have known there'd be an investigation."

"Better a Felis investigation that he could steer and monitor instead of Prosser calling in the feds over her reporter buddy going missing." I winced for both of us as I shifted to another area. "Want some drugs?"

"I got it." He snapped the lid off the generic bottle of painkillers and dry-swallowed two pills. "It's not too bad."

"Says you." I moved up to work on the gouge just above his hairline. "I saw the room. You put up a good fight."

Bran touched his left eye and the growing bruises. "I opened the door like a damned fool when he identified himself. Bastard launched himself right at me without warning, slapped the cuffs on and dragged me out."

I scowled at the matted hair. "You're going to need to get into a shower. It doesn't need stitches but with you rolling around in the dirt it'll need to be cleaned out."

His hand landed on mine, rough and tense. "Join me." A brush of his fingers across the back of my hand sent goose bumps up my arm. "We need it."

There was something in his voice, a connection between us that hadn't existed before.

I nodded. "Could use one myself." My back ached at the sight of the claw marks.

Bran stood up and started stripping in silence, leaving a trail of clothing on his way to the shower.

I did the same after rolling up his shredded shirt and jeans into a bundle and tossing them into the wastebasket—they were beyond saving. By the time I got into the bathroom, steam had already started to pour out of the shower stall, the shadowy figure inside waiting for me.

"So now what do you do?" Bran winced as he reached for the tiny sliver of hotel-issue soap. "What do you tell Jess?"

"The truth." I gestured for him to turn around so I could lather his back. "The Pride's going to figure out how to cover it all up. Are they too integrated with the locals? Hell, yes. Felis on the town council, Felis on the police force—something like this was bound to happen with the opportunity for corruption and to use the family to hide it." I shrugged. "But that's none of my business now. My job here is done."

"Did you learn anything?" He kept his back to me.

"I learned that I really, really love French fries in my sandwiches, not on the side."

This earned me a snort as he ducked his head under the water. "And?"

I frowned. "And what?"

Bran shrugged and reached for the minute tube of shampoo.

I felt a cold wind wash over me. I'd missed something and I wasn't going to get a chance to guess.

I washed up as quickly as I could and stepped out.

"Don't forget to let that heat soak into your muscles."

The grunted reply didn't do anything to make me feel better.

I wandered around the suite wearing the thick,

plushy white towel, trying to ignore the pair of duffle bags neatly set on the floor. I wasn't sure if I was about to be thrown out of the room or out of Bran's life or what.

All I knew was that for the second time in my life I felt totally alone.

It hurt.

"Reb."

I spun to see Bran standing there, the cream-colored towel tucked around his midsection. The gashes on his midsection still looked terrifying but at least they'd stopped bleeding.

"Come here." There was no mistaking the commanding tone.

I put my hands on my hips and walked over, meeting and locking my eyes with his.

"You trying out to be my Dom?"

"Smart ass," he replied. A short step brought him closer, our noses almost touching. "Do you have any idea how worried I was about you when I was facing down Carson?"

I choked back a laugh. "Me? Why the hell would you worry about me? You're the one who went toe-to-toe with a Felis and lived to talk about it." The trembling in my voice betrayed my fear. "You could have been killed."

"And what would they have done to you if I'd died there?" Bran snapped. "They would have come up with some bullshit story about my death and made you play along for the sake of protecting the family. Hell, they could have kept you here, talked Jess into letting you stay—making you stay to keep their fucking secret." He rolled up his fingers into a fist and shook it at the wall. "Bastards were so quick to write Hancock off, they'd do the same with me. And with you."

"No." I said the word but my heart wasn't in it. I didn't want to begin to go down that path, of helping the Pride not only cover Carson's tracks but also dealing with Bran's death. "They would have made Carson pay. The hunt would have gotten him eventually."

"Then what? They auction you off to the highest bidder to keep you quiet about me being gone?" The rage in his eyes was building, reaching terminal levels as his voice rose. "Give you to Trace in some sort of arranged marriage to keep the peace between the two Prides? Keep Jess happy?"

The breath caught in my throat as I realized what this was all about.

Us.

Or, to be more precise, the possibility of not-us.

I reached out and touched his hand, the bruised knuckles still tender from the handcuffs.

"That's not how we work. It's never been that way." I lowered my voice, hoping to defuse his anger. "Hell, can you imagine anyone telling Jess what to do?"

Bran's lips twitched for a second before settling into a thin smile.

"So this is about us?" I ventured, going out into uncharted territory.

"It's all about us," Bran retorted. "It's always been about us. I just never saw it before." His voice dropped down to a whisper. "I didn't figure it out until I was there with Carson, facing down those claws. I may not be Felis but I realized what you need. What I need."

I shook my head, letting the damp blond strands fly free. "I don't get it."

"Right. Let me explain it." Suddenly he spun me around and pressed me face-first against the wall. My hands flew up, slapping the pale blue wallpaper over my head. "Let me lay it out for you so it's clear to both of us." One hand went to my hips and yanked the towel away. "I'm done asking what you want, what you think. I'm telling you from now on. And you belong to me." His hands settled on my waist, gripping with newfound strength.

The snarl burst from my throat, unchained. "What?"

"You belong to me." His teeth came down on my earlobe, the sharp tug sending my pulse into triple digits. "And I, unworthy human that I am, belong to you."

"I don't…" Confusion buzzed in my ears, threatening to drown out any coherent thought.

"Shut up," Bran whispered. His hips thrust forward as his hands pulled me back. "I may not be a Felis but I sure as hell am a man. And you are mine. No one else's."

Teeth moved lower, brushing over the back of my neck. A short nip sent a rush of heat down my spine.

I gasped as he yanked me back against him again, the towel around his waist scrubbing against my bare skin.

"You feel what you do to me?" He rotated his hips, letting me feel his arousal. "You know I've wanted you since you left with Trace? I wanted to punch him out and throw you down on the bed, take you right there in front of him. Tie the bastard up and let him watch me make love to you hard and long, make you scream over and over again."

My cheeks began to burn at the mental image of Bran grabbing me from behind, lunging forward as I gripped the headboard for support.

His lips landed again on my earlobe, tugging and pulling. "Do you know what you do to me, what effect you've had on my life? How fucking lost I was, coughing out mindless pieces of fluff because I didn't have anything in my life, anything to keep me going?"

I shook my head, too choked with emotion to answer.

"Say it," Bran demanded.

"What?" The oatmeal formerly known as my mind sloshed around.

"Tell me I'm yours. Tell me you're mine." His fingers tightened on my hips, guaranteeing bruises. "Tell me we're going much further than just 'hanging out' together until someone better comes along."

The tension in my shoulders returned. "You know we're together."

"No." The teeth returned to the back of my neck, sharp and demanding on the exact same spot. "Say it."

"I love you." The words burned my throat, the raw emotion threatening to drown out my sanity.

"Not enough." Another nip, this one harder and longer. "Love and devotion. Say it."

I tried to move. Bran pinned me against the wall with another long, leisurely swivel of his hips.

"Say it," he whispered. "Give me all of you. All of you, all of the Felis in you."

The fire was burning me, tearing me up from the inside. Three months and I'd hit the wall. I couldn't go forward and I couldn't go back without losing part of myself.

It was time to make the kill or give up the hunt.

"I can't leave you." It was the best I could muster.

"Sure you could." His tongue danced along the tortured skin. "You could walk out of here right now and drive to the airport. Be back in Toronto in two hours. Go home and never have to see me again."

"I won't leave you," I gasped, feeling faint.

"That's good to hear. But not enough." His lips moved along my earlobe, dropping light kisses. "Say it," he whispered. "Say it, Rebecca."

"You belong to me." That much was easy to say, easy to devour.

"And…"

I closed my eyes and surrendered.

"I belong to you. All of me."

"Yes." Brandon kissed me on the cheek. "Only yours. Always and only yours."

My pulse drummed in my ears, pounding faster and faster. He didn't move back. His fingers stayed on my hips, locking me in place.

"You spoke about Felis women scratching their men, putting their mark on them." I could feel his smile against the back of my neck. "Do the men mark the women?"

A shiver rocked me from tip to toe.

"Yes." I heard the shaking in my voice, unable to stop it. "They do. With their fangs."

"Where?" His hand slipped away from my waist. A sharp tug and the remaining cream-colored towel fell around my feet.

"Anywhere they want." I was burning up. I was frozen in place.

"Hmm." The teeth landed on my back, on the left shoulder blade. "I don't have fangs but I think I can make do."

The ivory whites closed on my skin, tugging and sucking, the sensation spiking my arousal to new levels.

"Been a long time since I put a killer hickey on anyone." The tension increased on the skin, threatening to break it. "I'll apologize if any of them bleed," Bran growled in my ear.

"Right back at you," I gasped, my fingernails clawing at the wallpaper and my surrender complete. "Keep that first-aid kit handy."

"Yes," the answering purr came, thick with lust. "Now show me what you're made of, Felis."

SIXTEEN

LISA DARNING LOOKED up from the medium-rare steak and eggs as we slid into the booth beside her. Plussey and McCallum sat on her right, each devouring their own giant slab of semi-raw meat.

"Got your message when we checked out this morning. Along with Bran's laptop and my duster." I waved at the waitress. "Two coffees, please."

Bran's knee nudged against mine. I didn't flinch. It might have been the only part of my body not aching. When we'd stopped by the hospital on the way to the diner to see Henry, the coroner had given me a curious look while drawing my blood. To say I was walking bowlegged would have been an exaggeration but not by much.

"No problem. Figured you'd want that back before heading out." Plussey's tone was casual, too casual. "We were wondering what you was gonna tell Jess." Plussey reached for the ketchup bottle. "Just curious."

I didn't buy the gentle words. Whatever I said could come back to bite me, quite literally.

"I'm going to tell them you fixed things up. The

Pride's safe, the family's safe and justice has been done." I eyed McCallum. "Hasn't it?"

The waitress arrived with the two mugs of coffee. She dropped a handful of creamers on the table before wandering away.

"Stanford's taken Carson into custody for mutilating a corpse and failing to render medical assistance, along with the corruption charges." He took a sip of coffee, eyeing Bran. "He's going down for a good long time."

I frowned. Felis weren't known for doing well in prison.

"We're figuring he'll plead out and we'll work out some sort of probation," McCallum offered. "After all, he didn't kill Hancock. Henry says it's impossible to prove who gave the killing blow so it's unlikely either of them will go down for a full murder charge."

"He almost killed me," Bran said in a low tone, almost a growl.

"True," Lisa agreed. "But that's just the official punishment." She glanced toward the window. "April's left him. He's lost his position in the Pride and his job. He'll probably end up running odd jobs on the farm for a living." She eyed Bran. "I know it's not what you want but it'll have to be enough."

Bran shifted and I felt his leg bob up and down, the nervous rubbing daring me to act.

"And Sophia?" I placed my hand on his knee and began a slow, steady stroke. The muscles clenched and unclenched under my touch, sending a tingling up my fingers as I remembered the workout they'd been given last night.

"She's going down for involuntary manslaughter, at the worst." Plussey studied his coffee, holding the mug close to his mouth. "Prosser's not thrilled but without evidence that Martin intended to kill Hancock there's little chance of getting a first-degree murder conviction. Woman's an emotional mess as it is. It's going to be hard to get a jury to buy that she set out to kill him. An accident's the most likely theory and one everyone likes."

"Is Carson going to testify?" I suspected I knew the answer but had to ask.

"Not a chance." McCallum stabbed a thick chunk of meat. "The last thing we want is him up on the stand. He'll work a deal, plead guilty to reduced charges, and disappear."

Bran's leg slowed and stopped.

"What about the club?" I opened up enough creamers to turn my coffee into a café au lait while Bran took his black. "Is it going to close?"

Plussey shook his head. "Patty's taking over as manager. We're acquiring it for the family."

I coughed on a mouthful of coffee, unable to speak for a minute.

Lisa gave me a half smile, seeing my confusion. "We're still enforcing the no-men rule as far as working there goes. But it's good for the community and if it adds more money to the family's coffers, well…" She spread her hands.

"I was right. You are definitely right for this Board," I mumbled around another sip.

McCallum cleared his throat. "You tell Jess that we're okay, we're under control and we're just fine without anyone else coming down and causing trouble."

I couldn't hide my smile. "I'm that much trouble?"

"And then some." McCallum grinned. His eyes wandered over to the side of my neck where a bruise spread out from under my loose hair. "I'm guessing in other areas as well."

Now it was Bran's turn to beam. I let the three men share a moment of macho manly bonding, looking at Lisa, who put her hand up over her face to stifle a snicker. She tilted her head to one side, eyeing Bran, and gave me a quick nod of approval.

"We've got to get to the airport." I slid out from the booth, wincing as my hips protested. "I'll let Jess know what went down." *If she doesn't know already,* I added mentally. I didn't put it past her to have connections all over the place—if not her, then the Grand Council.

McCallum stood up and extended his hand. "Thank you for coming down. I know it wasn't what you expected and we might not have been the best hosts, but…"

I shrugged, letting my tiny hand vanish in the giant's grip. "So it goes."

He turned to, Bran who stood beside me, and put his hand out.

Bran didn't hesitate, grabbing it in a death grip.

The two men stared at each other for a long, long minute. I saw Bran's knuckles turning white, the half-healed cuts and bruises from the clearing more pronounced.

McCallum stepped back, relinquishing the field. He pressed his lips together, the tight smile passing for approval.

I nudged Bran. "Car. Go home."

He nodded and turned away from the table. I gave the three Board members one more glance before joining him in the rental car.

"What do you think is going to happen?" Bran drove out onto the highway.

"I think no matter how much things change they'll stay the same." I stifled a yawn. "Jess'll want a report when I get back to the office."

"What are you going to tell Jess?"

I rolled my shoulders, feeling the tension disappear with each fresh mile. "They found their killer. Case closed."

"About us, I mean."

"She knows about us," I offered, ignoring the silent question. "I think she suspected we were heading for a crossroads."

"Ah." He swerved to avoid a small crushed creature in the road. "Think she'll be upset at the path we took?"

"I don't care. She lost the right to say anything years ago."

"Hmm." The single word held a world of emotions.

"Don't start." I raised my hands and flexed my fingers. "I can still scratch, claws or not."

"So can I. And bite." He eyeballed me, a sly smile on his face. "I believe I made that clear last night."

I dropped my hands into my lap and put on my most innocent look. "You're no fun."

"That's not what you said this morning in the shower." He drew a deep breath and cleared his throat. "In fact I do believe it went something like…"

I felt the heat rise in my cheeks as he paused, waiting for my response.

"You don't play fair."

"And you're just figuring this out now?" He chuckled. "When we get back to Toronto I'll drop you off at your house and go collect Jazz," he replied. "Along with fresh clothing."

I eyed him, noted how he kept his back straight, away from the car seat. "And some bandages?"

He chuckled. "Might want to keep those in stock."

"Hmm." I shuffled closer to him, cursing the restraining seat belt. "I'm still not giving up my house."

"I'm not giving up my condo." His right hand crept onto my thigh. "But we'll make it work."

"Yes." I relaxed into his touch. "Yes, we will."

ONCE I GOT home I spent a good hour sorting through my clothing, tossing anything that smelt of Trace to one side and stuff I meant to wash and keep to the other.

The front door slammed shut as I studied my shoes and pondered if they were salvageable.

I glanced at the clock on my bedside table. It was too soon for Bran to be back with Jazz and food.

I picked up the baseball bat from behind my bedroom door and crept down the stairs. I wasn't in any mood for a fight but if there was going to be one I was ready.

"Rebecca." Jess was waiting for me inside my office, resting her feet on my desk.

"I don't recall giving you a spare key." I dropped the bat on the couch, strode by her and went to the kitchen.

"You didn't." She watched me from the chair, rocking back and forth as I filled the kettle and plugged it in. "But I'd love a cup of tea."

I resisted the urge to throw the Brown Betty teapot at her head. Instead I fished out a pair of teabags from the battered plastic container and tossed them into the pot.

"If you're here for my report you'll have to wait a few hours longer." I strode out and stood by the desk. I'd be damned if I'd sit opposite her in the visitor's chair.

"Pssht." She made a dismissive wave. "The Grand Council's happy, I'm happy and from the look of things, you're happy as well. We don't really need the paperwork." A smirk appeared. "You seem to be doing well at mixing work and play. I heard he's moved up from boy toy to mate." A soft smile replaced the steel grin. "I like."

"None of your business and I wasn't looking for your approval," I snapped.

She got to her feet in a flash and stepped in front of me, so quick I shuffled back a pace. I'd forgotten she wasn't some old cat, lying in the sunbeams and dreaming of better days.

"It's all my business," Jess said. "You're a valuable asset to the Pride and the family." She paused a second before continuing. "And I don't want to see you get hurt."

Her words held a hint of something else, something beyond professional concern.

"Thanks but Bran and I have worked things out. Without your help. We know how to keep secrets." The kettle screamed from the kitchen for attention and I backpedaled, glad for the escape.

"So do we," she murmured, just loud enough for me to hear. "At any cost."

My hands shook as I filled the teapot. I drew a deep breath and turned, prepared to confront Jess about Bran and my future.

She wasn't there.

Jazz trotted into sight. She hopped onto the desk and lay on her side, sprawled across the varnished wood. She lifted her head and trilled at me.

A cool breeze blew in from the open door. I made a mental note to change the locks, again. Although

I suspected Jess could get in any place she darned well pleased.

"What's up?" Bran stepped in, carrying grocery bags. "Jazz couldn't wait to get out of her carrier so I just left it outside…" His voice trailed off as he saw my face. "What's wrong?"

"Jess was just here." I moved past him into the front yard. The brown grass held no footprint and the silent street kept its secrets.

"And now she's not." Bran finished my thoughts as he moved behind me, putting his hands on my shoulders. "What did she want?"

"To thank me. And approve of you."

"I like the first and to hell with the second." His fingers tightened for a second before shifting to rub and massage my back through the leather duster.

I turned and walked back to the purring cat. An envelope stuck out from under her pale pink belly.

Three thousand in small bills.

Far above my usual going rate.

"Payment for services rendered?" Bran shut the front door.

"And then some." I tossed the wad on the desk. "I'm not complaining. We earned it."

He tugged the jacket off my shoulders. "I like the way you said 'we.' Sounds sort of nice."

"I'm not adding you to the letterhead." I closed my eyes and tried not to think of Jess's expression.

It reminded me of Ruth, the woman who had raised me after my parents had died.

It reminded me of my mother.

"Stop that." Bran pinched my earlobe. "You think too much."

I tossed my head around, whacking him with my ponytail.

"Fine, then." Bran wagged a finger at Jazz. "See, this is what happens when I let your big sister be on top."

"When you don't want to do the work," I replied with a smile. "As usual."

"Well if we've started keeping count…"

Jazz stretched out a leg and began washing herself as Bran grabbed me around the waist and hefted me up over one shoulder.

"Hey." I smacked his butt.

"Hey, yourself." He headed for the stairs. "I think I need to up my count on some particular positions. And check some of those bandages."

I relaxed. Jess and the family could wait, the bills could wait. I was in the right place at the right time with the right man, and that was all that mattered.

For now.

* * * * *